THE REMAINS

OF REALITY

Dvita Kini, Vedha Kodagi,

&

Ava Mandhare

DEDICATION

TO LIFE, FATE, AND DEATH
-WHERE IT ALL BEGAN.

INTRODUCTION

I suppose we owe our biggest thanks to the worst teacher we have ever had. Her class ensured we went from 'school' friends to 'bond-over-our-shared-hatred-of-a-teacher' friends to 'YOLO-let's-write-a-book-together' friends.

Our process of writing this book started in the depths of the Covid-19 pandemic. We had ignored our online classes, opting to FaceTime and tune the teacher out as we gushed over the recent Marvel movies or our latest reads. It was at this remarkable time that one of us had- out of the blue- suggested, "Hey, we should write a book together."

It was that simple, offhanded comment that spiraled our trio into a long three year journey.

Unlike most of our ideas that usually were forgotten after a day or two, the passion we had for our project only grew. Our thirteen year old selves had opened up a 'brainstorming' document, and then began our incoherent word-vomit of ideas. Originally, our book had been completely different. There had been different characters, different problems, and frankly, no solution. We had over confidently made a plan that we could each write three chapters a week, resulting in a total of nine chapters. At that rate, we would have been done with a horrendous book in two months. To be fair, it felt like a sound plan at the time. I don't remember when our immature mind-scramble of a plan had turned into a very complex, chapter by chapter schedule, but, boy, are we glad it did.

The first six months or so were purely dedicated to FaceTime-ing while we discussed possible journeys the characters could go on. It was here when we started to experience the ups and downs of creativity, vision, and teamwork. This half year had to have been the longest six months of our lives. It was here when our motivation slightly started to slow, but that was the benefit of having three authors: one of us was always randomly motivated. Someone was always saying, "We just need to get through the chapter planning, writing will be so much easier."

Turns out writing a book was not 'so much easier'. The next year was both the most grueling and most rewarding experience. The farther we got into writing this book, we would have another brilliant idea that we simply had to incorporate into the book. Just like before, anytime one of us entered a writing slump the others wouldn't hesitate to remind them until they wrote.

After a seemingly never ending year we were left with a 600+ page book. It was at this point that we started to realize that just maybe the book was too big. After several long discussions, we came to the conclusion that the original book would have to be a duology for the sake of the reader's sanity (you're welcome!).

After this decision we found a place to split the books, and thus began the next most difficult part of the writing journey. Now that the book was two, the once coherent thoughts started to make a bit less sense. We had to spend months trying to fix new problems and diluted plots. But, hey, we did it.

We took just as long to edit. The final year of editing was the disadvantage of writing a novel. We were incredibly unmotivated, unnecessarily drawing out the time period before publication. It took us too long to realize that if we wanted this book published before we approached our eleventh grade year, we'd need to put in the effort. After all, we couldn't have our years of work go to waste, but, more than that, the incredible characters of this book deserved to see the light of day. The ball was rolling then, and we ended up with the product you see today.

I suppose that about sums it up. This journey was long and grueling, but we are so glad that we got to experience it with each other. And how could it not be worth it when we get to see others just as excited about our characters as we are?

4

Well that's *our* story. Now may we introduce theirs.
Happy reading!

CHAPTER ONE

DEATH

*I*nhale.

He couldn't breathe.

Death adored new things. Whether it was a new sparring move that Fate learned, a new species Life created, a new prank Chaos set up, a new story Retribution had to share, or a new cookie recipe Balance invented.

He loved the brief stumble of recognizing and adapting to the change, laying there as a gentle reminder that they weren't perfect. That they didn't need to be perfect.

Death looked up at the outline of The Library of Lucror that had suddenly turned blurry. He swayed slightly in the cool night air.

Exhale.

This was new.

Death clenched his eyes shut. This wasn't a good new. This was foreign. No amount of training could prepare him for this.

It was as if a piece of his own self was being torn from him. Death clawed at his chest.

Lucrians shoved past his quivering form, throwing quick looks over their shoulders.

The pressure crushed down at his lungs, leaving him gasping in gulps of air. His hand lunged out, gripping the cobble stone fencing, pushing his body into a straighter standing position. Death's brows pulled together, a bead of sweat dribbling down his face.

This 'new' had been alien to Death. However, whether willingly or not, in the last ten years, 'new' had slowly started to become more and more familiar.

The First War had started a ripple effect of new events.

The first attack, the first bombing, the first fall of a kingdom, the first empire, and now?

Death stumbled forward, clutching his stomach. His hands shook. Each heave of his chest felt excruciating, as if a blunt dagger was lodging itself deep into Death's ribs. He stumbled past bustling figures.

Rain pelted onto Death's figure. He raised his gaze, searching.

Lines of coffee stores and bookstores lined the streets of Lucror central. The once clear figures of bustling people had now turned into faint blurs of movement.

Death stared through his lashes at the pelting rain.

It was nearly dark now. The stuttering glow of the city street lamps casted dancing images of fire onto the cement pavement.

He shut his eyes, plowing through the crowd.

After the war started, 'new' started to have a different connotation for him. New wasn't baked goods or harmless pranks anymore.

'New' was war.

He staggered into a pitch black alley way. The echoes of laughing women and yelling men bounced off the walls.

His features contorted into one of pure focus.

"Breathe-" He muttered quietly. His palms covered his ears, his eyes still tightly shut.

His lips moved to mouth out a word. *'Focus'*

His surroundings stilled, blurring into a muddled, distorted canvas. Flashes of light flew past his closed eyelids. He couldn't think. He felt light; he was weightless. The ground felt malleable under his feet. He held his breath. The floor disappeared from under him. His knees momentarily buckled from the force of the teleportation as he slammed into solid ground.

He didn't think. He couldn't think. So he ran.

Piercing light forced itself into Death's gaze.

The sun.

Different time zones.

He widened his strides desperate to reach there faster, squinting his eyes to see through the taunting heat. A quaint house came into view. Colorful flowers sprung from the beds surrounding it. They looked unusually sad and dull as if they knew something Death didn't- as if they were pitying him.

Death felt his legs slow. His muscles contracted painfully under his pale skin. He heaved in deep breaths.

A bluish flower wilted near Death's boot. His gaze darkened as he lifted his head to glare at the flowers. He felt a chill run down the center of his spine, dissolving near his lower back.

An ugly brownish shade seeped in from the sides of the flower, wilting the stem as a few shriveled up petals fell from the center.

He tore his gaze away from the flower, disgusted. Death.

He felt hot tears trail down his cheek. The still unfamiliar pain ripped through Death's chest again.

In a jolt, he ran. He ran through the garden, roots digging into his ankles, the tough ivy clung to his feet like a lifeline. He stumbled and tripped over beds of roses ridden with thorns that pierced his skin. Yet, he didn't flinch. How could he even think of a few thorns when the unimaginable had become a reality?

He took jagged breaths, when a choked sob ripped from his throat. Tears streamed down his flushed cheeks.

"No... please-"

Bruises and cuts bloomed on his exposed legs. Leaves flew as plants fell under his feet. He crashed through the front door, pain blossoming onto his shoulder at the contact.

"Balance?" Panic crashed over him "Balance, where are you?"

He strode to the closest door. He flinched at the bang of the wooden door hitting the wall as he flung it open. He looked around the dining room.

Fresh flowers lay in several glass vases around the room, as if preserved. As if amidst all of the destruction, her flowers would be there as perfect as ever, mocking him.

Death pivoted, harshly wiping tears off his face. He turned, banging through another wooden door, his wrist aching.

"Balance?"

His throat felt raw. His vocal chords screamed for relief. His heart screamed for her.

Her bedroom was empty. Her sheets lay in pristine condition, every fold and curve made with precision.

Death's gaze flicked to the mirror above her bed.

He looked awful. Death's lip curled. His hair laid in a tangled mess from all the times he tore his hand through them in the past minutes. His lip was red and swollen from the anxious biting, perfectly pairing with his red puffy eyes. A glossy sheen lay on his cheeks.

He glanced away quickly, leaving the room.

"Balance! Where are you?!"

Death strode back, curling and uncurling his fists, his eyes darting. He crashed through the door to the living room, hissing as he tripped over something-

Tripped over someone.

His eyes widened as he froze in shock.

"No...no no no please-"

There she was. Her porcelain skin was tight with dried tears. Her face was one of complete peace. Her monolid eyes covered half of her irises. Her lips at rest in what Death begged was a small smile. She layed in tranquility. The eye of the hurricane. Almost as if the universe took a picture.

9

Death dropped to his knees, tears clouding his vision. His cold hands clutched Balance's colder ones. She looked pale-deathly pale.

He looked into her eyes. They looked dull- devoid of color. They looked empty.

Death closed his eyes trying to reach her, begging to everything that this wasn't real. He begged for her to wake up and yell, 'It's a prank!'

He begged for her to come back.

Blood pounded in his ears. He didn't wince when the unbearable ringing in his ears somehow got louder. Nor did he wince when he faintly registered raised voices around him.

Fate's aggravated snaps, Retribution's venomous whispers, the stillness of the air. However loud they could've been, the voices sounded faded, muffled, as if he were under water. Death couldn't make out a single word.

A soft thump sounded in front of him.

Death looked up, trembling.

Chaos kneeled on the other side of Balance, his face unreadable.

He felt bile creep up his throat.

Death felt a soft hand rest on his shoulder.

"Death?"

He shivered, the wet clothes on his body finally spreading the cold to his bones. He couldn't hear. His mind was a minefield of clutter.

In a sharp movement he shrugged the hand off, scooching closer to Balance, tenderly cradling her head in his lap.

He heard Life shuffle away, her voice dissolved by Fate and Retribution's tones.

Death raised his hand, brushing a few stray hairs from Balance's porcelain face.

"Balance?" He whispered, his voice hoarse. His skin prickled at the contact of his against hers.

Death's brows drew together, as his fingers dragged up, shutting her eyes with the most gentle touch.

He winced as a loud voice rang out, though he couldn't make the words out.

This wasn't supposed to happen. He looked down at their intertwined hands.

One second passed.

Then another.

Death's eyes widened. The patches of her skin on his itched uncomfortably. Her usually pale complection seemed to grow paler. Her face looked almost translucent.

"Balan-?"

Balance's hand fell from his, as light as a feather as it slowly touched the ground.

Death blinked as if attempting to clear his vision. Her hand had fell *through* his.

"She's... fading?"

The argument around him subsided as all eyes trained on Balance. Everyone stilled with disbelief.

Death's hand was suddenly clutching nothing. A painful silence swept the room.

Exhale.

Death stared at the carpeted floor where Balance lay not seconds ago.

He lurched up, backing up into two figures.

The room was spinning and he couldn't get it to stop. He stumbled out of the room, his hands boring into his head. A strangled breath left his lips, as he ran down the halls and out of the house. He gasped as his surroundings started to mix again, becoming blurry. Death stumbled as he lost his footing. His eyes shot open.

He had teleported.

He looked forward. His face lit with recognition. He stepped closer, his mouth parted ever so slightly.

He remembered this.

A shrieking laugh causes Death to spin around, a wild grin on his face. A girl tumbles into his arms and Death lifts her back up, laughing as he backs her into the tree. The branches of the willow tickle their faces and a pond kissed with lotuses glimmers in the background.

"I have a present for you, Balance." Death reaches behind him pulling out a brown, leather box.

Balance looks up at him, gently plucking the heavy box from his hands. Her hands skim the lid. Death keeps his eyes trained on her, a small smile decorating his features. Balance's hands delicately lift the lid of the box, uncovering a block of wood. On the wood an intricate pattern of Death and Balance sitting next to each other is carved in.

She lets out a small gasp, clutching the wood tightly.

Death holds Balance's other hand, his smile widening as he sees her grin grow. Balance stares down at it awestruck, her finger tracing the engraved details.

"You made this?"

Death smiles softly, "yes."

"For me?" She grins.

Death rolls his eyes, "No for Retribution- yes for you!"

Balance grins looking back at the wood, "Oh, It's amazing Death."

She places the figure back into the box and gently sets it at the base of the tree, amongst the flowers.

Balance suddenly breaks out in a run giggling as Death doesn't hesitate to run behind her, grinning. The wind sweeps her hair behind her. Death trips and tumbles onto Balance. The pair bubble with laughter. Death lands on top of her.

Balance goes rigid under him.

"Balance?"

Her skin felt cold unlike its usually warm feeling.

12

Death's eyes met Balance's.
They were dull, devoid of color.
They were empty.
Death whipped his head back up.
The air had a bitter chill to it.

The once glimmering pond was frozen over, the lotus flowers limp and dead.

Death glared at the base of the tree, dragging away a stray tear running down his face. He looked to the horizon, wisps of smoke uncurling in the distance. His gaze softened as he looked back at the barren willow tree.

She had always wanted him to open up, to learn to accept help. He had always made sure to be rigid, and never let his guard down. He learned that love was strong, like pollen. She told him that they would live forever. Yet here he was, clawing at his face.

And her?

She was gone.

"Please- please don't be gone…"

I need you.

CHAPTER TWO

FATE

It was common courtesy, Fate had believed, not to begin an argument the moment after losing someone. *Shockingly*, she didn't care to voice that thought.

"You could have saved them all. The humans on Cadere, Balance-"

"Humans are meant to *die*, Retribution." Fate almost laughed.

"The Protectors aren't." A third voice interrupted.

Retribution's jaw twitched, giving Chaos a cursory glance, "He's right. Is the point of Balance's existence to end?"

Fate paused, "Perhaps it was."

Was. Retribution's mouth twisted at the use of the word.

A sharp laugh burst from Fate's mouth, "And don't act like you understand the way my ability works."

"Oh? So you can't see the future? You can't use that to help the world?" Retribution interrogated.

When she didn't respond, he shook his head,"What, exactly, does your ability entail?"

"Foretelling. Though it's a little more complicated. I'm afraid you wouldn't be able to wrap your mind around it if I told you."

Retribution threw his hands up in the air and scoffed, "However it works, it allows you to-"

"Cheat arrogant men out of money I have no use for while gambling?"

"*See the future.*" Retribution glared at her. His body was tense. His eye was slightly twitching, Fate noticed.

"Yes- to win a game of Parieur." Fate snapped.

"No, no," Chaos interjected from Fate's right, "Retribution surprisingly has a point. If you could have looked a little closer into the future, we could have bypassed my major headache." He looked at her, disappointed, and whispered, "Do you need glasses?"

Fate shoved him, "Do you need common sense?"

Chaos scoffed, stumbling dramatically.

This conversation was a frequent one. Every time a conflict arose in their planet Cadere, the blame seemed to fall on her. Those in the past were small misfortunes- a street fight in Hikma, a public execution of a Lucrian spy in Riqueza, the loss of hundreds of lives during a tsunami in Fortem. Ever since the First War fell upon Cadere, tension seemed to tear a crevice between Fate and the others.

Heping was declared under Riqueza's rule minutes before Fate had felt the lurching pain in her stomach and a strange, overwhelming pull towards Balance. Balance had held on for nearly a decade, her face losing color as time passed, but with her fall came the rise of utmost turmoil. The war was tipping dangerously in Riqueza's favor.

Retribution slumped down in defeat in one of Balance's pristine armchairs. Balance's cottage had always been decorated that way, comfortable, yet elegant- every item perfectly in place. She had kept *them* in place.

Now that Balance was gone? Fate felt...well...what did she feel about her cessation?

She inhaled deeply, focusing on the cabin rather than her thoughts.

The front part of the cottage had two wide windows on either side of the door, allowing Heping's early light to spear through; it grew increasingly harsh. A mahogany cabinet was placed on her left. Dust wasn't powdered over the top, but it should have been. Balance had been frail the more the war's influence grew. The past years, she couldn't summon enough strength to even teleport to attend their progress meetings. Even rising from a seat would have been more energy than it was worth.

Wearily, Fate eyed some white flowers sprouting from a vase perched on the cabinet. The flowers glowed under the sun's light, living and cared for. Yet as the flowers flourished, Fate had witnessed Balance fade mere minutes ago. The way her edges had blurred until she melted into the shadows-

Fate's hands shook.

The question was, *was Fate to blame?*

Grimacing, she pushed her shoulders back and placed her arms ready at her side- ready for another surprise. She was used to having the world's future in her hands. She knew every possibility of a decision someone would make, every card an opponent could and would place, every fail and success. And she liked it that way, unless she was in for the thrill of winning parieur without her ability. Then, she would simply choose not to see the dimensions of probability in her mind.

Unfortunately she didn't have that option for the other protectors. Abilities didn't work on them. Fate could only predict- and although it was oftentimes accurate- she didn't have peace in truly knowing. But this- Balance's cessation- was far off from any assumption. She hadn't even known it was *possible.*

Would she have played the game differently if she would have known? Or was it their destiny? After all, balance in a world, as most humans understood, was always a doomed concept.

She scoffed at herself. She sounded like some philosophy textbook Death would read.

A small movement pulled Fate's eyes to Life who stood over the rug with an almost unnoticeable sway. Waves of gold covered her face as she looked at the spot Balance and Death had been.

Fate tore away from the sight, facing Chaos instead.

"You seem to be enjoying this. You thrive off of chaos, don't you?"

Chaos titled his head and feigned a pout, "How did you know?"

"When balance is rid in a world," She blinked at him, "what is left?"

He looked around the room, bored. "Uh, us?"

At Fate's glare, he rolled his eyes. "Havoc, *Chaos.* Is that the answer you wanted?*"*

She scowled.

"Even if I gain something from *whatever* is going on, I can't control it. You, however…" Chaos broke off looking infuriatingly calm, but it was all he needed to say for her to tense.

Retribution interrupted, clearly not enjoying their conversation, "Chaos, that's enough."

Her eyebrows shot up. She was sure he would have taken Chaos' side and created a lengthy argument. Maybe that's what she had been hoping for. A distraction. The feeling of exhilaration and strength that came with debate. But, Retribution, she guessed, had learned early enough that it was pointless to argue against her; it would take things nowhere.

He pushed himself from the chair and glanced quickly at Life. She made no effort to move at the side of the rug, staring at the floor as if Balance would miraculously materialize if she only stood there long enough.

The slight upturn of his lips and the glimmer of affection in his expression sent Fate's eyes upwards. She crossed her arms and gave Retribution a cool look.

"We need a plan." Was all he said.

As if that helped anything.

"Do we now?" Chaos muttered.

Retribution ignored him, "It may be too late," He fixed his eyes on Fate, "But it's still our sole duty to protect this planet and the people of it."

Chaos nodded his head fervently, brown curls falling into his eyes, until Retribution turned away to face Life. He hid the roll of his eyes from Retribution's sight.

"I believe it's our main priority to resolve the war." He continued.

Chaos gasped, still unmoving from his position against the wall, "Oh! Whatever gave you that idea?"

Retribution took a deep inhale, "I need to speak with Time to see how to further proceed."

Fate sneered at his words. Time- the creator of the universe, the creator of the planet, the creator of *them*. And yet, they'd never seen his face, with, of course, the exception of Retribution. Time hid away in who knows where, offering no help whatsoever to the problems on Cadere.

It was really quite comical; if he really was as powerful as her and the others grew to believe, where was he when they needed him? Why could he not cease the war and return peace and Balance to the war-ridden world? Except for occasionally offering superficial advice that wouldn't save a soul- through, who was now their official liaison, Retribution- conversing with Time was pointless. He would tell them that Balance's cessation was a natural process- although they'd never heard of it since they had been created- and convince them to move on and grow from it. Like an adult consoling a child whose pet had just passed.

She turned back to Chaos who seemed unaffected by Retribution's statement. His eyes flicked lazily over to hers. She understood that with Balance gone, he took control of the social scale, but did he have to act so unbothered? She stilled suddenly.

The same could be said about her. There was no will in her, to dive into her feelings. Was there guilt? Was there remorse? Was there *some* sympathy for Death as he fled from the scene of Balance's cessation?

She hoped she would never find out.

"And what will we be doing?" Fate finally asked schooling her features into her usual look of indifference as she caught Retribution's somber gaze.

A shadow of a smile passed his face, "Keeping your eyes open."

And with that, the spontaneous gathering was over. Chaos pushed himself off the wall as Life blinked out of sight without a single word, followed by Retribution and his iconic crossed arms. As they left, a long stretch of silence- pure and wretched silence- tore through the room as sunlight danced upon the wooden stakes of the high-tented ceiling.

Fate couldn't bring herself to talk, but her mind was spiraling, or in better words, creating contingencies; she was planning. This was her forte- seeing all the sides of a situation.

What would happen now? Maybe Retribution would have them force alliances between the countries, maybe they'd create peace treaties, maybe they'd kill King Casimir or, *maybe,* more plausibly than the previous idea, they'd utilize the Rebellion. Fate knew the last thought was very…*risky.*

She didn't want to be seen by the Rebellion again, especially the Krasaviyan branch. There were certain people she was hoping to avoid. Certain memories. Either way, it had been heavily impacted from the end of the Krasivayan Queen's reign and had yet to strengthen again. There was no leader, no order, no *chance* if she came to them.

The Riquezan rebellion was secluded, to say the least. The time it would take to gain their trust would be much longer than Fate had the patience for, or longer than she believed the world could survive. With those out of the way, the only logical option was the Fortem Rebellion.

Chief Sarki, *oh may the Altar help her*, was someone she could get on her side, although she'd probably be ready to punch him within a minute of laying eyes on the man.

Sarki aside, the Rebellion wasn't a horrible plan. All the branches had been 'alive' for at least a decade. Whether or not they had any real intention of banding up and starting a war against Riqueza, she didn't know. She…couldn't tell?

She was probably just exhausted- a different type of weariness than humans experienced. It was a decade's worth of memories, fears, thoughts, and emotions weighing down her shoulders.

She let the disturbance in her abilities go.

She couldn't help but think that Retribution and Time, to no one's surprise, wouldn't support using the Rebellion. The unstable and illegal group of powerless citizens fighting a ruthless, clever monarch was asking for an exponentially large death toll. They wouldn't risk it. But Fate knew what the Rebellion, clearly established, was like firsthand. She wouldn't count it out, if it were her.

"Well, what are we waiting for?" Chaos finally asked, interrupting Fate's thoughts.

"*We?*" Fate scoffed.

Chaos gave a wry grin and mocked her earlier patronizing tone, "To discard the problem, to find peace, what is the first step?"

Fate looked at him in annoyance, "Root out the cause. The chaos."

"Precisely my point." He paused, "So we head to Riqueza."

He winked as if expecting her to understand some joke.

They had been there often enough, seeing as it was now his home, but she felt no joy in returning.

He grabbed Fate's arm without giving her a chance to pull away, he dragged them into the exhilarating falling sensation of their teleportation ability. Fate willed any thought about Balance, any guilt, and any remorse to stay behind as they disappeared from the cottage in Heping.

***

Fate's feet hit the pavement as Chaos' pressure on her arm was released. She scowled as she pulled her arm back, wishing for some time alone. She wasn't even sure what she'd do with that time rather than savor the silence for seconds, immediately lose interest, appear in a gambling hall, and play parieur with anyone willing to compete against her skill.

Her eyes tilted up from the hidden alley streets to the skyline. Shadows of purple and blue mountains climbed into the clouds behind hundreds of buildings. Thousands of feet under the peaks, lay the capital, Encima, of the kingdom of Riqueza. For such a destructive kingdom, its lands were a sight to behold.

Ornate buildings with gold borders and sculpted marble statues were at every turn. The grand complexes had even taller spires that could have touched Cadere's atmosphere. Huge-tiered fountains sprouted from the ground in front of important buildings-the banks, the colleges, and any wealthy businesses. Smoke vines spilled from chimneys and twisted into the cool autumn air. People strode through the paved streets in business fashion on their way back from work.

Amusement flashed across her face. Encima had changed drastically since she had been there last. It had been smaller, the architecture less extravagant, and the air had seemed lighter. But two things stayed the same. First, the dragon statue that the king had made, and second, the city flaunted its wealth.

Wealth- it was Riqueza's flaw. Without wealth there was no power here.

And the wealthiest, who led the country, were often the most ruthless and self-absorbed of them all.

A passerby, a young woman, with dark hair to her hips peered at them as she strode past. Chaos flashed a grin, an assurance that he didn't dream of robbing anything. At least not this time.

After the woman had passed, Fate followed Chaos out of the alleyway, which they had appeared in to prevent people from dropping from heart attacks.

The most jarring part of the city were the guards patrolling the streets, ears twitching in alert. Their skin tight uniforms held hidden armor threaded into the suits and was patterned with red and green stripes running across the shoulders. On their hearts was a blazing dragon, the colors matching the shoulders and striking against the black.

Her pace quickened in an attempt to reach Chaos' side, but he paused anyway at an unlit lamp post that had too much metal detailing for its purpose.

He was playing with the watch around his wrist when she reached him.

Fate could have just visualized her home in Mahana and left, but she didn't. She followed Chaos through the streets, the crisp air smelling of nothing but faint fragrance spray. She supposed that maybe- just maybe- she didn't want to be alone. Even if Chaos had never received the hint to keep his mouth shut in his existence.

It wasn't particularly surprising. Out of her fellow protectors, Chaos was the one she was closest to. They'd tormented their family for centuries- a team of destruction.

Chaos titled his head back into the sky, his eyes exploring the clouds merging with the smoke. His hand twitched at his side a subtle sign that he was craving movement. She smiled, a twisted smile; his wandering eyes and his pause told her everything she needed to know.

"You don't have a plan, do you?"

"Of course I do."

22

"And that is?"

A smirk.

He was waiting for her to *ask*.

Fate glared at him, turning on her heels to walk away.

"Patience." He said with a feigned sincere expression, then he flashed her a grin and dragged her down three blocks.

***

Finally after more than thirty minutes, Chaos' feet came to a slow halt. The lavish city's length didn't seem to spread to this part of Encima. The suburbs, she guessed. On paved gray streets, instead of ornately designed complexes, were now racks of shabby housing buildings. The air seemed thicker here, and it seemed a *touch* less jovial. People sauntered down the streets carrying briefcases and somber expressions. The working class. Although the sky hadn't darkened, Fate felt a looming shadow over the city- a heavy feeling of exhaustion rippling through the air.

What were they doing here?

She glanced at the building he had stopped at, a scowl turning her lips. It was a shorter building flanked by a housing building and a textile store- its clothing sleek and sharp unlike the vibrant threads they wore for festivals.

Their destination had a wooden sign nailed to the dark gray door. The Riquezan language engraved on it labeled the building. The display windows showed lined wooden tables packed with citizens and the flurry of cards and dice. It wasn't a housing building. It wasn't a market, or a restaurant. A slow smile crept up her face.

"Is this where we will root out the cause?"

"Most definitely." He said, as he pulled open the peeling door and strode into the gambling hall.

***

23

They both solved their problems in different ways. Fate preferred drowning them in a game of Parieur, and it seemed Chaos was trying out her method.

She *knew* there had been an ulterior reason for Chaos bringing her to Riqueza. He didn't care about the war or ending it. He didn't care to follow orders. He didn't care for anything at all. And neither did she as she placed her winning hand down.

She leaned on the table, resting her smug face on her hands. Chaos dropped the two cards he had been dealt.

He leaned back in his chair in defeat, with a frown.

Hours had passed and Fate had won every single game. An upturn of her lips proved her triumph, as she leaned over the wooden table and grabbed the coins on the center of the table.

Clinks of coins and hearty laughs erupted from the front of the hall, near the distribution counter, that drifted to the back left corner where they sat, along with the suffocating smell of cigarette smoke.

"Could you put an ounce of effort into defeating me?"

"It's the only reason you're winning."

Fate rolled her eyes and placed down more cards.

"What's your wager?" She asked him, her hands picking up the pile she gave herself.

"This is new." Chaos leaned back in his chair, "Fine. How large can I go-"

"Shut up, Chaos."

A corner of his mouth twisted into a challenging smile, "I win and you tell me why you didn't care to inform us about the rising probability of the war."

Fate's eyebrows shot up from behind her fan of cards, dropping her hand and the cards along with it on the wood.

"I already told you." She smiled coldly, "It's human nature to begin a war. There is no point in stopping the inevitable. Besides," She shrugged, "I would have gotten blamed either way, since Retribution so wonderfully believes that I create every calamity on Cadere."

Chaos groaned, "You're such a liar."

Liar. People often accused her of lying, and more often than not, their claim was incorrect. Chaos, however, was correct each time.

"A half-truth, sure. You couldn't have gone from caring to utter disinterest in a matter of days without some sort of *event*." He added.

Fate's face fell slack as a party erupted into laughter somewhere to her back, "It's perfectly reasonable. Humans are utterly useless. We don't serve them. If that's why you pulled me here-"

Fate made a motion to stand, but Chaos just leaned back against his chair, arms crossed.

"You get angry when proven wrong. Know that, Fate?" And he continued, "Besides, I believe you asked *me* for a wager."

Fate's jaw tightened but immediately paused at her motion to leave. A familiar tingling feeling threaded through every vein in her body, but it was so small, so seemingly irrelevant she could've passed it off for a shiver. If she hadn't known better. If not for the change in her dimensional outlook. It had been so long since her future sight slid over her eyes like lenses. Her ability had never worked the same since she foretold the war.

She stood up abruptly, the chair under screeching against the checkered tiling. Her hand motions swept the cards off the wood and they flew through the air sprinkling over the tiles, yet the other customers with their scruffy beards and tattered clothing seemed unfazed. She understood why- it was quite normal to experience a fit of intense emotions at a gambling center.

Chaos' head snapped up to look at her with a small scowl.

She threw a few coins onto the table.

"We're leaving."

Chaos stayed put.

"It wasn't an offer."

Rolling his eyes at her, he pushed from his own chair, not bothering to pick up the cards from the floor and table. Not caring enough to give him a second glance, she pushed away and darted past the tables and occupied chairs as Chaos followed at her heels. Her mind was set on one destination- the docks at the mouth of Kinara Bay.

She swung open the door, ignoring the passing looks, as the cold wind bit at her face, and strode past the textile market, past the array of housing buildings, past a grocery market, past a boutique, and led Chaos into an alleyway.

"Where to?" He asked so nonchalantly as he sauntered into the shadows. He acted as if it was on a regular basis she rushed *away* from a gambling hall.

"The docks outside the capital."

"Taking a nice swim?"

Fate managed a scowl, and the feeling of falling enveloped her again.

***

Her boots were greeted by soft grass as the frigid sea wind supplied a chill she could feel in her bones. Salt coated the edge of her tongue as she blinked open her eyes to find Chaos peering at her. Ignoring his raised eyebrows, she looked beyond the shadows of the arching oak tree to the raging ocean beyond. The waters were several shades darker than the pale blue above, and several times more aggressive. Curling fists of waves slammed into water, dispersing at the sandy shore. It was a miracle the wood docks that fanned from the coastline were still holding. And visible, less than a fourth mile away lay the beginnings of Encima with its spires like spears to the air.

But besides all of that, she had come here for the three ships. The large and wide naval ships were multiple stories high staying stoically still as unwelcoming waves crashed into them. She knew how massive they really were, but to any spectators on shore, the far away ships seemed as small as rowboats. Above them flew bronze and cobalt flags- flags that had been set to disuse after Riqueza had conquered them -the colors splitting the rectangular shape into triangles. Between the two colors was an image of a sword point blade side down, its hilt fitted with a scale. A scale for justice. A hundred row boats dotted the waters, floating empty, following the water's current.

Fortem, a fallen country, had come to attack. But she was too late. Fortem's soldiers had already dispersed into the city.

And the noise of a bullet shattered through the air.

'Frank.' Fate mouthed the curse.

"Just to inform you," Chaos drawled at her back after a moment of shocked silence, "if they come nearer, you will be my shield."

It was clear he was annoyed about her abrupt exit. She didn't know why that was still on his mind. It was as if watching an attack on a capital city was nothing remarkable.

Her eyes fell to the city as she stepped out of the tree's drooping branches. It was ridiculous, she thought, attacking Riqueza, with its combined armies and extensive security. Their country had fallen to Riqueza, but that didn't stop the Rebellion.

Fortem's Rebellion soldiers stepped from the shadows, all with a determined expression plastered on their faces.

She knew how this was going to play out and still, no sympathy bloomed.

She swallowed.

Their fate was written this way and it was to play out. More humans would be born to Cadere. These losses weren't important. And yet....

She sneered at herself.

There was no use feeling pity when they would leave the world eventually.

"They won't come nearer." She said it with so much surety, she could feel Chaos behind her falter.

"They won't." She repeated, turning to face him, her voice calm, "Because *they'll* kill them all."

She didn't have to point for understanding to cross Chaos' face. The black uniforms lined with red and green at the shoulders, a blazing dragon over their heart as they discarded their posts within the grand city. They each carried a weapon, whether it was a rifle or a gleaming blade, and ran with undying loyalty in every step.

Riquezan soldiers.

She and Chaos did nothing as the city was devoured by smoke and Fortem men in blue and bronze were led away in chains. Red ran down the streets that day, poisoning the land with a defeat at the loss of hundreds.

Lives she could have saved.

CHAPTER THREE

RETRIBUTION

H e bit at the inside of his cheek, grimacing at the metallic taste.

It was a restless habit he'd recently acquired, usually reserved for when he was overwhelmed.

He was glad he had left Balance's cottage. He couldn't exactly think sanely while Fate argued endlessly, which was exactly why he should've followed in Death's footsteps and left earlier. He should've allowed himself time to accept their loss. More importantly, he should've allowed himself to *mourn*.

A part of him was terrified to admit her cessation, and a part of him was terrified to show them how he really felt.

After leaving the interior of the cottage and a quick discussion with Time, Retribution hadn't gone far. He couldn't force himself to speak with the Protectors again. He felt too hollow- too close to crumbling. He would have never guessed something like 'death' could happen to someone like *them*.

Retribution looked up and quickly scanned his surroundings, his heartbeat obnoxiously drumming in his ears. His eyes locked on the woods behind Balance's cottage. With a sigh, he pushed off the stone house and walked towards the trees. The sight of the canopy of greens made his stomach fall back into knots. Balance loved this forest. She would have spent every moment of every day there if she could.

If Retribution was in less stressful circumstances, perhaps he wouldn't have reacted so *poorly* to finding her motionless on the ground. His lips curled into a deep frown. This was Fate's fault. She should've warned them a long time ago, back when things could've been changed. Been avoided.

The green trees reached out wide over him, allowing a few rays of the warm sunlight to shine through. Birds and smaller critters skittered around the forest floor, rustling through bushes around him.

He wanted to forget it all.

The cessation of Balance.

The war.

Time's mission.

He was grateful to Time, of course. After all, Time was their creator. He had given them everything- existence, a purpose, a family- but, Time expected too much from him, so Retribution's weariness was somewhat justified.

Although, even *he* couldn't push the thought out of his mind that he was the true problem. Yes, Fate would have foreseen it, but with common sense, they all could have stopped the war long ago, especially him since he was the closest to Time.

He'd never understood Fate, or even Death's, dislike for the Creator. Not that Death had ever out right expressed his discomfort. Death always said that he liked Time, and appreciated his work, but he never stayed on the topic for too long. Fate on the other hand wouldn't hesitate to talk for hours about her disdain for the Creator. It was overwhelming.

Retribution wandered along the crumpled leaves littering the grounds.

He needed to see her. She cleared his head.

His mind pictured the scenery of Krasivaya. Wildly overgrown flowers and vines- a perfect hint of chaotic nature on a rocky bridge. Life had taken to inhabit the late queen of Krasivya's castle. The west side of the building had collapsed from the forces of Riqueza back when they had attacked Krasivya during the start of the war. Not that Life minded. The castle was magnificently large. Far too large for her to use. She gave the west side to nature. She had eagerly told Retribution how she had interwoven vines through the rubble.

He shut his eyes tightly. The floor abruptly disappeared beneath him. His feet slammed into new ground, his body tingling with the familiar feeling. Was this how Balance felt? Was this what a cessation felt like? As simple as teleporting? The image of Balance's sickly body dug into Retribution's mind. He felt frozen in place, clenching his knuckles. He gasped in a deep breath, forcing himself to step forward.

Retribution opened his eyes. He let out a breath and strode over the bridge. He stepped up to her engraved door and knocked on it.

Silence.

He breathed in shakily.

The doors opened heavily and Life's flushed face came into view, creased with lines of worry.

"Ret?" she whispered. She swallowed hard. "What happened?"

It had been a few weeks since he had come to her castle in Krasivaya. Retribution was focused on the exhaustion on Life's face.

"Nothing. Just wanted to check on you. Are you okay?" He whispered.

She smiled sadly, "Are any of us?"

Retribution cast his eyes aside, opting to stare at the wall.

"Come in," she said, as she turned around. He followed after Life's retreating form.

The castle had tall walls adorned with portraits of Krasivyan monarchs. Retribution always wondered why Life never took them down- to which she always responded, 'she appreciated the history.'

Retribution squinted as he turned a corner allowing the golden light to blind him momentarily. Daylight was the only thing lighting the stone castle. Krasivaya never lived to see the technological revolution, so at night, Life relied on candles.

Retribution turned another corner leading to a living space. A couch lay pressed against a tall window. In front of it was a circular coffee table. Retribution lowered himself onto the plush sofa.

"Sad… isn't it?" Life started, staring out the large window.

He moved his gaze to stare at Life. There were too many things to be sad about. Life handed Retribution her cup of tea and sat down next to him, her head ever so slightly leaning on his shoulder.

"Balance's cessation," She muttered, barely audible

He looked away from Life and nodded numbly. Life tilted her head to peer at him.

"You know, it's okay to take a break." She told him.

Retribution immediately shook his head.

"I know. You need to focus on your mission with Time, but only do what you can manage. Time will understand."

"Yes, I know I-" He paused. He wanted to tell her. He knew she would understand. He knew she wouldn't judge.

"I just have a lot on my mind."

He wouldn't drag her into his mess. He lazily threw his head back as she got more comfortable in the crook of his shoulder.

"Can I ask you something?" She questioned quietly.

Retribution nodded.

"What exactly happened to Balance? I thought we couldn't die."

He let out a long exhale and looked out the window again.

"I'm not entirely sure. I spoke to Time a while ago, wondering what would happen if she continued to get…worse. He said that the amount of violence and destruction is unnatural in the war, and it caused a heavy impact on Balance. It ate at her being. In simple terms, she faded because of a lack of balance in the world. The abominable consequences of the war." He couldn't breathe.

"I miss her." Life whispered.

"I know." His gaze flitted to look at her hand. "I know."

A part of him yelled to reach out and hold her hand, but he didn't give in.

She shook her head. "I feel so bad for Death."

Retribution couldn't- wouldn't begin to imagine what Death must be going through. His urge to hold Life's hand increased slightly.

"No one else can die. There has to be something we can do." She whispered.

He took a deep breath. Even if he wasn't mentally prepared to see the others yet, the mission came before any personal feelings. The short meeting with Time had just been to discuss a plan of action, but it was enough to, hopefully, fix the blow of Balance's loss. Fix the emptiness he felt.

"Yes." He looked down at Life. "We need to find Death."

***

The Kingdom of Lucror.

"Come on. Let's check his house first." Life said to him.

He nodded, following her through the roads, as she held his hand and guided him.

Night had long crept onto the streets of Lucror. The roads were grim and dark, streetlights illuminated a dull glow. Fog settled in, hovering over the top of the brick buildings, casting a cool breeze over the town square.

Death didn't live in the heart of the city. He had opted for a quiet life- or however quiet Lucror could get.

The pair walked quietly. They turned into a small, uphill, one way road.

"Do you think he'll be at home?" Retribution questioned.

"Where else would he be?"

He shrugs, "Balance's home?"

Life shook her head, "Everyone's trying to forget or distract themselves. I doubt that he would want to look around and see memories of them."

They came to a pause in front of Death's house.

They were met with the sight of a tall, dark stone building. The walls were crawling with thorned ivy. Death lived in a historic part of Lucror. Everywhere they turned there were old buildings that weren't renovated- aside from electricity of course. Lucror wouldn't hesitate to boast of its success in the electrical revolution.

Lucror was not the kingdom to start creating electricity and technology. However they were the first to quickly incorporate it. After all, Lucror was a kingdom of spies. They caught wind of the technological revolution and didn't hesitate to profit.

A dim light shone from the thick windows, and shadows of movement could be seen.

They climbed the creaky, wooden steps and glanced at each other briefly, before knocking on the wooden door.

No answer.

He sighed and cracked his knuckles again, ignoring Life's glum look. He closed his eyes.

His fingers tingled, tugging the visualized strings in his mind, giving the usual emergency meeting sign to the other Protectors.

Fate.

Chaos.

Death.

Retribution winced. He could feel an emptiness. The familiar call to Balance he normally sent never came.

Each thought of their name gave him a rush through his body and when he opened his eyes, they stood in front of him.

"So what about the attack- " Chaos started. Despite the exhilaration from the argument, the two looked worse for wear.

Fate gave him a murderous look, "Not now."

34

Retribution rolled his eyes. He couldn't care less what they bickered about; it seemed to be endless, anyway.

Death opened the door to his house and stared at the group.

He looked horrible. His face had a dull gray look to it. His eyes had slightly hollowed and his features had adopted a more gaunt look.

Life stepped towards Death, her hand reaching to clutch his. Death gripped onto Life's hand tightly. He leaned into Life as she whispered to him, though his expression was unreadable.

Death nodded as he stepped to the side, letting everyone in.

Death's house had always been slightly cluttered. He always insisted that the clutter sparked his imagination, though now, the state of his house was a mess.

Old letters, newspapers, discarded clothing, and who-knows-what littered the floors and desks.

Life sat next to Death on a brown leather couch while Fate and Chaos stood in front of them.

Thick silence spread through the group.

"You shouldn't have left." Retribution didn't realize he had said anything until the room turned to stare at him. Death slowly looked up at Retribution.

"You should have stayed so we could figure out what to do."

Life stared at Retribution, her eyes blown wide. Chaos' gaze flitted between Death and Retribution while Fate's gaze stayed trained on Death.

After a few seconds of tense silence Death opened his mouth.

"Please tell me you're joking."

Retribution narrowed his eyes, "Our first and foremost priority is the protection of Cadere and its people."

"Retribution, you may have a few honorary abilities as Time's second, but don't think you can lecture me about my *conduct*. Especially when it comes to my personal life." Death's

35

voice had changed into an unfamiliar sneer. With anger or distraught Retribution didn't know.

Retribution softened his voice. "Listen, Balance's cessation is horrid and should never have happened, but that's not a priority right now."

Chaos whistled quietly as Life flinched at Retribution's word choice.

He didn't know how to talk…'empathetically'. He was resorting to what he knew best- business- whether it was a great time to discuss it or not.

"Well, it's a bit too late for fixing the war is it not?" Death's voice came out deathly calm. He tore his gaze away from Retribution, looking up at Fate and Chaos. "I felt a larger than usual death toll today."

Fate curtly nodded, "There was an attack on Riqueza by Fortem."

Retribution blinked in surprise, "What?"

"An attack took place in Riqueza led by Fortem." She spoke slower, mocking his inability to understand.

"How do you know?" Life asked.

"We were in Riqueza when it happened," Chaos responded.

"Ah." Death clapped his hands together softly. "I was right. The war's worsening. How much longer until another one of us has our cessation?"

To the group's discomfort, he laughed. It rang of pure agony.

"Casualties?" Retribution whispered, the chill of the noise sharp against his spine.

"A lot." Chaos helpfully concluded.

"267." Death muttered.

"Frank-" He cursed quietly, "We need to figure out how to stop this-"

" Really? What an ingenious idea, Retribution," Fate snapped.

"Do we?"

All eyes turned to look at Death.

Death didn't look up. He nudged the carpet with his foot, watching as it rolled and unrolled.

Retribution's gaze moved to throw Fate a questioning look.

"I mean-" Death laughed bitterly, "What's the point anymore? Balance is gone." Death looked up to stare at Retribution. "And she isn't coming back."

He leaned back into the couch, "If there's no balance, then there's no resolution to the war. There is no reality in which we win."

Fate narrowed her eyes slightly before turning to look at Chaos.

Life shook her head, "No. No, we can fix this. This all happened for a reason. There is no balance on Cadere anymore, which is the reason Balance faded. But, if we bring peace back-"

"Balance comes back." Fate finished.

"That simple?" Death scoffed, his voice was so quiet that Retribution barely caught it.

Retribution nodded, stepping forward, "It was bound that conflict would arise. Balance was destined to be overthrown. Now we have to think about-"

"You think you're invincible, don't you?" A bitter smile curled onto Death's face. He turned to Chaos and Fate, "How much do you want to bet that justice will fall in six month's time?'

"That sort of thinking never got us anywhere, Death-."

"Oh, save your *mighty* speech for another time, Retribution." Fate snapped.

He scoffed in reply "We are wasting time! We need to act now."

"This isn't getting anywhere." Life announced. Retribution studied her face briefly, before dragging his gaze to the floor.

"Like you're doing anything to help." Fate scoffed.

"I'm doing the best I can, Fate." Life argued.

"Which is?"

Retribution's gaze hardened, "Fate-"

"We are the ones doing most of the work Retribution. All you're doing is galavanting around Riqueza with your idol, Time." She rolled her eyes, walking up towards him.

Retribution scoffed loudly, "*All I'm doing?*"

"You heard me."

Death abruptly stood up, "This conversation is ridiculous. A waste of time for me and for you all."

He roughly shoved past Retribution as he left the room in a tense silence, while the Protectors stared at his retreating figure. After a few seconds, the sound of a door slamming signalized Death's departure.

Retribution's fingers came to brace his temples, "Fate and Chaos, you two will go to Hikma and try to convince the president to create a new alliance with Lucror to take down Riqueza. We can't risk the cessation of anyone else. Deaths right, if Balance faded away due to the lack of harmony in Cadere, who's to say that someone else couldn't fade? We need to intervene."

Fate let out a sharp laugh, "Who put you in charge?"

Time.

He shook his head, "Do you have a better idea?"

Fate's lip curled at Retribution.

"Talk with the leaders of each country and settle this war." He added. "I will talk to Time and discuss further actions that we should take."

Fate turned to look out a window, over a stormy city, muttering something about Time.

Life stood up from the couch. "What can I do?"

"Find Death, I'm sure he could use someone to snap him back to reality."

She nodded.

Without another thought Retribution turned around, striding out of the room.

His gut churned. They were running in circles. There was no chance that two Protectors who looked to be in their early 20s would convince the kingdom rulers to create alliances. As for Death-

Retribution's lip curled.

Not that he was going to question Time's direct orders, but he needed to speak with him. He didn't know what he would say, but he knew he needed the guidance- the structure.

Retribution shut his eyes. He pictured Time in his mind. He sighed as the floor vanished below him

Chapter Four

DEATH

Death slammed the door, striding out of his house.

Blood pounded in his ears. He balled his hands up, fingers digging into his palms.

He tripped over a protruding stone, cursing under his breath.

Everything was too loud- too bright.

He looked around. Men and women with briefcases and bags alike rushed around, shoving past him. Children darted past his legs.

Death shook his head. His lip twitched downwards into a frown as another rough shoulder bumped past him. A tall man with an ugly sneer glared back at Death.

"Move. I don't have all day." Aiming a spit to the pavement next to Death, the man stormed off.

His head was spinning. The world was spinning. The world kept spinning. No matter what happened, it never stopped. Not for anyone, and certainly not for Death the Protector.

Did he expect it would stop for him? He frowned. Was he wrong to? This was the first cessation of a Protector. This wasn't supposed to happen. It was impossible.

Death trembled slightly. He tore his hand through his hair. He didn't realize when his vision blurred. Nor did he realize when he wasn't standing in Lucror anymore.

A warm breeze brushed past his hair. The sun kissed his cheek. A green, seemingly endless, field stretched out all around him. He heard the faint sound of water. Bliss surrounded him.

He froze.

He knew where he was.

It wasn't the tall structure that gave it away, but the berries.

Death inhaled deeply, shuddering slightly.

Oh, how he missed the berries. He missed Retribution walking in with a basket of them to share. He missed Balance baking them into pies. He missed seeing Life try coloring her hair with them. He missed seeing Fate and Chaos' clothing stained with them after a spontaneous wrestling match.

Wisps of grass tickled his ankles. The alluring smell of the berries dragged him forward. He could almost taste them melting in his mouth. His gaze flicked up, climbing higher and higher. Death's eyes widened in recognition.

A magnificent manor stood tall in front of him, welcoming him back. Tall vines of ivy wove their way through the cobblestone walls. A few stained glass windows that the six of them had once painted cast dancing rainbows on the grass.

Death felt his hand travel to rest on his forehead. His shoulders relaxed, welcoming the familiar wave of comfort.

Death wasn't on Cadere anymore. He was in a middle ground. He was in their old home.

Death had found the Altar. It had finally let him back.

He scanned his once home. He could perfectly recall him and Fate sparring in the far fields, him and Life playing board games in the large window, him watching Chaos and Retribution bickering near the statues, or him and Balance-

Death's smile fell.

He missed it. He missed all of them living harmoniously. He missed all of them living.

41

The Altar had been his haven. All of their safe spots. Until the day it wasn't.

Death perfectly remembered the look of desperation and panic on all the Protectors' faces when they had realized that they were locked out of their home, forbidden from returning. Yet here Death was– back where it all started.

Death turned his head, staring at a field of white figures. Statues.

The statues were what Death remembered the most. The way the marble carvings perfectly sculpted the most important moments in each of their lives. Like photographs.

Death stood in silence. Life's statue stood tall, her flowing hair abundant with flowers, mimicked perfectly by the marble. Her chin was raised, and her skin seemed to glimmer like the sun. A subtle smile graced her features and her hand opened outward towards him.

Death stared.

He had always wondered what phenomenon caused these statues to exist in the Altar in the first place.

He had always had a fear- a childish fear, in Retribution's words- that one day, the Altar would simply cease to exist; Or just not let him back which obviously ended up happening- for a couple centuries, he corrected himself.

Death couldn't fathom how the Altar had only now let him back. He pushed the thought away, slowly dragging one foot in front of the other, forcing himself to tear his eyes away and walk forward.

Retribution.

The statue of Retribution stood tall, a challenging look in his marble face. The marble Retribution gripped the hilt of a dagger firmly in his hand, his stance defensive.

Death raised his chin slightly, his nails dug red crescents into his palms. He tilted to the right, peering over to the next statues.

Fate.

The marble Fate seemed to have the same air of superiority surrounding her as the real Fate did. Her hands were curled into fists, always ready to jump into the action. She stood tall with a taunting smirk on her face. Death continued walking.

Chaos.

Needless to say, it was chaos. The Marble Chaos had a teasing grin. His hair was thrown haphazardly over his forehead and his wrist bore his signature watch.

Death moved forward.

Death.

He stared at himself, his eyebrows pushed together. He had changed. The marble Death had his shirt sleeves pushed up to his elbows. His hands were crossed and there was a grin on his face. He looked... Death couldn't recognize himself. He turned away, walking forward. He froze.

Balance.

She looked beautiful.

Death couldn't help but gawk at the statue. The marble Balance had her eyes closed. Her silky hair was braided up into an ornate bun, decorated with flowers.

Death felt a wave of sickness overtake him... he missed her.

She was everything.

Was.

Death winced at how easily his mind switched to past tense. Only a few days ago they were laughing together. Whispering secrets into each other's ears at meetings. Now he was referring to her in the past tense.

Death felt bile rise in his throat. He ripped his eyes away from Balance's figure, walking towards the Altar pond.

The Altar looked like a canvas. Red, orange and purple hues of the sunset bounced off the pond painting the grounds like fire. Blues and greens from tainted windows reflected onto the

43

ground like an ocean of fluid tears, dancing with the destruction of fire.

A perfect *balance.*

Death bent down, dipping his hand into the crystal water. His jaw unclenched as he cupped the cool water. Reaching forward he gently plucked out a white lotus. Tenderly, he shook some of the water out of the roots. Death walked back to Balance's statue, rolling the velvety flower in between his fingertips.

He stopped in front of Balance. He leaned up and placed a gentle kiss on the forehead of the cool marble sculpture. With nimble fingers he delicately placed the flower in her opened hands.

With that he ,tore his eyes away from the marble figure, and walked towards the familiar, welcoming doors of the Altar's manor.

CHAPTER FIVE

FATE

Mahana was a facade. The stone streets were brushed with varied colors and hues, revealing liveliness. If Fate hadn't known better, she wouldn't have noticed the equally prevalent mischief underneath.

The citizens had an identical feel in their expressions. If one were to find themselves in a good-natured conversation with a Mahanan, they would later be horrified to discover their wallet and any valuable items gone. A kingdom of loyalty and thieves, and to Fate, it was home.

As Fate and Chaos made their way through the crowded bar, people stared. Not because they were recognized, no. People stared at their apparel. Fate wore a traditional Mahanan lehenga, the yellow-orange blouse short and the deep maroon skirt twisting with gold tendrils pulled high, and accented with a scarf over one shoulder. Authentic gold jewelry was clasped against her chest and dangled from her ears. Contrasting her traditional attire, Chaos wore a suit, the angles sharp and perfectly ironed, adorned with his silver watch on his left wrist.

They *looked* expensive.

"Do you think they're drooling yet?" Chaos whispered without subtlety as they slid onto the high bar stools at the counter.

Fate rolled her eyes, "Why are we this dressed up again?"

"Oh please, like you don't revel in the attention."

"Luck will have graced us if they decide not to kill us instantly and pocket our valuables." Fate pushed her hair behind her shoulder, her eyes focused on the wall. Bottles of different size and height, filled with liquid ranging in color, hung in an up-down pattern. The dim illumination provided enough lighting for the bottles to reflect the scene behind them, including the bartender nearly prancing around the packed round tables to serve them.

Fate felt something looming at the back of her mind, casting a large shadow over her thoughts. Something weighing on her shoulders. Something she brought them here to escape from. But it was impossible to escape from her tie to their planet, Cadere. Their plan to save the kingdoms of Cadere from colonization and destruction was inevitable, and much as she pushed it from her mind, she knew it was destined to occur. It was what she was *made* to do. Protect the people of Cadere from themselves.

But if they were to cease the war, she wasn't going in blind.

"Do we have a plan, or not?"

Chaos, sensing she wasn't referring to their alcohol intake, groaned. "When have we ever needed a plan? Just appear in-"

"In where?"

"And speak to their ruler-"

"Tell them what? As who? Two young adults with no status?"

"Convince them to attack Riqueza and force Casimir to yield his own attacks."

"That's a horrible plan. Riqueza has the most resources so any mortal with an ounce of common sense wouldn't agree. Hikma is never involved, Lucror stays in defense, Mahana is allied to Riqueza, Fortem and Krasivaya are in ruins and their people are conquered, and the people in the Aontaithe Isles fall when their home country falls." Fate hissed, keeping her eyes on the granite counter to keep from drawing attention from the incoming bartender.

She wondered if he would notice that she excluded Heping- Balance's kingdom- from the list.

"So it is." Chaos turned, his back now facing the counter.

Fate caught his smirk as he gave a wave to the bartender. She turned her head to see the bartender making his way around the counter, ignoring the others waiting. His lips were curled into a subtle victorious smile as if he had won the lottery, but was expected to keep the news quiet. His black Mahanan kurta shimmered in the mellow lighting, reminding Fate of the night sky behind the open door of the bar.

"Susandhya," He greeted in Mahanan. *Good Evening.* "Your days are going well, yes?"

"Quite." Chaos replied airily.

As if the weight of the planet was no longer on their shoulders.

As if Balance's body hadn't faded.

As if Death hadn't run off.

As if tensions between their group of protectors couldn't be cut with a knife.

Fate nodded, her lips graced with a placid smile.

"Hm, and what would you both like?"

Fate turned back to Chaos and he spoke, "Anything."

The bartender grinned. He turned to the back wall, reaching for and unclasping a tall bottle of liquid the color of Fate's blouse.

"I will not be surprised if we never wake from those drinks." Fate straightened, a smirk playing on her lips.

"Your country really is ruthless, isn't it?"

"It gives me pride."

Fate and Chaos watched as the bartender reached for a precarious tower of glasses and grabbed two. He poured the drinks, and pivoted to face them. Placing the drinks, which she guessed was scotch, so elegantly on the counter, he strode away to serve the others.

Fate stared at the amber color in the tumbler glasses, reminding her of Balance's eyes-

Suddenly the bar seemed like a cage, nauseating, tight —*too tight.* Her heart beating rapidly in her ears, Fate turned abruptly and fixed her gaze on someone she had noticed earlier while walking into the bar.

Fate watched the Mahana woman, her face flustered for the wrong reason. The woman sat on a stool, her hair long and sharp to the small of her back, dark like the color of kajal. She didn't seem to be drinking anything, but instead gazing through the window lost in thought.

Chaos' attempt to grab Fate's gaze was futile. She continued watching the woman like an engrossing play.

"Go on, speak to her."

Fate could hear the smirk in his voice.

"Fraternizing with humans should be done on a minimum-only when necessary." Fate mocked Retribution's words, relieved he had not questioned her off behavior.

"You're right."Chaos nodded solemnly, then proceeded to say, "You speak to her, or I'll do it."

"Not a chance."

"An immortal being of control, scared of a mortal? Who would have known?"

"As if, Chaos. It's only impolite; she already seems properly situated."

Chaos shrugged.

Fate, turning back to the counter, finally picked up her drink, swirling it. Looking away from the tumbler glass uneasily, she caught a wry smile on Chaos' face.

"Is it good?" He asked as she sipped the malty liquid. The cool liquid ran down her throat, bringing her out of her stupor.

"No." Fate placed the alcohol back on the counter. She knew Chaos wasn't going to drink any. He didn't exactly have a great history with drinking.

"I've been pondering our *dilemma.*" Chaos grinned, a lopsided grin that only meant his next words would be ludicrous.

Fate narrowed her eyes at him.

"Solution one- we kill Retribution." He paused, then spoke hurriedly, "That was the only solution I've created. Any strategies?"

Our dilemma seemed to mean the work they'd have to put in to bring Cadere to peace.

"Who? Me?" Fate feigned offense, "You truly believe me to be so- so traitorous?"

She pushed her drink to the front of the counter, then dropped her voice to a conspiratorial whisper, mocking Chaos' absurdity.

"His weakness- a being with hair the color of dried grass, ironically, having the power to revive dried grass."

Chaos gave a wicked smile, "Time may also be an option. I can't decide which one Retribution's more in love with, Life or Time."

"Hadn't you heard his speech to Balance and Death the other decade? 'Our existence has no place for love.'" It was true, he had said that, but he had come around, not without an earful, however.

Chaos snorted at her mimicking tone, "Time and Life didn't reciprocate his feelings, did they?"

Fate turned away against the wall to hide her grin. When she turned back, she shrugged at his amused expression as he raised his glass in mock toast, "Perhaps they had no room on the bed together."

Chaos sputtered. He slid the glass back and forth on the table. He shook his head as if he had had enough of this conversation. Which she knew he hadn't.

As their conversation slowed, she could hear the soft static of a radio playing in the background. *"Riqueza's government is chillingly violent. Forty peace protesters were executed in Time's Square today-"*

49

Fate's heart jolted. When had that happened? Why had she not known?

A setback.

It *had* to be a mistake.

No, no, no, no.

Her hands shot up to her head, as if searching for her power. Fear spiked up her back as her hands dropped at her side.

Knowing came so easily to her- like breathing- and she reveled in it. That way she was in control. There were no surprises. She could play the future like a game of parieur. The loss of it while in presence of the other protectors was barely tolerable. But with the humans...

There was no possible way it could abandon her now.

Her head pounded.

Her eyes burned.

She felt a hand on her shoulder.

Her ears rang.

Breathe.

The hand shook her lightly.

Was she asleep?

A nightmare.

A muffled voice cut through the fog.

"Date."

The date?

183,729 days since creation.

"Fate!"

Her name, her name, her name.

The hand dropped.

It abandoned her too.

A sob bubbled up her throat.

BREATHE.

And, for once, she complied.

She took a breath.

The sharp, bitter smell of alcohol burned her throat. Her eyes focused on a boy. His eyebrows were pinched in worry. His skin was gold, a kind that wasn't tanned from the sun's harsh rays. His hair was a mess of chaotic curls.

Chaos.

The ringing in her ears faded at the sight of him.

He wasn't gone. He hadn't abandoned her.

Not like *she* did.

Not like Fate had abandoned her duty to Balance.

Of course.

It was a punishment.

She had a last chance with her ability after Balance died and she did *nothing* as innocent people fell at the hands of war. So it hadn't been a fluke when her knowledge about the Rebellion's plans hadn't come to her naturally.

Another breath. This time she could feel her white-knuckled hands twisted in her skirt. Her hands clawed into her thighs.

Her vision whipped around the room.

She wasn't asleep.

She was still at the bar.

The moonlight spilled from the display window, the booming laughs echoed off the ceiling, clinks of glasses rang high, the voice of the bartender obnoxiously flirting with some woman on the opposite side of the counter rose above all the other conversations.

She felt a cool hand on hers. She glanced down to see her hand trembling against her knee, Chaos' hand over it, a futile attempt to stop her terror.

It was gone.

Her power was gone.

And if she wanted it back, she'd need to prove her ability was in good hands.

To whom, she didn't know.

But she knew how- and there was only one way.
She'd have to bring back Balance
And to do that, she'd have to end the war.
Fate fixed her eyes on Chaos' horrified expression. Her voice speared through their silence, frigid and sharp like ice.
"Get up. We're going to the capital."

***

"You've been prone to fits recently."
"How kind of you."
Their voices were the only sounds that carried through the cool midnight breeze. She could hear Chaos' indignation at not explaining her recent outburst. She had instead slammed crumpled dhan, the Mahanan currency, on the counter next to their unfinished drinks and stalked out of the bar as Chaos followed in an attempt to match her pace. She had given him a brief layout of her plan on the streets and dragged him to Naseeb, the capital, and appeared right before the royal castle's grounds.
"Are you going to tell me why you've had an amazing revelation about having good morals and trying to stop the war?" Chaos drawled as she plotted the castle's grounds from their hiding place behind a couple measly bushes and a stick of a tree. She stiffened at his words. Did he know?
No. It was impossible.
"It was our mission." She spoke carefully, not daring to glance back at him.
Chaos snorted. He didn't say more. She exhaled softly in relief.
"There is a representative meeting tonight, we'll enter when they leave for intermission."
She turned to him as she spoke, only seeing Chaos' eyes glinting beside her. It was unusually dark; the moon seemed to have hid behind a blanket of fog.

Fate strained her eyes, peering around the line of castle guards, protecting each entrance. Lights as bright as the sun spilled from windows around the castle, leaving the white castle with a diaphanous glow. The castle was made of white stone, embellished with gold borders around windows and openings. It seemed to spread forever, and its height made Fate nauseous only glancing at it. It was majestic; turrets spiked like multiple crowns above the castle. There was no mistaking royalty lived in Naseeb.

"Are you checking the time?" Fate demanded.

"Do you think I am?"

"There is a reason you always wear a watch, yes?"

"One minor issue, I cannot see the watch."

"Teleport near the royal castle and check under their ridiculous blazing lights."

Chaos groaned, disappearing. In seconds, Chaos reappeared beside her.

"This is tiring. I'd like to be sleeping right now."

"The time?"

"One minute past the outset of their intermission."

Fate shot him a glare, "See that corridor? We go to those rooms on the side. This way no one notices our sudden appearance."

Chaos peered at where she pointed, "The washrooms?"

Fate gave him a pointed grin, knowing he couldn't see.

"We have no disguise." Chaos glanced down at the suit he had worn to the bar.

"Why else would we be breaching Queen Aahi's security? Besides, I said I had a plan, didn't I?" Fate snapped.

Ignoring the scowl she could tell Chaos was throwing at her, the feeling of falling enveloped her, dropping her feet against tile. Her eyes flicked open, the harsh light a burning difference from the endless black. As she took in the washroom stall, reaching for the metal clasp holding the door shut, a body materialized beside her. Fate flinched slightly, not expecting him.

"Oh, I'm in the women's washroom." Chaos blinked his eyes, and threw Fate an appalled expression.

Fate's eyes narrowed, "You can only teleport somewhere you've been in or can visualize."

"Mhm." Chaos smiled innocently.

"You aren't going to get any men's uniforms here." Her voice came out calmer than she felt.

"Maybe someone in a masculine uniform will walk in. Will one?" Chaos shot her a hopeful expression.

Her finger curled into her palms planning her next words carefully, "No, Chaos. Now leave before someone walks in."

He glared at her while mumbling, "How was I to know which one was the men's?"

He departed swiftly after.

To be fair, she had just guessed as well.

The washrooms were quite some distance from the representative meeting room. Which meant the one of few who ventured far enough, either to use the washrooms or to splash frigid water on their face to keep from feeling drowsy, could be a lucky victim. Why they were conversing so late at night was absurd to her.

She carefully unhatched the lock of the stall, swinging the light blue door open. Her eyes fell on a mirror that hung over the opposing wall, right above a line of taps, and she frowned, patting down a stray strand of hair. Remembering what she came for, Fate turned to the washroom's entrance. And she waited.

Anyone could come through that door, at any time.

All she could do was wait and hope.

And she hated it.

Her stance stiffened at a ready position. Her hands itched at her side, wishing for the daggers she had always kept tucked at her hips. That was before she was accustomed to her power- also when she had just preferred their security- but that was centuries ago.

Her lips quirked into a soft smile. It had been so long since she had done something so exhilarating that wasn't winning a game of parieur. Well, it was exhilarating only when her ability was in disuse.

However 'exhilarating' it felt to be trapezing around without the constant knowledge of every being's decisions, she would go insane another day without her ability, much less an eternity.

It was an addiction. The more she grabbed control, the more at loss she would be without it.

That was what it was. She didn't feel amiss merely because she was devoid of her power. It was because she felt human. What made her who she was, what made her the powerful being they worshiped, was gone.

She was just like them. Forced to make decisions just as they would. Feeling the pull of addiction as humans did. It felt so trapping. This space between the past and the future was all she could reside in.

Fate swallowed her clawing emotions, dusting off the side of her maroon skirt.

Minutes passed of her eyes boring into the polished wooden door that separated the corridor and the washroom. Thankfully, seconds before she resorted to demolishing the washroom, the door swung open.

A young woman about Fate's presented age strode in, her hands wrapped around a large textbook. Thick midnight hair was cut to her shoulders, resting on a rich purple blazer. Over the blazer's left side was the Mahanan flag decorated with two swords on one side, two on the other, and one straight through the middle. In the center was the face of a tiger and forming a ring around its head were two snakes.

Fate's heart pounded in her ears as the woman raised her eyes to glance at her.

Fate offered her a tilted smile, "Could you help me with this zipper?"

Hesitance flashed through the woman's dark eyes, but she placed her textbook on the counter, walking over to Fate.

"Oh! You're a representative? From what district?" Fate gushed, as she cocked her head to urge the woman to the zipper at the back of her blouse.

"North-west." The representative seemed slightly more pleased, "Who are you?"

She glanced at Fate's lehenga, noticing it wasn't akin to the blazer she wore.

"Invitation from Queen Aahi. General's niece." Fate gave a sheepish smile, "May have gotten a bit lost."

"No worries. The first time here, I swear to the others I almost ended up in the Queen's quarters." The representative's hands were now sliding down the back of Fate's blouse to find the zipper.

Fate could hear confusion in the representative's voice when she spoke, "It's already zipped."

A grin flashed across Fate's face. The representative was just a scholar. Scholars were the only Mahanans incapable of misdemeanors or anything remotely deceptive. It made her job easier than it should have been.

Her leg swept under the representative's feet. The representative shouted as she fell, twisting to land on her shoulder which resulted in another startled cry of pain. Fate twisted to the representative on the floor, dropping to her level. She placed a knee on the woman's abdomen, sticking out her bottom lip as she loomed over the woman's trembling frame.

"You'll forget when you wake up." She spoke in a placating tone, as she whipped her hand at a nerve in the woman's neck. Within seconds, the representative was unconscious.

Fate scoffed. Nothing she did today could be traced back to her; she had no DNA, nor did she have any identification.

After taking a few deep breaths and watching the slight rise and fall of the woman's chest, she proceeded to peel the uniform from the woman's body, undressing her and dressing herself. Not to scare the woman when she woke, she fitted her own outfit, that was now a crumpled heap next to the woman's undressed figure, on the representative. After dressing her, Fate winced, dragging the unconscious body to the far wall, leaning her against a stall. As soon as everything was in place, she brushed off the uniform, glancing at herself in the mirror.

Frowning, she checked the pockets.

The woman's ID was missing.

She *needed* that ID.

"Frank." She cursed. She gave one last look at the woman's unconscious body, knowing she would wake soon.

Done with her recent abundance of misfortunes, Fate pushed the door open with her side, as she burst into the corridor. She blinked at the opposing wall that reflected her image. A glass window. She concluded it would have been pleasing to look through...at any other time of day.

She continued walking, following the faint human voices.

She turned multiple corridors, growing increasingly annoyed, eyes searching, until-

The corridor to her left was packed with representatives, chatter filling the air, their matching purple suits making them surprisingly difficult to tell apart. She noticed most of Mahana's representatives were of Mahanan heritage, but those with backgrounds from other kingdoms were scrambled in the mix. They still had one thing in common; they were scholars. Pocketing a badge would be almost *too* easy.

Forcing her expression into wide eyes and a saccharine smile that could have dripped sugar, Fate strode through the representatives. Her eyes inconspicuously ran through their uniforms, hoping for a sign of a badge. At last, they fell on a young representative, standing near the middle of the corridor, a blue ribbon showing from one of the suit's pockets. Her hair, in raven curls, draped over her face which seemed to be shoved in a textbook.

Continuing her brisk strides, Fate dodged the others, heading for the representative. Passing by the woman, Fate's shoulder brushed the textbook she held. It fell with an echoing sound, loud as a clap of thunder, but the dropping of textbooks seemed to be normal; hardly anyone stopped to look. Turning around the woman's side in feigned horror, Fate's hand slipped swiftly into the suit's pockets, gripping the badge and slipping it in her own pocket as the representative dropped to gather her textbook.

"Oh! I'm quite sorry!" Fate leaned in to the representative, her hand on her chest and her face a facade of concern.

The few representatives watching had their eyes on the representative on the ground. She stood, her delicate face flushed and she shut the book, placing it under an arm to her side.

"No worries." She assured Fate, her eyes shifting away after a brief eye
contact.

"You are not hurt, are you?" Fate frowned, her eyes still forced wide.

"No, no." The representative said. At this point the others had trained their focus on other things. Offering a small sheepish smile, Fate walked away at a brisk pace hoping to find Chaos, but not without her lips twisting into a smirk. *Scholars.*

She found herself at where she began after continuous turns: the washrooms. She leaned against the walls by drinking fountains, tapping her feet impatiently. She swore she could hear a clock in her mind ticking as she stood.

Fate's head whipped at a muffled terrified scream coming from the mens washroom. She rolled her eyes and barged through the door.

"I only need your badge...and your uniform." Chaos' reason echoed through the washroom as a young representative gripped the walls as he fit himself in a corner. The man frantically glanced at the mirror, releasing another shrill scream, upon seeing Fate. He seemed as if he would render unconscious even without their assistance.

"Oh, Frank, " Chaos rolled his eyes, his hands flying in the air.

Fate scowled at Chaos, constructing a spontaneous plan. She disappeared and reappeared beside the representative. Tilting her hand, she whipped it at his neck. Instantly, the representative's eyes rolled back, and he dropped at Fate's feet, laying sprawled on the tiled flooring.

"Do you not remember a single move from the years we spent learning combat?"

"I tried the diplomatic approach."

"You know it's quite noticeable trying to steal clothing from a conscious man's body, yes?"

Chaos leaned over the man's body, shooting her a look that was equal parts amused and annoyed, pulling on the man's blazer and leaving his own over the representative's dress shirt. Why hadn't *she* worn a suit?

He pulled the bright blue badge from the man's neck and slipped it over his own.

And as Fate walked over to place her hand over the man's forehead, pulling the memory from his mind, Chaos straightened, "What now?"

Fate swallowed her shaking desire to cease the war at this moment as she stood and glanced at Chaos. She took too long debating whether her earlier back-up plan was worth pursuing. On one hand, more than half of the Fortem Rebellion's men had recklessly attacked Riqueza so the group must have been heavily impacted. On the other hand, she had *lost* her powers and she needed a solution. Fast.

There was no absolute way she was trusting *Chaos* with diplomacy after the stunt he had pulled today. *Clearly,* he had no idea what diplomacy meant. Which meant *she* had to ally the countries, and he would try reeling in the Rebellion. Whether this was a back-up plan or one to support the Hikman and Lucrian alliance against Riqueza, she wasn't quite sure. She just knew it needed to work.

"We'll split ways. I have a job for you. Then I head to Hikma."

As Chaos frowned in protest, she wondered if he would ever understand that she had decided to follow the idea she shut down earlier about allying the kingdoms. She smirked as she felt her surroundings blur.

"What job? *Fate?*"

Fate ignored him. She'd explain soon enough. She was more focused on the horrid excitement building.

They were going to save the world. She would be fixed. She just had to wait until dawn.

CHAPTER SIX

Life

Before the First War, the tensions in Krasivaya were already high. The people hated their government. The young queen was corrupt and powerful. Perhaps that's why Riqueza decided to annex them first. The people of Krasivaya never cared too much for controlling forces. Talk of overthrowing the queen quickly spread, so the Krasivyan government took precautions. In the lowest room of the castle the late queen hid an arsenal filled with one of the world's first bombs and firearms.

It ended up being used but not for its intended purpose. Late one summer night Riquezan forces attacked with no warning. Krasivya put up a fight, but they weren't stupid. They had no time to prepare, they knew they were going to die, so they decided to die with some dignity.

Before the Queen was captured by the Riquezan forces, she ordered that the room be blown up.

She would rather her subjects die than have the castle fall into the hands of Riqueza.

Life blinked at her weathered castle. There were more vines than walls at this point. The castle was almost completely caved in. It was a wonder how she managed to live there.

The demise and discord. The destruction of the kingdom and of the Krasivyan castle that had become her home after the Altar had evicted them.

Tree trunks lay on the ground, restricting passageway through the never-ending trails of dirt and pebbles.

She frowned. It felt like the world was spinning too fast, and she just wanted it to stop. Memories replayed in her mind of the past couple of days. Balance, Fate, Death, Ret... she felt anger course through her veins. She was furious with *everything*. More than that she was scared. Death was right. Anyone of them could be next.

She shook her head. In times like these she often wished she was more like Fate. Strong enough to stand up for her opinions. Strong enough to stay alive.

She reached her hand up to grab onto a tree trunk to hoist herself over a fallen stump. She continued to follow the trail, a part of her wanting it to never stop so she could wander till her limbs constricted in.

Birds chirped in the distance. She kept her gaze forward. She found her mind drifting to Balance.

The scene replayed, everyone's faces ridden with disbelief. Silence filled the room as Balance faded, turning a sickly shade of gray in the process.

She remembered Death's trembling form, hovering over Balance. It was unbearable to think about. She felt her vision go slightly blurry. She wanted to curl up and cry on the forest bed, releasing all the built up pressure in one loud scream. She let out a long breath and sat down on a nearby log.

She knew her 'task' was virtually impossible. If Death didn't want to be found, he wouldn't, and she had a sneaking suspicion that Retribution knew that as well. Nevertheless, Retribution and Time may be sending her in circles, but that didn't change the fact that she still needed to find him.

She clenched her eyes shut. She felt her jaw unclench and her shoulder relax. She felt a sweet breeze rustle past her hair. It smelled too sweet for her forest. Confused, she opened her eyes.

Her jaw dropped. A sense of awe washed over her.

"How-" she started. A bird whizzed past her ear, chirping gleefully.

She absorbed every little, familiar detail about the place she never thought she would find again. She wasn't in the narrow little dirt trail anymore, instead she was in the most alluring place she ever laid eyes on. Marble statues stood overlooking the gardens of greenery. She noticed rugged stone paths that wound around each statue. The place felt ancient. More ancient than she could ever process. She made her way to the first couple statues near her.

"How?"

All she knew is that she wasn't on Cadere anymore.

Life along with the other Protectors had once lived at the Altar. Before them, Time inhabited the manor.

One day they tried to get back and the Altar refused. Death always said that their once home had a funny way of making the Protectors see that they needed to grow outside of the safety net.

Life's eyes caught a statue on her right.

The statues were there even when she had lived there, but there were many more now. The marble figures represented the important and not so important moments in their lives.

She exhaled sharply and made her way over to the statue with her features. She studied her own statue, trying to take it all in. Her hand was stretched forwards. She looked elegant and confident, nothing like how she currently felt. The white marble was slightly cracked in the ends of her hair, falling in waves over her shoulders.

Where was she now?

Where was Balance?

Her shoulders drooped and she tore her gaze away from the statue of her and looked in the other direction. The opposite of Life's statue stood Death's marble figure, his stern expression with his arms folded. She felt her face break into a small smile.

"Life?"

Her head whipped around at the sound. Her jaw dropped. Death stood behind her. His face was no longer gaunt, the eyebags had disappeared from under her eyes, yet Life could still see the mourning clear in his demeanor. The caved in posture, the glazed over eyes...

Maybe she wasn't completely hopeless in her task.

She took a few steps toward him.

Life's brows drew together, "You've changed so much."

She shook her head, "It's only been a day?"

Death's voice came out steady, "Healing works differently here. You know that."

She did know that. She couldn't even count how many times her broken bones or scraped knees mended in just days. She didn't know that mental wounds counted.

He sat down at the base of one of Chaos' statues, "Feels strange, doesn't it?"

"What feels strange?" She asked, crouching down beside him.

"Everything... the war, this-" he gestured around the Altar field.

"Balance-" for the first time during their interaction, Death's voice faltered.

Life's brows creased. The two of them were always close, no matter how ironic it was that Life and Death would walk side by side together. They fell into a silence that was only interrupted by a few birds chirping and the familiar frogs croaking by the pond a few meters beyond them. In this moment, silence said more than any words could. He stared down at the ground as she studied his fidgeting hands.

"What will you do?" she finally asked, breaking the stillness.

He took a deep breath before replying. "I haven't decided yet."

Life knew him better. He wanted to be alone- grieve alone. She didn't blame him, but she also didn't want to face Retribution's subtle annoyance towards everyone.

She frowned. She was supposed to find Death and tell Retribution. She cringed slightly. She couldn't tell him now. Death was healing. Retribution would just throw a wrench in his efforts.

"You have to come sooner or later though, Retri-" she tried saying before Death's hands abruptly stopped fidgeting at the name. She fell silent.

"We can bring her back once the war finishes," she said, a glint of optimism in her tone.

"Don't give me false hope, Life." He swallowed. "I know she won't. I've accepted it."

"I'm sorry…" She quietly told him. "About everything…"

"Don't be. It's no one's fault. We are all mourning."

She looked around the room once more, noticing the vines and willow trees dancing with the breeze. She rested her pale hands onto Death's. She felt his muscles relax.

She shut her eyes. When she suddenly felt cold she knew she could open her eyes again. The familiar twisting trail welcomed her back. She brushed off her clothes and sighed as she started making her way back to the castle.

***

Hikma.

One of the two kingdoms that hadn't been annexed by the allied Mahana and Riqueza.

It felt bright and alive as people busily hurried by her. The humid air plastered her hair to her skin. She saw the little market place that engulfed the place in all of its different smells. One thing she appreciated the most was how they managed to not let the war stop their everyday lives. It reminded her of when things were normal. It reminded her of everything she had.

Had.

She shook her head. She was here to distract herself, not worry even more about the war.

She smiled at the people in the square, the children running around and giggling at each other.

Life's smile flickered. Life often found herself wishing she was a mortal. Being a Protector was exhausting despite all their autopilots doing most, if not all, of the work.

When The Altar had kicked them out the Protectors all had the same fear: *what if the autopilots stopped working?* The population was too great to manage without the autopilots.

They wouldn't break.

They couldn't break.

Yet, it was exhausting. She sighed and continued her walk to the warm sidewalks that guided her throughout the city of Azhar, the Capital of Hikma.

"Pastries! Fresh Pastries!"

Life tilted her head to look at a raggedy man sitting behind a makeshift booth.

It wasn't like Protectors needed to eat to survive, but Life didn't mind indulging in a sweet treat.

"How much?" Life asked as she made her way to the raggedy man behind the food cart.

"Twenty Naqud." He replied, monotonously holding the pastries in his hand.

"Twenty? That's a little much, don't you think, sir?"

"It's twenty or nothing, madam. I don't have all day." He told her in a thick accent. She pulled out the twenty in the small pocket of her white dress.

"Here." She gave him the money and in return got a few baked pastries, smelling strongly of fruity syrup.

The man grinned for the first time during their interaction.

"Sayih." he sneered.

Tourist.

She rolled her eyes and turned around, making her way downtown to the heart of Azhar, munching on the creamy pastries as she studied the people around her. It took around twenty minutes to walk to the busy central streets.

She looked up and was greeted with the huge sights of buildings and trees lined with sidewalks and roadways. Carriages and horses galloped alongside motorized vehicles through the streets.

Hikma was currently in the midst of their vehicular revolution. Horse and carriages were now automobiles and steam engines.

Life remembered when people used to greet each other warmly at cross roads. Everyone was paranoid after the war started.

After a few lefts and a sharp right, she soon found herself in the midst of the city and was greeted by the sight of a white, marble-bound fort of the president. There was a border wall, decorated with silver specks, gleaming against the marble. Nine guards stood at attention in front of the wall. Her eyes wandered away from the soldiers and found itself settled on the huge pole proudly waving Hikma's blue and yellow flag.

Life smiled at the building.

Hordes of people in groups walked around, staring in awe at the building.

Hikma was proud of their presidential fort. It was a must visit place for tourists, and she decided that for a day she would be a tourist.

Life froze, frowning. She squinted her eyes at two new figures standing in front of the fort stairs, merely three yards from where she was. Were they there before?

The pair dressed in unforgettable dark purple and blue blazers. They were in Mahanan colors.

She tilted her head. Mahanans were allied with the Riquezans. What were they doing here?

One of the figures turned around.

Life's eyes widened.

"Frank." She cursed, lunging behind a tall oak tree.

Chaos scanned his surroundings then disappeared before reappearing next to Fate. With a slight nod from Fate, they walked up the stairs.

"Excuse me, what's your name?"

Life's eyes widened.

They were stopped. Life leaned over the curve of the tree to peer at Fate, Chaos, and the guards glaring at them.

Fate calmly flashed her ID card. The guard in the middle glanced at the guards at his sides before he grunted and let them in.

Life bounded up the steps as soon as Fate and Chaos disappeared through the door. Just as she was about to step through the wide double doors a guard stepped in front of her.

"No tourists allowed today."

Life blinked at him. "Oh... Oh no, I'm not a tourist, sir. I'm actually..." She desperately scanned her surroundings. A man in yellow and blue stepped out of a car.

"I'm a representative! For Hikma." She grinned nervously at the guard's unimpressed look.

"No tourists." He concluded curtly.

She needed to get in. She could help.

Life bit her lip as she turned around and walked down the steps and instead opted to walk towards the pavement that surrounded the walls.

She couldn't be near the front in fear that the guard would recognize her and arrest her. She walked along to the back of the building. Soldiers guarded every side. She pretended to gape in admiration at the building everytime a soldier's gaze trained onto her, not wanting to draw any attention to herself.

This was wrong. She shouldn't be breaking into a highly protected presidential building, but she couldn't stop herself. It was as if her body had a mind of its own.

Her eyes traced every single wall for an entrance all around the building. She scanned the doors that lined up in the very back of the fort, hidden by the shadows of the buildings and trees.

She tilted her head. There were no guards positioned at the doors. The entries were presumably what the help used to get in. She walked up to them and tried to open them all one by one.

Locked.

Her brows furrowed.

Now what? She asked herself, looking around for guards.

Suddenly, the doorknob turned and the door flung open, with a maid's back propping up the door, while she hauled the bag of trash behind her.

"Frank," Life cursed quietly. She quickly sprinted away from the door, hiding herself behind a dumpster, while keeping her eyes trained on the maid.

The girl cursed under her breath, lugging the bag inside the dumpster opposite from where Life was hiding. She kicked the ground then grumpily scanned her ID and pulled the door open, disappearing inside.

Just before the door closed, Life lunged, grabbing it just before it shut. She released a surprised puff of air and quietly slipped inside.

It was a small room, filled with gray aprons hanging from walls and wheeled carts filled with cleaning supplies. The room was dark with some sunlight coming from the open entrance that led into the main hallways of the building. She stepped towards the wall of aprons and grabbed one, quickly putting it on. She then picked up some liquid cleaning spray and a towel, then left the room with a new sense of surety.

As she walked the halls, people in black suits and traditional attire didn't even pay her a glance. They all walked with a sense of determination in their step, too proud to spare a glance. She shook her head and continued on walking, trying to look as normal as possible.

She made her way to the glass railings and peered down, seeing rest lounges with couches, tables, and people buzzing around. She then looked up at the high roofed ceiling and saw a magnificent chandelier, dripping down and spreading its tinted light. She saw all around her the banners of the Hikman flag, with their signature yellow and blue dazzling the building. Her eyes bulged at the astonishing wealth and beauty that it was glittered in.

Without warning, a hand grabbed her shoulder and turned her to face the person.

"What are you doing? The room you're assigned is the waiting room of President Ayad. And I'm sure she does not want dirty windows and tables giving her a bad impression on the representatives." A severe looking woman sneered. She had a perfect, slicked back bun, glasses, and a blue blazer to contrast with the yellow button up shirt.

That was perfect. That was probably where Fate and Chaos were. A perfect place to help them rather than pretend she was still out searching for Death.

"What are you waiting for? She has an exact five minute break. Go!" The woman seethed as she looked down at her clipboard then back at her.

"What-? Oh! Yes, I can do that."

"Well, you better hurry up then!" And with that, the woman strode down the hallways, leaving Life to navigate her way to the waiting room.

The waiting room was bizarrely different from the rest of the building. Instead of the bustling halls there was a front desk with a woman sitting down behind it, and there were rows and rows of chairs, filled out by representatives of the countries, and everyday clients waiting for their appointment with the president in silence.

"The president states that she is agreeing to have a conversation with the Mahanan Ambassadors now," A woman said near the door of the office.

"Ah, not the best timing for me." A familiar voice chimed. Chaos.

Fate nodded at Chaos who casually glanced at his infamous watch.

"I'll join you soon, just give me a minute will you?"

The secretary spluttered, "Well- I- Madam president doesn't wait-?"

"Something came up." He turned to look at Fate and rolled his eyes, "Just go."

Fate brushed off her clothing as she turned to enter the hallway leading to the president's room.

Life watched Fate enter into the room while catching a glimpse of President Ayad's office, which was filled with windows that stretched to the ceiling.

A window cleaner's nightmare

While the door slid shut, Chaos looked around at the empty hall before blinking out of sight.

Where was he going?

Life frowned. She wasn't going to get far with following them around anymore. She didn't know what she was hoping to accomplish by following them around *this time*. Clearly, they already had a plan that seemed to be working.

Putting in her two-week notice, she brought up an image in her mind and let the ground sink under her.

CHAPTER SEVEN

CHAOS

He was doing the most effective thing he could think of to find a secret organization: yelling their name in public. If he couldn't find them, he'd get them to find *him*. Unless he'd discover some Riquezan enforcers who'd arrest him for acting like a drunk lunatic and even daring to suggest there was a rebellion.

Fate had given him a job, and essentially kicked him out of the alliance-party-planning-committee.

Find the Rebellion in Fortem. Gain their trust. She had told him that them alone as insignificant ambassadors weren't going to change anything and they'd have to take the unconventional way. A coup.

That sounded like a great idea to him, which was why he was now asking a suspicious old woman about the organization.

"The Re-*bell*-ee-on, Ma'am."

"I heard you." The woman snapped, peering at Chaos through her cat-eye glasses. She turned around to pick up an orange from the box placed on the street vendor's stand, "I just don't care."

"How much?" He dropped his voice to a whisper, leaning in. He put his hand over his pocket, making it quite clear what he intended to give her. Not that he had any geld, Fortem's currency, on him at the moment.

"What?" The woman whirled on him, yelling into his ear as he backed up, his vision turning at the sudden noise.

"Fine, don't tell me." Chaos snapped, rubbing his ear. He ignored the dirty look the vendor was shooting at him as he surveyed Chaos. Chaos was used to it. One- he was untrustworthy. Two- he was Riquezan. Seeing as the kingdom had declared war on every single country in the Anatol Coalition, Riqueza wasn't exactly the most loved among Cadere's people.

He scowled, dodging a bicycle tearing through the road at his back.

"Oh no, boy. I just couldn't hear you."

Chaos groaned, dragging his hands down his face. He sighed shortly, putting an obviously fake grin on his face, "Enjoy your day. Hope you find your wallet, Ma'am."

It hadn't taken him long when he had leaned into her to slip his fingers into her handbag.

"Hope I find my *what*?"

Chaos was walking backwards from the woman with her graying coily hair pulled to a slick bun, when he put his hands to his mouth, "Your *walle-*"

At this point he was too far from her to hear what she was saying but when the vendor started chasing after him, his braids flying behind his head, Chaos had the hunch *she* had heard *him*.

His eyes widened, but he grinned, starting up in a run. The city air of Abavukeli rushed past his face as he took care not to fall into the busy streets or run over the walking citizens along the pavement.

At some point, after taking about fifteen turns, he ended up in a more secluded part of the packed city. It was darker there, but he wouldn't have said it was more peaceful. Rather than bustling streets full of unbothered civilians who spent their evenings shopping among the outdoor market, these people spent their evenings begging for change. Fortem wasn't in the best shape after the First War and its annexation, but this part of Abavukeli was horribly shabby.

Strung around the peeling lamp posts were paper cut outs of Fortem's symbol of the dagger and a scale on its hilt. He guessed it was fairly new because the paper was still a shocking white and it hadn't been burned down by Riquezan enforcers yet.

The people were stubborn that way.

He shoved his hands in his pockets, striding through the cracking concrete, not exactly sure where he was going. It was eerie. His skin prickled as he walked, feeling eyes on the back of his neck. It was either from the families forced to compact in makeshift tents with patched fabric in the alleyways or it was the ghost of Retribution.

"Please." A feeble voice stopped Chaos. When he glanced down, a young boy was coated in dirt, wearing a small coat and newsboy cap over his close-shaved curls. The boy's cheeks were gaunt, not full of youth as they should have been. His dark eyes were wide and blank. He sat curled against a grocery store, the dim lights flickering from the inside.

"Geld." The boy pushed out through his thick Fortem accent.

Geld- the Fortem currency.

Chaos hesitated, slowing. Something urged him to keep walking, but he reached for the wallet he had stolen from the old woman.

He kneeled down by the boy, handing him the entire wallet, somewhat awkwardly.

The boy took it gently, looked down at it with wide eyes, and up at Chaos.

Then he smirked.

"Impindezelo kunifikele."

Retribution has come for you.

Before Chaos could question his statement or snatch the wallet back from this weirdly frightening twelve year old, he felt something hit the back of his head.

And suddenly he could see nothing.

***

"An undercover enforcer?"

"That's ridiculous. He looks far too young. Do they employ under eighteen?"

Chaos' head throbbed. He felt like he was playing the children's game where they whacked plastic rodents with a mallet. Instead the rodent they were whacking was him.

When he tried to open his eyes, he still saw nothing but a black void, making it painfully clear he was blindfolded. It was only after regaining consciousness for a couple of minutes that he had noticed the biting metal around his ankle and wrists. Either this was the old woman's entire scheme all along, or he had just gotten on the Rebellion's bad side.

"I'm *twenty*." Chaos snapped, his voice raspy. Sure he was five centuries in human years, but time worked a lot differently for immortal beings. Technically, he hadn't been lying.

"You're conscious." Said a cool voice. This voice was new.

"How can you be sure I'm not just possessed by the gods? Which one was it again? Oh yes, Retribution." Chaos leaned back in his chair, "'*I am vengeance.*'"

"Actually," A female voice who he recognized from who was speaking earlier corrected, "Vengeance is just exacting revenge, whereas retribution is the consequence a person deserves based on an action."

"Shut up, Esi." A male voice groaned.

"Well there you go, Kasim, giving away my name!"

"You just did the same!" The masculine voice sounded appalled.

"At least if he hunts us down and kills me, you'll come along."

A pause.

"Can he even hold a weapon right?"

75

"I find it differs depending on if I'm blindfolded or not." Chaos drawled, lifting his chin to signify the cloth around his eyes.

"Silence." The cool voice was more of set ice rather than a refreshing stream now.

It was effective, because both Esi and Kasim stopped bickering and muttered in unison, "Apologies, sir."

Chaos could feel the man's presence near himself, crouching down next to him. He smelled faintly of vanilla which was a curious choice for a man in power.

"This will be quick, understand? You tell me why you've been asking for a rebellion, and I'll send you on your way."

Chaos wasn't deterred, "On my way to Death? Or back home?"

The man didn't need to know it was somewhat the same thing for Chaos.

He scoffed, amused, under his breath, "You catch on fast, boy."

Chaos could tell he was surveying the part of Chaos' expression he could see. It wasn't because the man was worried about Chaos possessing weapons. That had most likely already been accounted for with a pat search.

Chaos smirked, "I won't overstay my welcome. I'm here because of a woman named Fate. She was with the Rebellion in Krasivaya."

When none of them answered to the name, he continued, "We want the Rebellion to join us- to aid us- against Casimir."

"Where is Fate? Why has she not come?" Esi spoke. Chaos could hear shuffling to his side, and suddenly his vision returned.

It wasn't fully functional yet, seeing as vibrant colors formed pulsing shapes in his view, but it was enough to see his surroundings. The building he was in was coated with dust and cleared to form a huge empty space. Fogged windows racked the side of the room, hardly supplying any of the sun's harsh gray light against the painted concrete flooring.

At the very far end were cardboard boxes of old bunsen burners, beakers, and plastic goggles. It gave the hint that the building must have been some old science facility.

His eyes finally rested on bodies belonging to the three voices that looked increasingly different than what he had pictured in his mind. Esi had a puff of coily hair around her head, with shorter strands in the front to frame her face. Her eyes were wide, making her appear innocent, but at certain angles, Chaos could see the glints of mischief underneath.

Kasim appeared to be of Hikman descent. He was tall and lanky, though his head was only an inch or two above Esi's. He leaned with an arm on her shoulder before she pushed him off. He straightened quickly, scowling and scratching his dark waves of hair. Both didn't look to be over twenty.

Their leader was a man with dark skin, just a shade darker than Esi's. He had close cropped hair that only accentuated his sharp angles. In other words, his presence at Chaos' side was quite terrifying.

"Fate couldn't be here." Chaos blinked, "Think of me as her lackey."

The man stood, straightening his back against his long unbuckled coat, "You do know who we are, yes, boy?"

"A pathetically smaller chapter of the Rebellion."

Chaos' hands had lost feeling.

The leader smiled, "You believe we would show you our entire group. You think of us as fools."

Chaos cocked his head at the leader, "Oh, really? So there are more of you? And here I was thinking that Riqueza killed all of you off during the raid earlier this month."

"Well, unsurprisingly, you'd be wrong. We actually only sent three-fourths of our people to that figh- ow"

Esi smacked the back of his head sharply, "There you go telling a Riquezan our business."

Chaos nodded, glumly, "He's not the smartest one, is he? Don't worry, I've got one of those too. But mine has a more grim name-"

The chief stepped forward, "How do you know about the raid? Riqueza keeps all the information classified."

Chaos smirked lazily, "I have communications. It's important to have ears and eyes everywhere. Now why don't you remove these restraints? Why not have a little trust?"

Esi cocked her head to the side, "A Riquezan boy asks of us on the streets. It's not exactly a trustworthy notion."

"How did you know that?"

Kasim grinned, drawing Chaos' attention, "We have communications. We have watch control. We sent the boy in to distract you after catching you with Mrs. Ruhlen."

Esi blinked, "It's important to have ears and eyes everywhere."

Chaos raised his eyebrows, "That kid was a Rebellion agent? I thought he was-"

The leader shook his head, "That part of Abavukeli is abandoned. Riqueza has destroyed us and left us impoverished."

Chaos gaped. A child had tricked him. He'd lost his dignity *and* that old woman's geld.

"Enough stalling." The man snapped, pacing. His footsteps echoed under the large ceiling, "What help do you need and what makes you think that I'd give it?"

Chaos smiled, "Well, there's power in numbers. I want you to fight"

Kasim scoffed, "What do you think we've been doing?"

"Not that pathetic fighting. I mean why would you believe that storming Riqueza's capital would be a good idea? No. I mean actually work as a team for once. Coordinate with the other Rebellion chapters and rally."

Esi shook her head, "It's impossible. In fact it's a suicide mission. Requeza has guards crawling all over the annexed countries. It's not worth the risk especially since it probably wouldn't work."

"But it would work," Chaos interrupted, "Riqueza is focusing their efforts on offense. Their defenses are weak. Take advantage of it."

The leader shook his head, "Even if we did consider your half-baked plan, what makes you think we'd do it?"

Chaos smirked, "Well, it's not exactly like you're thriving."

The man's gaze darkened, "No, we're not, which further fortifies my question. Why would I risk it?"

Chaos sighed comically, "How about I give you something in return?"

"What could you possibly have to offer us?"

"Nothing right now, but I've been told I'm quite accomplished at the art of thievery."

The chief raised his brow, "Fine, you say you want help? We can offer it."

Kasim and Esi exchanged bewildered glances.

Chaos just leaned back and waited.

"If you can get our team plutonium, we'll discuss aid."

Kasim's head whipped to look at the chief so quickly that Chaos was sure we could have broken his neck.

"Chief Sarki-" Esi interjected, crossing her arms.

He silenced her with a glance.

Chaos hesitated, "Why do you need plutonium?"

He'd heard of it before. Well, by that he meant he had skimmed over the name once while reading a textbook at the Altar for their studies. It was some sort of elemental material.

"Find it, and get us enough to sustain, and *then* we'll discuss." Chief Sarki smirked, clearly proud of himself.

Chaos wasn't quite convinced, knowing this man was about to send him to look for something as hard to find as a piano at the bottom of the ocean.

"You know, it sounds like you're trying to get rid of me. It shouldn't be too difficult, yes?" Chaos asked flatly, glancing at Esi and Kasim for an answer.

"No, not at all. It's an incredibly rare element sold only at low quantities for more money than you can muster. I bid you good luck." The Chief told Chaos, patting his shoulder.

Chaos was under the impression this man should have been named Chief *Snarky* instead.

Esi winced as Kasim waved, his hand stained with dark brown designs Chaos hadn't noticed him having.

Chaos raised his eyebrows at their reaction but didn't have to wait for long to understand.

"You might feel some pain."

"Wha-"

The Chief punched him in the face.

And Chaos saw nothing again.

CHAPTER EIGHT

FLASHBACK

"*It's important to check up on these every 57.5758*

years. To keep the order." Death mocks smoothly, standing tall next to Retribution. Both walk in striding paces.

Retribution scoffs as he crosses his arms.

"Where to first?" Death questions, turning his head to look at Retribution.

"Riqueza. It would be best to check Chaos' autopilot first. Things are getting a bit too quiet."

"So be it." Death grins at the thought of Chaos' autopilot.

"Why are we walking? Why not teleport? We were given those abilities for a reason." Retribution grumbles, a flicker of annoyance passing through his features.

Death lets out a sigh, "Keeping Cadere safe is our purpose. To fulfill this, we need to take the well being of our humans into account. How better to do that than see for ourselves?"

Retribution turns, his eyes scanning the city they were currently in.

Death merely shakes his head, chuckling, and continues walking.

"So…" Retribution starts. " What's going on between you and Balance?"

Death trips over a non existent stone, his face flushing.

"I have no idea what you're talking about." He grumbles, praying to everything that Retribution can't see the deepening blush on his face.

Retribution smirks watching the humans conversing.

"As long as it doesn't interfere with our job, I'm sure it's fine." Retribution turned to look at him. *"Plus if you were to ask her... I'm almost completely sure she would say yes."*

Death's eyes widen, he meets Retribution's gaze. *"Ask her what- I mean... I don't know what you're talk-?"*

Retribution chuckles, *"Don't you see the way she looks at you?"*

Death shakes his head.

"We're at the border, teleport to the autopilot."

Death stares at Retribution, *"Wait continue your senten-fine."*

Death closes his eyes focusing on the familiar sinking feeling. His feet hit the ground hard, his eyes flying open.

"She looks at you like you're the brightest star."

Death looks away.

Retribution flicks his gaze forward, scoffing, *"It's baffling how oblivious you are."*

Death raises his chin, continuing to walk, *"You're one to talk."*

Retribution's head snaps to look at Death. *"What's that supposed to mean?"*

Death furrows his eyebrows mockingly, *"Absolutely nothing. Oh look we're here!"*

Retribution drags his eyes away from Death's face, squinting to scan their surroundings. Searing heat, burns their backs, their faces, everything.

"Chaos' is always the worst. Well let's get this over with." Grass tickles Death's ankles as he steps a foot forward, looking upward at the bubbling volcano.

82

"What did Time want us to talk about?" Death can practically hear the boiling lava.

Retribution straightens up, answering almost mechanically. *"Make sure the autopilots function, and go over their purpose"*

"Purpose?"

"Yes. Why are they important, what happens if they stop working-"

"Right" Death turns around, facing Retribution. *"Autopilots are important because they do most of our job, in the sense that it does our whole job, just ten times faster, and more efficiently."*

Retribution narrows his eyes. *"They lessen the burden of-"*

"If they stop working then us protectors will have to do everything ourselves, and that would be virtually impossible with this population size." Death interrupts, a bead of sweat rolls down his face. *"It's really hot here isn't it?"*

He waves his hand, fanning himself.

"It would break the natural cycle of-" Retribution starts.

"And the autopilot seems to be working perfectly. Shall we move on?"

Retribution glares at Death. Death rolls his eyes, *"Good. Fortem next?"*

***

"But it was so perfect!"

Balance grins as she nudges Chaos' leg in mock disapproval, *"Hey, I had to wash my hair at least ten times to get all the powder off."*

Retribution scoffs, *"I don't think it's out of my hair yet."*

83

Life grins, wickedly, *"That's what made the prank so amazing; it had an impact."*

Chaos throws Balance a lopsided grin. *"Plus, it cheered you up!"*

Her smile flickers slightly. Her gaze moves down to her hands.

Life frowns, placing her hand on Balance's knee, *"Hey, he was in the wrong."*

Balance nods, smiling weakly, *"I know. I just feel like the whole argument could have been avoided."*

Chaos scoffs, *"Yeah, Death was just being irrational."*

Chaos leans towards Balance, suddenly serious, *"If you need Life and me to prank him, we can make it happen."*

Balance throws her head back laughing, *"I'm not mad at him, Chaos, but I'll be sure to keep your offer in mind should the need arise."*

The group turn their heads at the sound of the door opening.

Death and Fate walk in. Fate has a pamphlet held over her mouth as she whispers something to Death, who nods in response.

Balance shoots a quick glance at Chaos.

"Balance," Death starts, his eyes flit to Life's glare trained on him. He cringes, *"I'm sorry."*

Chaos snorts as he readjusts his watch.

Death frowns and turns to shoot a desperate look at Fate who merely shrugs in response, sitting next to Retribution on the couch opposite Balance, Life, and Chaos.

"I'm not mad at you Death, you know that."

Death frowns, staring at his feet. *"I know, but still I'm sorry. I should have told you I was staying out late. I didn't mean to keep you waiting for me."*

"And...?" Life pushes.

"And I'm sorry for snapping at you when you asked me about it." Death finishes.

Balance smiles, "Well, I forgive you. Now, come sit down."
Death steps forward and settles himself on the couch next to Fate.
Fate grins as she waves the pamphlet in the air. "I've got news."
Balance quirks her brow while Chaos and life lean forward.
"Fortem is now a fully functioning kingdom. Do you know what that means?"
"No?" Life muses.
"Well, spit it out Fate." Chaos groans.
She rolls her eyes, chucking the Fortem pamphlet at Chaos, " It means that there are now 6 kingdoms, which happens to be the amount of protectors here. I say we each choose a kingdom." She finishes proudly.
"Choose a kingdom?" Retribution frowns.
"First good idea you've had all day." Chaos grins, "I call Riqueza."
Fate raises her hand, "Mahana."
"Krasivaya." Life chimes.
Death bites her lip in thought, "I'll take Lucror."
Retribution tilts his head to look at Fate, "Which one is the new one?"
"Fortem."
Retribution shrugs, "I guess I can take that one."
Balance smiles, "Then I'll take Heping."

***

"I say we set a plague loose."
Retribution turns to stare at Fate, appalled.
"A plague?" Life snorts.
Chaos pushes off the couch.

85

"That's the stupidest idea I've heard today, Fate, and I've been listening to Retribution all day." He shrugs, a lazy grin spreading on his tan face, *"That says something."*

Fate spins around to glare at Chaos. Her sharply cut hair whips at her shoulders.

"At least I'm doing something, Chaos." She bites back.

"Barely." Chaos scoffs.

Fate's eyes narrow dramatically.

"Back to the topic." Retribution cuts in, his hand skimming over his tight curls.

Fate sits back down, glaring at Chaos.

Retribution's hands place themselves firmly on the long rectangular planning table. "As Death was saying, we are getting dangerously close to overpopulation. Does anyone have any ideas on how to stop this? Preferably not a plague."

"Why doesn't Death just kill more people?" Chaos shrugs.

"It doesn't work like that." Death chimes, repaying the information for the tenth time.

A girl with silky brown hair creeps forward until she stands at Death's side.

A smile spreads onto Death's face as he crouches a bit lower.

She leans towards his ear. "How long do you think before Fate and Chaos start arguing again?" *A teasing smirk plays across her pale face.*

Death grins as he turns to whisper in her ear, "50 pecunia they're fist fighting in 5 minutes."

"Oh, you're on!" She whispers, straightening up.

"Balance. You're all about stability. You must have a solution." Retribution declares abruptly, addressing the Protector by Death's side.

Balance smiles coyly, " This isn't really my area of expertise. I mean-" *She drawles,* "We could always make Life stop making humans."

86

"I said that! Great minds think alike, yeah?" Chaos grins, nudging his elbow into Balance's ribs.

Retribution turns away from the pair, rubbing between his eyebrows.

"Is anyone going to pay attention?" Retribution questions exasperatedly.

"No." Fate answers simply.

Balance laughs as she steps forward, gathering the attention of the near arguing group, "Okay, guys-"

She pauses, swaying slightly.

Death's brows furrow, "Something's wrong. A whole mass of humans just died."

Chaos rolls his eyes, "Yeah, I'm pretty sure that's what mortals do-"

"No, more than usual." Death shifts his gaze to Retribution. "I think something happened."

Retribution's brows pull together in thought.

Death turns to look at Balance. "Balance, what-?"

Balance's eyes flutter shut.

"Balance?" Death steps towards her, reaching forward only for her to gently push his hands away.

Death's eyes fly to his right, briefly making contact with the other Protectors.

"I'm fine. I think it's just a minor disturbance of peace. Must have just been some bar fight." Balance chuckles, stepping forward towards the center table.

Her knees buckle.

Death lurches forward, catching her mid-collapse. He gently lowers her to the floor

"Balance?"

Retribution steps forward, helping Death prop her against the leg of the table.

Life peers over Retribution's shoulder now flushed in panic as she stares, stricken with fear.

87

Chaos bites his lip, *"What's going on? What's wrong with her?"*

"Balance... Balance?" Death whispers, shaking her shoulders gently.

Fate sits next to Death, her eyes wide as she stares at Balance's slack form.

Retribution turns his face slightly, "Someone needs to go down to Cadere and see what happened-"

"I'll go."

Retribution turns his gaze to stare at Life's unwavering expression.

He frowns. He closes his mouth, then opens, then closes again, hesitating.

"Life, something dangerous is happening on Cadere," He turns to look at Fate, "Fate has more fighting experience, maybe she should-"

"I can do it." Her eyes flit to Balance before training back on Retribution. "I can protect myself. I can fight. You've seen me do it."

Retribution shakes his head, indecision written clear on his face.

"You don't control her, Retribution." Fate snaps.

Life's back straightens. "I can do it."

Retribution tears his eyes away from hers, nodding.

Life disappears.

Retribution turns back to Balance.

Chaos' eyes bore into his, a rouge flush lays under his brown skin. He repeats his question, "What's wrong with her?"

Retribution frowns, "I don't know-"

Death raises his head, staring at Retribution, "The only way this could have happened is if something happened on Cadere- amongst the humans. Something that stopped the peace so intensely-"

"Is she going to be okay?" Fate interrupts.

A beat of silence passes.

Death's gaze moves back to Balance's face.

Retribution looks between Chaos, Fate, and Death, "Let's just wait for Life to come back. She may have an answer-"

Balance's eyes shoot open. She lurches up, coughing and sputtering into her hand.

"You're okay- you're fine." Death places his hand on her knee wincing at every horrible hack that left her lips.

Balance grabs his hand in a vise-like grip, forcing his full attention onto her face.

"The war."

Death shakes his head, "War? There's no-"

"There is," she winces, clenching her eyes shut.

Death closes his mouth as he grips her hand tighter.

Balance turns to look up at Retribution.

A chill passes through the air.

"The first war has begun."

Chapter Nine

Fate

"Allies?"

"Yes, President Ayad. I understand that your country is at a minimum with the resources-"

"If you understood, then you would not be asking to bring together the only security I possess and fight on the offensive side *against* Riqueza." Her eyes narrowed in discontent. Fate knew that Hikma was surviving by a thread, but she also knew that without her cooperation, any attack they tried would fail.

Hikma may not have resources, but their wits alone could strategize attacks. It would be the eastern equivalent of Mahana, in the sense of serving the war.

"Resources," Fate huffed, "No. The others can provide… fine. Strategy?"

The president narrowed her dark eyes as she straightened in her seat. She was flanked by two guards, two at the grand doors at the front, and Fate knew more were lined outside the office. It wasn't that she couldn't attack them. She could fight 50 of them and still win, but it was important to keep a low profile. This was her only opportunity at having a viable chance at winning the offensive.

"Will you be our strategists?" Fate cleared.

"I'm sorry," Fate braced herself for Inaya Ayad's rejection, a reaction that felt completely foreign to her, "who are you again?"

Fate's eyes widened in character, "Mahanan ambassador, North-West sector. Kahani Mehra."

Fate had gotten a representative uniform, but it all looked the same to an outside source. It was possible to be both an ambassador and representative in one.

Inaya tilted her head back, her dark coiled hair falling behind her shoulder, and let loose a disbelieving laugh, "Do you know why I accepted your request to visit, Kahani?"

"No, Madam President."

"A Mahanan ambassador appears at my door to construct an alliance opposing her home country and *their* alliance. I merely wanted to see how this would proceed."

"Well, I assumed you were well versed on Mahanan ideals, forgive me. Our country believes trust should always be questioned. There is no exception, nonetheless in politics. Once Riqueza has captured all, who will they turn to next? War is inevitable. Their alliance will crumble. But before they can capture your country, before they can capture Lucror and Mahana, they must be taken down." Fate's fingers wrapped into her palm under the desk. She sprouted lies on behalf of Mahana, but it was a legitimate concern. One that Aahi seemed to keep covered to the public. She just hoped it was believable enough to convince Inaya.

"Of course, it is like Aahi to put her country above all else. She couldn't have come to this realization a decade ago? When it comes to the safety of her country," President Ayad gave a sharp laugh, "Then she considers the lives of others. You know," She continued, "I had the luxury of meeting her and her mother while I had just recently become a politician. Though, Aahi had always been much younger than me, so she had just graduated from primary school. This was a decade and a half ago, however. Her mother was an incredible woman; she cared for all. She was always traveling to other countries, strengthening their partnerships, their entente, if you will. She gave and others gave back. She was loved. Aahi does not seem to have followed in her footsteps."

Inaya's brows were pushed together against her dark skin. She was angry. Hikma and Mahana had history to say the least. Something along the lines of toxic waste and murders.

"Please. Her Highness' motives may not be for the greater good, but it will save your country as well." Fate pressed.

"What will stop her from building up another empire then?"

Fate pressed her palms against the dress as the guards at Inaya's side gripped their weapons, "Your country is on the verge of falling. We have offered you an alliance. Will. You. Join?"

Hikma's president paused, her eyebrows nearly merging.

"Fight or fall. Both ways will call upon death, but there is a chance of survival while fighting. If not for you, then your country. For your people." Fate's jaw tightened. She could hear the clock's isochronal ticks. Resounding. Closer and closer and *closer.* She could win. She could become whole again.

Inaya's lips twisted, "You bring up a valid point, ambassador Kahani. Very well."

Fate's shoulders slumped in relief, until President Ayad opened her mouth yet again.

"On one condition," Inaya straightened her black suit around her curves, fitted with blue and yellow across her cuffs, "Lucror joins the coalition and, along with Mahana, they supply the fighters. Any rebel groups hiding from Riqueza's attack will do so as well. Our country is at a low, as you very well know."

A small, dark smile spread across Inaya's round face, "You convince them to join, and our service is yours."

CHAPTER TEN

CHAOS

When something was referred to as 'rare,' it was usually a sign that Chaos could find the material somewhere a little less conventional. A secret underground trade center made only for selling illegal items for example.

The Night Market was known as the largest illegal trade center on Cadere. Chaos had been begging to go for centuries, but no one knew exactly where it was unless you asked the right person. That, and he was too busy following useless orders at the Altar and 'saving' people's lives. Now that those two goals coincidentally aligned, his reasoning to travel to a place selling all sorts of hallucinogens, weaponry, severed body parts, and maybe even the collector's edition of the *Invincible Individuals* comics, was justified.

After Fate's success, if they could call an impossible bargain a *win*, in Hikma, she had started planning for Lucror. It left Chaos to take his own methods of achieving his goals. A free period before he was dragged to see King Favian.

He'd get a headstart at scoping out Lucror since the Night Market was also in the kingdom. The only thing that he needed was to find Death. If anyone knew Lucror, it was the kingdom's Protector. Unfortunately, he didn't know where Death was after he had fled from Balance's home in grief. Life, who had always been close to Death, probably knew and was just letting him mourn on his own. Though, he had to give her credit going against Retribution's orders.

Chaos was here to find a way to destroy Death's peace.

"Life." Chaos knocked on the door softly. He tried his best not to get the splintered wood in his skin, "I know it's considered improper to teleport in a house without warning so consider this one."

"*Life.*" He repeated, louder.

Chaos stared blankly at the peeling wood. Life, wanting to live in greenery, decided that the overgrown ruins of the late Queen Katya's castle was perfect. It was also sort of a hazard.

The door swung open, revealing Life cloaked in a knee-length white skirt, embroidered with a flower rim. She wore a loose brown sweater over it, hiding her curvy figure.

"Chaos." She addressed, surprise clear in her face. The warm wind brushed her hair against her round face, acting as a barrier between them.

"Life! Fantastic. Let's have a little chat." Chaos nodded to get her to agree.

Life looked unimpressed.

Chaos hadn't been expecting her to consider his statement but she just watched him. Sure, Chaos could have thought about Death's location for more than two seconds, but he wanted to speak to Life. See how she was doing.

"I have something on the stove. Come back later."

Chaos frowned at the implication her castle would burn down if she didn't walk away at this very moment, "What? I assumed ruined homes were in your favor."

Life scowled, "It's not ruined."

Chaos nodded, with feigned fervor, his eyebrows raised.

"Are you upset with me?" Chaos questioned. "I know I have a skill of getting under people's skin but I don't recall how I've bothered you- recently, of course."

Noticing her unwillingness to speak, he tried another strategy. He strode forward and plopped down on the small half circle of concrete before her door. He leaned back against the wall and looked at her with a smile.

"We can speak now or later. Your choice. I'll be here. Bring me some *Medovik* while you're at it."

Life blinked seven times before she yielded, carefully not answering his previous question .

"What is it?"

He decided to ignore her lack of a response. Chaos grinned, slipping his restless fingers in his pockets, "Do you know where Death is?"

Life's fingers were tapping against the door but they went slack at his question. Her eyebrows raised instantly, her mouth parting to supply a response.

"How would I know? We both saw him leave, Chaos."

Chaos almost rolled his eyes. The other protectors had no business being so horrible at lying.

Chaos scowled as the birds chirped cheerfully above the cracking stone of the castle, "That's been your only task. You must at least have a guess."

Life hesitated, but Chaos was adamant.

He put a hand over his chest and frowned, wiping off imaginary tears with his other hand, "Come now, Life. I just *have* to see him with my own eyes. I have to know he's doing well. He's a brother to me. I can't bear to see him so *pained*-"

"Have you told him that? I'm sure he would love to hear it." Life widened her eyes in innocence. Her lips tilted in mockery.

Chaos' face fell flat.

Life sighed, raising her eyes to the sky, then landing back to Chaos, "Have you checked the Altar?"

She narrowed her eyes, but the corner of her mouth twitched in amusement at Chaos dropping his facade. He scrambled up.

He was not returning there, and she knew it.

"I'm not-"

"Save it," Life held up a hand at Chaos' sulky tone, "I don't know, Chaos."

Chaos leaned against the vines climbing up the walls. He tilted his head up at the bright blue above, the dancing rays of the sun against his face. He stood there so long, he was sure Life had shut the door and left him on her doorstep until she groaned in annoyance.

"Couldn't you try calling him? Like how Retribution does for our progress meetings?"

"How would I-"

"Figure it out, yes?" She told him sweetly, then slammed the door in his face.

He blinked. He was *not* asking Retribution for help. He wasn't even sure Death would answer if Chaos had called. Perhaps Chaos would just have to flood Death with requests until he was summoned, an angry grief-stricken mess.

He was content with the idea, deciding he'd figure it out later. Remembering that he'd rather spend an evening at the Night Market than Life's unnervingly peaceful home, he headed to Lucror.

***

Chaos had spent the past two hours searching through the wreck in his mind, only to find a row of taut strings as his answer.

Their bond was held together by thin thread?

That meant that each of these four strings had to belong to Fate, Retribution, Life, and Death.

The problem was, it wasn't exactly obvious who's string was whose. There was a faint labeling when he focused on the string. Each had its own feel, matching the aura of the protector, even the empty space to the side. It must have been the absence of Balance's thread.

Fate felt like the tip of a blade, the sharp side of her smirk, the edge to her words. Retribution was unwavering, a sort of unwavering that was seconds from snapping. Life's had a bouncing feel to it. It was her flowy clothing, bright persona, the ripples of her mood.

Death's string was more of a bridge, a support in his mind. It kept him alive, but it was the same thing that made sure the entirety of him collapsed. It was protection over rocky waters, but left him more vulnerable if the tide rose too high.

Chaos pulled that one. The string vibrated, sending shock pulses through his body. After waiting for a couple of minutes, he tried again. And again. And again. And again.

He opened his eyes, feeling his mind shake with the string's impact. All he had to do now was wait. Well unless Death never showed. Then he'd have to pull the string again.

If Fate ever asked what he did this evening, he'd have to say he had been playing with an imagined string. The worst part was that she wouldn't have questioned it.

Chaos was sitting in Death's home. It was a large building on the side of the road, but more than an apartment, it was just multiple smaller versions of a two story home in a single building.

He was completely disregarding propriety. Knowing Death would most likely appear in a familiar surrounding, he'd decided nothing was more familiar than seeing an old friend, with a knack for trespassing, in your living quarters.

He was waiting inside, leaning back on Death's extravagant office chair, his feet up on the desk. Chaos had switched on the lamp to the side due to the dark skies. It cast a dim light over the mahogany desk and the shelves and shelves of leather bound books across all four walls. From the large window to his side, he could see the lamps hooked over the roads, dim spheres in the black, and the civilians trudging along the pavement to get to their homes.

He rolled his eyes as he glanced at his watch on his crossed arms. He nearly fell off his chair when a panicked voice spoke.

"Chaos? What is it? What happened?"

Chaos lifted his head and grinned at the figure in front of him. Death's eyes were wide with alarm, his body terse, protecting himself against Chaos' next words. His face only lost the edge of horror after he noticed Chaos' sheepish smile.

Death flicked his eyes down to Chaos' shoes, "Get your feet off my desk."

Chaos dragged his shoes off, bringing a stack of sprawled-on parchment and a dip pen along with his motion. Death tracked the movement, but didn't so much as flinch. Instead, a shadow was cast over his expression. He inhaled and spun around, scowling.

"Oh, don't leave so soon. I have a question." Chaos scrambled up, pushing back the wheeled chair.

He hadn't spent two hours for Death to leave again. Perhaps he should have rehearsed this in his mind to seem more convincing rather than heading straight into his favorite topic that was criminal activity.

Death tipped his head back and groaned, "Ask someone else."

Death seemed to be waiting, though. A chance for Chaos to justify pulling him from his daily seances with Balance. To be honest, it was probably more like *hourly* sessions.

Chaos stilled, hesitant to ask again. He rubbed the ring on his pointer finger with his thumb to fill the expectant silence. He opened his mouth, and then shut it, wincing.

"Please."

Although the weighted word was softly spoken, Death spun around slowly. His eyebrows pulled in, quizzical. He crossed his arms- for support- Chaos guessed.

98

Chaos exhaled, not quite making eye contact with Death. His hands were at his sides, resting on the desk as he proceeded to ask his brilliant question.

"Where is the Night Market?"

"The *what?*"

Chaos kicked the cabinet, annoyed at Death's slow comprehension. Death only frowned at him.

"Are you just emphasizing or did you not hear me?"

He found that the old woman from Fortem had really questioned his way of thinking.

"*What?* Of course I heard you." Death looked bewildered as he rubbed the side of his head wearily.

"Then tell me where it is."

Death paused in utter confusion, "You mean the illegal trade center in Lucror?"

"Yes. What else would it be?" Chaos snapped, straightening, and crossing his arms.

Perhaps the lack of social interaction was affecting Death's memory or his common sense.

The soft lamp light filled Death's face, making the hollowed portions of his cheeks and under his eyes seem more prominent. Chaos waited for the argument- for the disapproval.

"Why do you need it?" Death scowled.

"Why does it *matter?*" Chaos plopped back down on the chair, unhappy at the length of the conversation.

Death glared at him.

"I need to find this element. Plutonium. It's for a friend."

"A friend?"

"Never heard of those?"

Death exhaled heavily, staring at Chaos as if he was deciding whether staying here and listening to the rest of Chaos' words was worth his time.

"Fine. I don't know where to get your *plutonium*, but I know the only way to the Night Market is through the Secret

System under Lucror. Tunnels under the whole kingdom." Death took a breath at Chaos' expectant face, "Only a few know those tunnels well enough to travel through them. You will find no map, no clues inside the maze as help. Luckily, I know a Traveler who has the entire system embedded in his brain."

Chaos felt his lips tilt up, "Who?"

"He's a librarian in the Library of Lucror, in Primor. Quinn knows more than I do about what you can and cannot find at the Night Market and its rules." Death gave a faint smile, turning to the window past the empty streets, "It will be hard to gain his trust. Tell him you know a-uh-"

Death hesitated, "-a Richard."

"A *Richard?*" Chaos gaped.

Had Death always been horrid at creating aliases? If the others hadn't been so adamant on keeping their identities a secret, he wouldn't have to refer to Death as *Richard*.

Chaos' mouth twitched to ask whether Death went by a shorter name, but Death, after noticing, interrupted, "Who exactly are you giving this element to?"

When Chaos didn't answer, Death sighed.

"Just humor me." His voice dragged, sounding exhausted.

Chaos glanced at him and tilted his head, "And you won't tell Retribution?"

Death took a breath, locking his eyes on Chaos, "No."

He said it in a way that was equal parts hesitant and in aggravation that Chaos had even suggested it was an action Death would commit.

"The Rebellion."

Before Death could press further, Chaos shook his head, raising his eyebrows, "What exactly is plutonium?"

Death's eyes shuttered, confused at the fleeting change of topics. He narrowed his eyes, "You don't know what you're heading into a crowd of criminals to find?"

At Chaos' shrug, Death's gaze turned cold, "You need to be cautious in there, Chaos. Do not tell anyone a single thing about yourself. Do not speak to anyone unnecessarily. Do not trust the vendors, understand? Those are well-knowledged criminals and you-"

Chaos' face flushed as he tore his eyes from Death. He didn't need to continue his sentence. Chaos already knew what he was going to say. He was going to say that Chaos was incapable of defending himself and, conveniently, also had a penchant for getting himself into situations where he would *need* protection.

"Chaos? Understood?"

"Thank you, you may leave now." Chaos put his feet back on the desk.

Death scoffed, "Not until you leave *my* house, I will not."

Chaos paused, debating ignoring Death. Sick of sitting in such a horribly decorated room, he stood up swiftly. Before he said something he would regret, he had to keep reminding himself Death had given him information, however measly, to find the largest crime organization in the world. Chaos could bring his anger down half a turn. He had to learn to leave his conversations on a good note.

Death's voice was softer as he turned to face Chaos. A sort of apology.

"And everyone else is alright?"

Chaos pushed past Death. The voice in his mind he had deemed Frank whispered something. Sparing no time for considering his words, Chaos voiced Frank's statement.

"Perhaps you would know if you weren't cowering somewhere."

Death had no opportunity to respond as Chaos slammed the office's door.

So much for learning how to leave conversations on a good note.

CHAPTER ELEVEN

RETRIBUTION

Retribution stood a few paces behind Time. His eyes darted, almost unsure where to look. He ended up choosing to stare numbly at the floor.

Time stood tall. His brown hair was combed back- slightly messy but still elegant. His face looked sharp, almost as sharp as his mind. His deep brown eyes wandered around the room almost lazily.

Retribution could tell Time's mind was working in a million different ways, one step ahead of every move anyone made.

"So Balance has had her cessation." Time paused and turned away from Retribution, opting to stare out a window instead. "Did you tell the others of their tasks?" Time asked.

"Yes. Life is searching for Death."

Time nodded, "Also ask her to check through Death's things for anything leading to where he is."

Retribution nodded.

"And what about Fate and Chaos?"

"Fate and Chaos are trying to convince world leaders to stop fighting and make alliances."

"Alliances never really worked all that well before did they?"

Time was talking about the League of Cadere. Until quite recently all the countries had a peace agreement: the nonviolence pact. The pact was decided on by the world leaders of Cadere in one of those League of Cadere annual meetings. Of course, Riqueza ended up violating that pact, bringing them back to where they were now.

Retribution shrugged, "There's little they can do. Why not have them chase down a possible thread?"

He hummed in response. Time stepped towards a large bookcase in the room. "The other countries, how are they doing?"

"Fortem and Heping have been struggling a little, but they're plowing on so far." He said. "Riquezan soldiers are in Fortem, supervising the people. With an incredibly strict agenda."

Retribution could practically see the gears turning in Time's head, working out plan after plan.

"Heping on the other hand, has been holding up stronger. The Riquezan enforcers have been dominating the southern region, but a lot of raids have been taking place." Retribution continued.

"The raids are minor. Like a mosquito bite. Annoying to Riqueza, yes…" Time's hand skimmed over a few books. "But harmless." He finished.

Retribution gazed out the window, children ran and played in the dry heat outside. "Why aren't the world leaders forming alliances? Wouldn't they be stronger?"

Time stayed quiet for a moment, thinking. "The countries don't trust each other. Not after Riqueza surprised the world by turning on Krasivaya and especially not when Mahana turned its back on the League mid-war and joined Riqueza, but what of the people? How are they adjusting?"

The dark hardwood flooring made hollow thumps as Time made his way back to Retribution. A dark look casted on Retribution's face, his mind replaying the conversation a few villagers had a few nights ago.

"Those Riquezans need to be stopped." One of the main villagers yelled on top of the bar.

The bartender peaked nervously at the man.

*"They have been tormenting us, kicking us aside as our
children are asking questions if they are gonna die. Is this what we
call justice? By hiding in the shadows?" The man slurred, clearly
having some liquid confidence surging through his veins.*

Everyone jeered, yelling their cheers.

*"We need to stand up and fight! The children of Cadere
need us, people to look up to! Our wives and children in distress as
they come and clear out our houses is unacceptable!"*

*Everyone cheered louder, lifting their beers and vodka
alike as Retribution leaned on a wall in the shadows, closely
watching the entire fit of passion unfold.*

*"They say violence isn't the answer. But you gotta fight fire
with fire!" Everyone hollered once more, cheering the man on.*

*"I say we start our own chapter of the Rebellion! A
Revolution to fight for our rights and desires! What do you all say?
Who's with me?" He shouted, beer dripping down from his arms
and the adrenaline sizzling in the air. They all cheered louder than
before, drunken smiles with hope and courage plastered on their
faces. The music immediately turned up, as they all danced around,
guzzling down beer after beer.*

*That was his cue. Retribution pushed off the wall, slipping
his way past drunk men and women. He breathed in deeply the
moment a breath of fresh air hit his face.*

"The Rebellion's influence is spreading." Retribution
voiced slowly.

"I suspected that much." Time mused. "Freedom at the
hands of the people."

"It was one night a couple weeks ago. They want justice."

"Good for them. What did they exactly say in this
meeting? Is there anyone who is actually willing to step up and
fight?"

"A well-liked man in the village stood on the bar, yelling
about how they shouldn't stay in the shadows, and that they should
fight for their family," He said.

Time nodded thoughtfully, "We need to settle down the people. Freedom doesn't come from mayhem. We almost have the control we need, it's just a few inches out of our grasp." Time turned to stare at Retribution. "With peace and control we can save everyone. We can restore Cadere back into order."

"But the revolution-?"

"A mosquito. The revolution can't do anything. But we can." Time looked at a clock perched on Retribution's wall. "Retribution, I'm counting on you to keep up with the information."

Retribution nodded.

"Also, take care of the other Protectors."

Retribution's brows furrowed as he nodded.

And with that, a blink of his eye was all it took for Time to diminish away, leaving Retribution with his thoughts.

Chapter Twelve

FATE

"This seems inhumane." Chaos whined as he leaned against Retribution's walls, which for some reason, were coated in some ridiculously elegant red and gold wallpaper.

"What does?" Retribution asked, placing the palms of his hands against the center table.

"The absurd amount of meetings we are dragged into."

"To be fair, are we not inhumane as well?" Fate leaned her back against the table, the overflowing paper on top crinkling at her position. She was feeling restless for some reason. Her stomach was even flipping- in apprehension or excitement, she didn't know.

After losing her ability, things seemed to be collapsing like a line of stacked bricks. One after the other. She could hardly process it. She was either on the verge of jumping headfirst off a cliff, or *worrying* about jumping headfirst off a cliff.

President Ayad had agreed, or to be technical, had given them a conditional. Either way it was a step closer than she had been. She was just concerned.

What if they couldn't get Lucror and Mahana to agree? What if she lost everything she had ever had, *ever been*?

The questions themselves were horrifying. How long had it been since she hadn't been able to slide the lens over her eyes and see the dimensions of probability? How long had it been since she wasn't sure of herself?

"That's not-" Retribution sighed at them, turning to the door, "Where is Life?"

He seemed panicked. Something close to a caged rabbit. His eyes were roving from corner to corner, a slight sheen of sweat glistened on his face, and he was continuously scratching the back of his neck.

Fate would've been doing the same, if she had been just as horrible as hiding her emotions as Retribution was.

"I went to visit her a while back. She wasn't particularly pleased." Chaos offered. He looked through the hole of the silver ring he was holding up to his eye. A slight purple shadow was visible right under it.

Thankfully, Retribution hadn't dared to ask about it. Fate had known exactly where Chaos had gotten it from. He had told her after his meeting with Chief Sarki, running into her apartment half-dazed. Chaos' efforts were more of a back-up, a fall back in case the remaining countries weren't daring enough to form an alliance.

Fate was planning never to resort to that option.

"She was at home?"

"What else is she to do with her time? While you assigned us to save the whole planet, she spends her time wandering and calling it searching. Could we finally know what *you* spend the days doing?"

Retribution smiled at him bitterly, "Cleaning Balance's home. You told me you would help. And where were you then?"

Fate watched Chaos' expression falter. His body went slack and he looked away from Retribution's sardonic expression.

"At least he's helping to cease the war."

Retribution looked affronted, stiffening, but said nothing. He glanced at Chaos, then relented, returning back to Chaos' previous question, "I've told you this multiple times before, Chaos. I have orders from Time. It's classified."

When Chaos turned back, it was like nothing had ever been said.

"A secret girlfriend-"

Fate coughed at that.

"No."

"A super weapon?"

"No."

"A secret that could shatter the universe?"

"No."

"A-"

"Enough." Retribution slid a hand over his hair, glaring at Chaos. Chaos just grinned in response. He seemed different. Younger. *Happier.* He was the only person who still seemed to feel that way each time the six- five- of them were brought together.

Retribution gave a fleeting glance to the open door revealing a silver of his curved staircase. Waiting for Life, Fate supposed. With half the team gone, the loss of Balance felt more real in the moment. Balance. Death. Life. Balance. Balance. Whatever they once had, was shattered.

When she and Chaos ended the war, they could bring it back. The fate of the world wouldn't burden her anymore. Her powers would return.

They just needed to convince Lucror. To be fair, if they couldn't overpower the humans, what were they good for?

"What happened in Hikma?" Retribution asked, treading lightly.

"They agreed to join our coalition." Fate replied smoothly.

She could hear Chaos' snort from the other side of the grand room. So she left out Hikma's terms. Retribution didn't need to know because they *would* succeed.

She glanced back to meet Retribution's raised eyebrows. "Don't look too surprised."

"May I ask how you managed to do that?" His eyes widened instantly, "Did you kill her?"

"Honestly, when she had told me what'd happened, *smiling,* I had thought the same thing." Chaos nodded mockingly.

Fate hid her smile. She twirled a pen in her fingers, "I tried the diplomatic approach this time."

She pulled away from the table, the one Chaos had once called "large enough to dine the entire country of Krasivaya." He had said it after the valiant country had gotten slaughtered and conquered by both themselves and Riquezan armies. Their group had been forced to listen to an *invigorating* conversation afterwards.

Retribution gave her a questioning glance before blinking his eyes, a reset to his mood. It was like he suddenly understood the implications of what they were saying.

"I'm calling an emergency meeting," Retribution told them, shutting his eyes, his brows pulling together.

Fate and Chaos exchanged a dry glance. Chaos pursed his lips to keep from laughing as he tapped the face of his watch. Fate shrugged back.

The silence was loud enough to morph into the ticks of a clock.

Tick.

Tick.

Tick. Tick. Tick.

Fate and Chaos had tacitly agreed to stare at Retribution as he waited, eyes shut, shoulders tight. His scowl deepened as time passed.

"Where are they?" His rough voice broke their silence. He opened his eyes and ran his hand down his face.

"Retribution, this may come as news to you, but no one wants to attend these meetings." Chaos drawled, propping his chin on a hand.

Fate noticed Retribution's fingers pressing against his palm,

"I'm going to go find Life."

And with that, his body blinked out of sight.

"How long is he going to pretend that this meeting was not about us, but seeing Life again?" Chaos groaned. He stumped forward, flopping face first onto the table.

"Seeing as he left, not long." Fate strode around the table merely to kick his ankle, "Stop sitting around. Let's go. We have work to do."

Chaos' voice was muffled from speaking against the papers, "You never let me take a break. After Lucror, I have to hunt down an illegal librarian that *Richard* is friends with."

"What?"

Fate decided against asking more, "We succeeded in Hikma so the plan remains the same."

"And," Fate added with a pointed look in Chaos' direction as he dragged himself up, "I do all the talking."

This was their non-anarchy related chance. She would take it in her own hands to end this war, prove to herself she wasn't unraveling- that she could still win.

Chaos feigned a frown, "What made you think I can't woo a king?"

Fate ignored him. She knew that being a Protector would make it easier to direct Cadere's future, so she wasn't worried. Lucror would come easy.

The only thing she was worried about was what purpose she'd have left once it was accomplished.

If her abilities did not return.

CHAPTER

THIRTEEN

Life

T he tree of life.

Life sat in the shade of her autopilot, thick branches intertwining with the leaves and blossoms. Each branch tilted up towards the sun, begging to get a glimpse of fresh sunlight. It was the only place that made her feel at home these days.

She wanted to sink deeper into the ground. The soft grass and tune of birds soothed her, but not enough to keep her mind from bustling with noise.

The first war started here. A violent invasion from Riqueza onto Krasivaya. The two power nations of the world at war. It didn't take long for the other kingdoms to quickly take sides. Yet the people of Cadere didn't like to think about it. War memories replayed in her mind, soldiers dying, buildings collapsing, women, men, and children crying and running into the forests. The image of Riquezan soldiers riding in with their daggers was burned into her mind.

She remembered telling the other Protectors about it, but their powers were useless as they all tried to stop it. The cruel unjustifiable actions that tore her home apart were gone. Balance was gone. She was gone.

Life stood up abruptly, pacing. She couldn't take it anymore. She closed her eyes.

Good wins in the end. It always does.

She needed good to come out of this mess.

It was her only sliver of hope left.

She imagined a bright ball of light coming from the palm of her hands. Her shoulders slightly tugged forward, her core clenched, and her insides felt like melting into one.

Her palms felt heavier, the ball of light becoming warmer and bigger. As she opened her eyes, to see the light of creation. She smiled. She bent down as she manipulated the light and warmth in her hand, and caved her hand out, reaching forward and spilling the rays of warmth into the soil. The light dissolved and a single white Hyacinth sprouted from the soil and quickly grew into a phenomenon of beauty. It was perfect.

The tree swayed in the gentle breeze above her.

After the feelings faded she began walking, letting her legs take her wherever it wanted. She wanted to see Death. No, she needed to. He always helped her think clearer.

She shook her head. Death was dealing with his own problems. Instead of going to him with her own problems, perhaps she should check up on Death. She was fairly certain he was still at the Altar.

She would check up on him eventually. For now, she had her own problems to deal with.

***

Lucror.

Life felt her knees pop, as they made contact with the ground. She looked around. She was alone in a back alleyway.

It was late afternoon, and the sun shined through the fog settled close to the ground. The chill of the breeze slightly brushed her shoulders and she gave a quick shiver. She began walking, talking the usual routes, and waving to the familiar friendly faces she'd met before. She crossed a couple streets, jaunted down the sidewalks, and made a few quick turns to find a stoned building crawling with thorned ivy. She walked up the wooden steps, hesitating a bit before knocking.

"Death? Are you in there?" She spoke out to him from outside the door.

No answer.

She wondered if he was at home or still in the Altar but she tried again, just in case.

"It's Life, by the way. I'm here if you need me." She said, as she gripped the door knob, twisting it to see if it was unlocked. Her hand slid all the way around.

Life frowned.

Why was it unlocked?

The door creaked quietly as she pushed it open.

"Death?" The silent eerie atmosphere stilled the room, making the dark room and stairs that were usually so full of warmth appear cold. She opened the door more, stepping to the door frame.

She straightened up, a memory coming to mind.

"Life, what are you doing?" Death stood at the door frame at his office while she opened draws and looked through papers.

"Death! I... uh- I-"

"No need to explain, I know what you were doing." He said, his expression stern.

"Death, I-"

"Life, why were you going through my things?" He asked placidly.

"It's just- I was bored and you always say to never enter your office and I was curious and-" She rambled before Death cut her off.

"Life, my office is off limits, you know this." He ushered Life out and shut the door.

"I made muffins" He said, "let's eat?"

She bit the inside of her cheek. Death was never a secretive person, but when it came to that room, Life couldn't count on two hands how many times Death told them to steer clear. Maybe if she found out what Death was hiding, she could help him and somehow stop the war, and she was curious. It was the perfect opportunity. She took a deep breath and pushed the office door wide open and walked in, the hardwood creaking with each step she took. She walked past his desk and placed her hand on the wooden double doors.

She held her breath, before pushing them open. Inside was another desk that was cluttered with objects and papers randomly splayed across the top and floors. Books piled on the floor, disorganized folders laid on shelves, and hand scrawled notes lay piled around random spots in the room. Two pairs of windows spilled daylight into the room, illuminating the dust particles in the air.

She didn't want to go in, but a part of herself longed for information. Anything she could get her hands on. Anything that could help.

"Death would want to stop the war." Life reasoned quietly before taking a deep breath and striding in. She quickly made her way to drawers and shelves, skimming over papers and folders. There were packets on the war, letters, and drafts on topics that she didn't pay much attention to.

She rummaged through cabinets below his desk and again on the desk when she saw a picture of Balance and Death… and a letter from the former. She slowly picked up the photograph and studied it.

Balance was beautiful, as always, and was smiling happily as Death's arm was wrapped around her shoulders, grinning. They were in Krasivaya, back before the war.

They looked happy.

She turned her focus to Death, his face frozen in a grin. She placed the photograph down and this time picked up the letter addressed to Death.

My dearest Death,

How are you? I heard you and Retribution went to check the autopilots. I hope they are running smoothly. I'm sure Retribution and Time would throw a fit if one of them was faulty. How are you doing though? I've told you to go easy on yourself. You work too hard sometimes. You deserve a break. Anyway, can you help me get everyone together for a little vacation! I promised Chaos that I'd take him on a trip for his birthday. How about a trip to Fortem? We could stop by at a beach! I know that you love to swim. I just want to spend some time with everyone together again, dear. After we left the Altar we barely got to have some time to goof off. See you soon!

Hoping you are well-
Yours forever,
Balance

Life smiled softly. Her hands trembled as she carefully set the letter back down. She slowly backed away from the desk, and just before she turned around, a certain book caught her eye.

Every inch of her being reasoned with her to turn round and sprint out the doors. She didn't know why it interested her, but she hesitantly approached it, and ran her fingers on the spine of the book. Her fingers brushed roughly over the leather bound book.

It was placed neatly between several other books, all lined up in a bookshelf. She glanced at the other book titles and all of them were different genres, mostly classic literature.

She glanced back at the book that had caught her eye and started to pull it out, when suddenly, the wall that the bookshelf was placed on started to turn.

She yelped, stumbling backwards. The wall creaked loudly as it spun 90 degrees, revealing a small compartment with thick cobwebs.

Her breath hitched. Almost mechanically she grabbed the book.

Similar to the others in the room, this one was adorned with more books than Life could count.

She rubbed the sheen of dust off her fingers as she splayed the book open, filled with what looked like faded writing. She picked it up, slowly digesting the words on the page.

Year 178 Day 36,

Tensions are rising. Time and I have been taking a lot of time alone of late, thinking about ideas as to why we are here and the sacrifices that lead us here. We are evidently here for a reason, and the quicker we figure it out the better. I'm growing restless. Arguments happen more frequently. It may take a while to finally figure it out. However, I'm almost certain we're destined for something incredible, and I should be glad to stand by it. We think that we may need to create more of us. Mortals, as we refer to them. Less powerful obviously. After having a discussion about it we ran into a significant issue. 'How do we do this?'

Regardless, what frustrates me most is that we have been thrown into this environment with absolutely no guidance, and we are expected to perform a miracle. Days have passed and we are getting nowhere. I personally think that however we do this, a price must be paid. It will most certainly drain a lot of energy from us, but I know that we are willing to take that risk. Can we even create life forms? Do we have the capacity to do it? If this goes wrong in any way, it could all go down in chaos. We still have much to plan, but even if a minor mistake is made, this may be the last time my handwriting will ever decorate this book. We will continue brainstorming but I am hoping all goes well. For all our sakes.

    Her brows furrowed. Her eyes quickly moved to reread the page again, and again, trying to make sense of it.

    She scrambled around for a paper, anything that had Death's handwriting on it. She looked through draws and cabinets, when finally she found a notebook, hidden under the study table.

    She flipped through the pages and saw scribbles of notes, all about the war. She didn't bother to read through it, but instead set it beside the diary, comparing both handwritings.

    Was this Death's diary? She gently touched the paper, the writing looked dull, as if it had aged for over a thousand years. It couldn't be Death's, could it? The handwriting was close, but there were still those small differences. The way Death dotted his 'i's with a slight flourish or the way his 's's were always slanted. More than that, the wording. Death didn't write like that.

Then what? Whose was this? It couldn't be Retribution. She knew Retribution. Not to mention Retribution didn't write down his thoughts. But whomever this belonged to, how come Death had it?

She closed the book abruptly and held it in her hands. She shouldn't have come inside. This was wrong.

She turned around quickly leaving the room, clutching the leather bound book to her chest tightly.

The book felt like it was growing more and more heavy in her hands, but she just couldn't bring herself to put it down. She shook her head. This never should've happened.

When she finally registered that she wasn't in Death's house anymore but walking on the streets of Lucror, her mind started back to life. She was replaying the same question over and over again like a scratched record.

What was Death hiding?

CHAPTER

FOURTEEN

FLASHBACK

The sun just begins to rise at the Altar.

Kick.
Evade.
Block.
Block.
Punch.

Fate rolls, recovering from the jab. She regains her stance as she drives her elbow into the side of Chaos' head. The impact sends a twisted smile onto her face.

"That's the best you got?" She taunts, the cheers of the other Protectors sounding muffled in her mind. She has only one thought consuming her at the moment.

Win.

Death leans down in front of Chaos' sprawled out form. Chaos looks up, his face twisted in frustration. Frustration aimed at Fate, at himself, at Death, at Life, at Retribution and Time, at everyone, at everything

"Get up." Death says plainly. "Is this what you would do in a real fight? Lay there as your attacker bests you? You need to be able to defend yourself. Where you lack you must make up."

Death speaks sternly, but softly. Yet, Chaos still glares at the ground.

"Well, I don't intend on getting in any more real fights."
Chaos quips sharply, as he shrugs the dirt off his clothes. "Why are we even doing this? I am currently being viciously attacked several times by my own family, and Fate keeps trying to kill me! Two times. I've tapped out two times and she wouldn't release me from her Franking choke hold!"

"We're doing this because you just got violently beat up by street trash, and you can't hold your own." Fate looks pointedly at Chaos.

"Well, if I had powers I-" Chaos mumbles.

"Well, Chaos, you still have time to discover them." Retribution interjects, "But we've talked about this. You need to know how to fight."

"Also, fights in real life are never fair- wait, did you just say 'Franking'?" Life interrupts.

"I like to use the names of my enemies as curses. It's quite catchy actually. Frank, you know? I'm sure it'll catch on soon."

"Okay," Death drawls, "Fate wins! Who's going next?"

"I don't see how me getting attacked is productive. This is actually quite traumatizing-"

"Life, how about you give it a shot?" Balance speaks up. Death turns to her, his gaze softening.

"Yeah, Life, give it a try." He insists.

Life steps forward, her hair falling out of a messy bun as she rolls up her sleeves, a sly grin adorning her face. Death backs away, as Life stands in front of Chaos' defensive form.

"Think you can beat me, Life?" He taunts jokingly, taking care to keep the weariness from his tone. Life's smile widens.

Punch.

Chaos winces at the blooming pain in his temple.

Twice. Two headshots.

Duck.

Block.

Life drops down and her legs swing forward, knocking Chaos off his feet.

"That was depressingly quick." Chaos groans at Fate's voice.

"Okay. Who's next?"

***

Flowers.

Death loves flowers.

"What brings you to this side of Lucror?" Death looks up as a man in a rugged flannel swaggers forward.

"Well, I saw a path of flowers and a sign about an art project and, well, I just adore arts and crafts so I couldn't resist.

"Oh, so you're here for the project?" A subtle glint of excitement lights up the man's eyes. "Oh yes, this way, sir, this way. We are so appreciative of every supporter." The man quickly ushers Death past him, following as Death makes his way down the flower trail lined by woods. "So what's your name sir?"

"Uh- D...erick" Death winces at himself. "What's yours?"

"Well Derick, names are powerful."

"Are you always this ominous?"

The man hums in response, as he leads Death further into the forest.

"So" Death drawls. "What type of crafts do you guys do?"

"Well our team, likes to make benefactions with what we have in nature." The man stated casually.

Death glanced up at the canopy of trees the man was leading him through.

"Oh, how resourceful and friendly for the ecosystem!" Death chirps. "It's getting quite dark here, how much further do we go?"

"Just a bit further. The thick of the woods is where the magic happens."

The man falls back into silence.

"So, Derick, what do you think about Death?"

Death pauses.

He couldn't know.

Could he?

"Um, like the concept or the Protector?"

"The god."

"Oh. Well, he's fairly good I suppose..."

"He is the superior god."

"Well the other Protectors contribute just as much to society like Fate-"

"Lord Death is the one who regulates the population. Without him we would be miserable."

Lord?

"We-They're not gods. They are here simply to protect the humans. As equals."

"Do you even worship Death?"

"Well-yes? Yes, of course I do."

Pull it together Death, you're supposed to be a Lucrorian.

"I just feel like he wouldn't see himself as a god or anything. I mean Death is humble and kind, and he's just here for the greater good."

"You keep saying 'He's here' does that mean you believe they live among us?" A beat of silence passes. *"You should know,"* He continues, *"The people you're about to meet are very passionate about Lord Death. After all, if we are generous enough to him, he will guarantee us eternal life. He said so himself."* The man says with a tinge of superiority.

When did I say that?

"If eternal life is what you seek then why not worship Life?"

"Because everyone knows that Death and Life are mortal enemies. Plus, Death promised us, not Life"

Death holds back a smile. Mortal enemies?

A thick silence falls again as the pair walk. "My apologies. I didn't intend to get so defensive. It's just that Death means a lot to my people and I."

"I understand." *Death sighs.*

The man stops. "We're at the first checkpoint."

"We are?" *Death questions.*

Checkpoint?

The man leans forward, his hand brushing over stone almost mechanically. His hand stills over a piece, hovering, with a sharp jab the stone pops out of place, revealing a pathway.

"That's quite a lot of security for an arts and crafts club meeting." *Death chuckles uneasily.*

"Some of the members have social anxiety." *The man answers quickly.*

"I see"

Makes sense.

"Just past this pathway."

Three more steps.

Two.

One.

The man steps to the side, allowing Death to go in front of him. Death enters a dimly lit circle, candles line the border, the flames dangerously close to the dense trees.

What peculiar outfits.

Must be a new fashion trend.

Several people stand in a circle, wearing long black cloaks that drag across the floor. All eyes turn towards Death as he entered.

"Everyone! This is Derick, he has humbly requested to join us. He has expressed to me that he shares our values, however he is still in doubt."

"Oh no, no doubts from me. I love arts and crafts. I do a lot of it in my free time! You know... clay work, painting, a bit of

123

*scrapbooking if I'm feeling bold-" Everyone's eyes stay trained on
Death, not a pair blinking.*

*"Nevertheless I expect everyone to give him a... warm
welcome."*

*"Where are the art supplies?" Death questions, laughing
anxiously. Cloaked figures step towards him. Harsh fingers cling to
Death, dragging him forward towards the center of the ring.*

*"What's going on?" A slight edge of panic seeping into Death's
voice.*

*The man steps towards Death, "It's truly nothing personal.
It's just that small sacrifices must be made for the gods."*

Is this not arts and crafts?

*"When Death speaks we must answer, and he is thirsty for
blood. He wants you."*

Where are they getting this from?

Wait.

This can't be arts and crafts.

Is this a cult?

A cult that worships me, Death, is about to kill me, Death.

*Panic fills Death's expression. "Sir I feel as if that would
be quite counter-productive-"*

*"Silence." With the wave of his hand, a man steps in front
of Death, unsheathing a dagger from his cloak.*

Nope.

*Death clenches his eyes shut. He calls for the familiarity
and it answers. The feeling of freefalling fills his senses as the dull
atmosphere and cloaked men morphed into one of piercing sunlight
and familiar faces.*

*"Death?" Retribution crouched down next to Death's
sprawled out form. Death quickly springs onto his feet, sending
panicked looks around.*

"What- you look awful." Fate deadpans.

*"I- uh." Death looks around seeing the eyes of Fate,
Retribution, Chaos and Life staring at him.*

Death brushes his clothes, "I went on a walk. Needed some air." He met Chaos' unimpressed stare.

Death clears his throat. "I- I should be going." He spins on his heels, striding towards the Altar's manor. He pauses and mumbles behind his shoulder, "Um, be responsible... yeah."

CHAPTER FIFTEEN

FATE

They had been standing before the throne room for

hours. It was an extensive process, to say the least, to even step foot in Favian's castle. They had been searched for any weapons, their identification badges were checked for any sign of forgery, and they were confirmed representatives of Mahana from some clandestine data the Lucrian spies provided the king. With all these procedures, it was clear how Lucror had kept out of Riqueza's clutches for so long. And she was here to ask them to step right into Riqueza's weaponized hands.

"Give him his wallet back, Avi." Fate muttered, glancing at Chaos' hands as he pocketed a hundred Pecunia. *Avi was* the name on his identification badge, though he insisted that Avi's childhood nickname was Kaos, *with a 'k'*, and that it was acceptable to call him as such.

"Sorry, sir." Chaos handed the wallet back to one of the guards assigned to watch their every move. The guards seemed to be quite awful at their jobs.

The guard, who appeared to be the others' superior based on his badge of ranking, snatched his wallet away. He pocketed it in his black uniform, with a scowl in Chaos' direction. He expected nothing more from a Mahanan, otherwise they would have been thrown into the dungeons in mere minutes.

A younger guard who stood at their left, his brown hair cut tightly against his head, walked forward to whisper something in his superior's ear. *Do we restrain him, sir? This is the seventh time he's done it this hour.*

Fate would have advised him to speak in anything but Lucrian, the world-wide spoken language, but it wouldn't have kept her from understanding. Protectors could understand every language spoken; it was an ability she only used to eavesdrop.

The superior spoke aloud to the younger guard, a threat clear in his words, "It's nothing but harmless antics, Finnian. His Highness will dispose of him soon enough for wasting his time."

The older guard shot Chaos a satisfied smirk, but Chaos merely placed a mask of innocence on his face. The two guards stationed on their right, kept their eyes off the scene, wanting no part in it.

Fate rolled her eyes and let them wander through the castle for the hundredth time. Lucror, in its seemingly endless gloom, was beautiful. Antique and dark structures lined every street, a preservation of time since life had been created.

The old Caderians had built this country as the first, integrating their language and history in many parts of Lucror. Many citizens believed the carvings engraved into Lucror's architecture and cobblestone streets told the secrets of the creation of the world. Unfortunately, very few spoke and could understand the old Caderian language. The language's disappearance didn't matter much because Fate knew the carvings were nothing but the tales of which woman or man they slept with at night.

The royal castle had the same ancient designs built of crumbling and weathered cobblestone, carved wood, and arches of glass. The door they waited to open was carved with a tale of the city's beginning along the bottom half. Above the kneeling citizens and the mountain line, was a carving of Death, his arms outstretched, as if claiming the city for his own.

Fate smirked at the horribly inaccurate carving. Death in actuality looked worse. For such a 'respected' being, he had no sense of style.

At the very top of the door, words were carved. *"Mors est praemium vitae."* Death is the prize of life.

Fate raised her eyebrows; the old Caderians were morbid people.

As she turned to show Chaos the amusing doors, they shook. Her heart dropped. She smiled, wide.

Apparently, whatever her victory smile looked like, was horrifying Chaos. He blinked at her, rapidly, as if he was checking to see if he was just imagining it.

With a swift motion, the double doors pushed open, freeing the frigid air from behind.

Finally.

"Go on." Finnian's superior spoke, raising his bearded chin in the air.

Fate switched to a subtler smile.

As they stepped forward, the doors creaked shut behind them. The bronze of the stripe on the Lucrian uniforms flashed in her mind, reminding her, yet again, that the world's fate fell on the most foolish king of all the centuries.

A black rug split the cobblestone flooring in two leading for what looked like half a mile to the dias, upon which rested a singular throne coated in genuine gold. The domed ceiling above was taller than it needed to be, displaying an unlit black metal chandelier. The only light provided was from the ten arched windows that nearly reached the ceiling, to their left side. Guards- more than Fate wanted to count- were stationed from the doors to the other end of the room, where King Favian sat, each holding a silver spear.

Favian.

The King had eyes dark and horrifying as dried blood. His dark hair was combed back in stark gelled rows. He stared at them blankly, a look on the edge of insanity.

Fate and Chaos exchanged raised eyebrows and continued forward until they were only 50 paces from the foot of the dias, and kneeled. Seering silence prickled the back of her neck as Favian's gaze fell over them, pinning them to the floor.

"Avi Nehru. Mahanan ambassador, South-West sector. Kahani Mehra. North-West sector." Favian's voice boomed through the grand room. "What is your objective for this conversation?"

"Your Majesty, we are so honored to be in your presence-"

"That is not the question I asked, *Ambassador*."

Fate clenched her jaw, the heat of fury climbing her face.

"Your Majesty, we come to ask you to join Hikma and Mahana's coalition against Riqueza's colonization." Fate didn't lift her head, but she didn't need to see to know Favian's disapproval of her words.

"Mahana and Hikma? Against Riqueza?" Favian spoke slowly through his Lucrian accent. He laughed, "*Mahana and Hikma?*"

Fate swallowed. She could have reasoned. She was good at it- or had been. Either way, Favian wouldn't have listened. His decisions were chosen randomly from a sack, made on a whim.

This was why she needed her abilities. To pick and choose her fights. To ensure that whatever she chose, she won.

The king hummed delightfully, then dropped his tone, "You know what I call that statement, Ambassadors? A lie."

Fate had to hold herself down. Her knuckles balled at her side and she spoke in Lucrian once again, "Excuse me, Your Majesty?"

Favian took a couple seconds to respond, "Are you not versed in the actions of your own country? Mahana works for Riqueza, and they are demolishing Hikma at this moment."

Hikma?

Her heart dropped. Her skin pricked with cold sweat. Hadn't she just been to Hikma? How had she not known? *How had she not known?*

At her silence, Favian laughed, sharp like whipping winter wind, "This war will not be won, girl. Whatever precious alliance you struck with Hikma will be forfeit, when the country falls. Do not ask me to fight against it, or my people will become nothing but ash and bones."

Hikma would fall.

Favian was right, Cadere would never prosper under an emperor.

They could never succeed. She would never fix what had been. Never- years and years and decades.

Decades and centuries and millennia and eternity.

Eternity.

Eternity fixing the ruin of a planet. Eternity without abilities, with then crackling tension, with a broken team.

Her vision seemed to blur. What had she waited for? What had she worked towards these past months collecting a coalition, when it was destined to fail? She had waited too long.

The mortal world moved faster than she had understood. Her breaths were getting shorter. How was she failing? How was she *losing?*

Fate couldn't speak, couldn't move, couldn't think. What was happening to her?

"There will never be a chance, girl." Favian stood from his throne, "Guards, escort them out."

Fate lifted her burning gaze to the king, and made a motion to move towards him. Chaos' arm wrapped around her arm.

She shot him a sneer, trying to pull away, but his grip was too strong. The guards pulled them from their kneeling positions, as Chaos whispered, shocked,"Are you insane? Did Favian rub off on you?"

Fate paused against the guard's motions, "You don't *understand*. This war needs to end. I need this war to end."

"Fate-"

"Leave me alone." Fate snapped.

Chaos wisely kept silent, but his expression darkened, and he turned from her.

The guards marched them through corridor after corridor, then leaving them outside the castle's grounds.

What would she say to the others? She had failed. But it didn't matter anymore. The world would fall anyway. She would watch as existence shattered. It wasn't like she had any means to stop it anyway.

She kept trying to keep herself from failing, but she already had lost. Her powers, Balance, her family. She had been a fraying thread away from losing herself in the process of trying to regain her purpose.

Now, there was no thread at all.

CHAPTER SIXTEEN

CHAOS

"Do you know a man named *Quinn*, sir?"

Chaos grinned when the man behind the informant desk made disinterested eye contact from above his glasses.

Chaos was hoping to finish this conversation soon. After Fate had snapped at him, she had mumbled 'find your librarian' before they split ways.A reconciliation of some sort. Clearly, they were both bad at apologizing.

Either way, he felt bad for her. Unfortunately, he was in the business of putting Fate's feelings before his own, so he had come to the Library of Lucror right after meeting Favian.

"A 'Quinn'?" The man drawled. His eyes were dropping so low, his tone so airy, Chaos was sure he was half-asleep. Perhaps sitting in a corner forced to watch the dim overcast skies for hours wasn't as thrilling a job as was expected.

Chaos kept his eyes on the man's wisps of blond hair that stood up around his head, "Indeed."

The man looked at Chaos. Blinked. Inhaled for what felt like dragging minutes. Then sighed dramatically, "Could you be any more specific?"

Chaos' eye twitched, subtly rocking on his heels on the tile. He could have reached over the russet colored counter and threatened to suggest comic novels were worthy of being placed in libraries. He didn't.

Chaos also inhaled, placing on a saccharine smile, before his thoughts escaped as words.

Hairless sloth.

"He knows a *Richard*, sir"

At this point the turning of the pages a corridor down was louder than the informant man, "I have a nephew named Richard."

Chaos laughed mockingly, then shut his mouth with a thin line. He placed his forearms on the wood and glanced down at the seated informant. His glasses were now aggravatingly tilted to a side.

Chaos looked down at the man's papers which were nothing but hourly logs to state he had worked. Only a dip pen and ink and a small hooked lamp lay to the side. No wonder the informant was drifting to do more exciting things- like shelving books- in his dreams.

The man frowned at Chaos' laugh, placing a finger to his lips. Even his shaking hands moved lethargically.

"I do know two Quinns that work here."

Chaos' eyes flew to the oval domed ceiling in frustration. After meeting with Death and Fate snapping at him, he was in no mood for this man's sluggishness. Nor was he in a mood to continue being in Lucror.

The painted pictures of the protectors around the bronze bordering and a large rustic pocket watch in the center were *somehow* more interesting than the man's spiked hair and the tall corridor washed in gray.

Of course there were two Quinns.

"Will you take me to them-"

"A Quinn Harris and a Waylen Quinn." The man finished without blinking an eye at Chaos' interruption.

The cold air smelling faintly of dust and wood was making Chaos' head spin. He should have asked Death for more information, but, unfortunately, he was too busy keeping himself from saying something worse than essentially calling Death a coward.

Chaos could have slid the informant some pecunia, Lucror's incredibly detailed currency, but he feared the man would not understand. That there would be no time to explain before Chaos cupped his hands around his mouth and yelled for a 'Quinn' while the man scrutinized the bill.

"Which one knows Richard?" Chaos asked through his teeth.

"Shall I make an announcement, sir?" The man scratched his wispy hair with the back of his pen. He seemed as unperturbed as a person could be.

Chaos' jaw dropped in disapproval as the informant pulled open a drawer and landed a small pulpit microphone on his parchment. He punched the button.

"No, wai-"

"May I have the librarian Quinn who *knows Richard* at the informant desk, please?"

Chaos cringed, thinking the voice was to boom around the library's lengthy halls and the center area with levels of shelves beyond this corridor. Thankfully, it was only announced as soft static, hearable, but not jolting loud.

He glared at the informant as the man neatly pushed the microphone into his drawers and looked up at Chaos' through his wire frames again.

"Anything else, sir?"

Chaos smiled through his seething anger, "That will be all."

"Pleasure." The informant blink's were becoming longer. He was no longer looking at Chaos, but beyond at the tall glass wall and the embedded door lined in bronze. What he found so alluring at the bland sky, the empty cobblestone streets, and the cloud-reaching buildings beyond that he most likely stared at everyday, Chaos didn't know.

But Chaos looked with him. That was until his eyes had also started to droop and his bouncing feet had stilled.

"You called for me, Waylen?"

Chaos flinched, his consciousness returning in a shock. What he found even more shocking was that the informant's name was Waylen. *Waylen Quinn.*

The informant had referred to himself when Chaos had asked for a Quinn, although it was quite obvious he had no idea of the 'Richard' Chaos was speaking of, so, in summary, there had always been only a *single* Quinn remaining?

Chaos' head was spinning. *Old fool.*

The informant didn't seem surprised at the voice, "I did. This young man wanted to see you."

Chaos dragged his glaring gaze from Waylen to a man with incredibly pale skin, as if he had never seen the light of day, which was on brand for a librarian. He had hair redder than his autopilot's lava and wore a navy colored sweater vest under a blazer. His eyebrows were raised at Chaos.

Quinn, Chaos knew now, put his arms in his pockets at his sides.

"I'm sorry, what is your name?"

"Chaos."

Quinn's eyebrows rose a fraction of an inch but said nothing about it, "Do I know you?"

Chaos grinned.

"I come from a man named *Richard.* He told me that you could aid me?" He placed on a cool expression, his lips tilted to a side. A sort of expression that should have signaled to Quinn that there was an unsaid meaning.

Quinn's face didn't budge, "I've met many Richards. Which one are you referring to?"

Chaos replied, fixing the sleeves of his coat, "Pale. Badly cut brown hair. Has never spoken a humorous statement in his existence."

Quinn paused at that and waved Chaos over as he walked. Chaos frowned, not sure why. When he glanced at Waylen, his head was dropped against his desk and his eyes were shut tight.

They walked in silence past the entrance corridor, and when they took a left the library's books were revealed.

Shelves spanned the four sides of the walls. There were three floors and on each floor, the shelves dipped into rooms, spanned those four walls, and back out again. Dotted along the shelves were colored leather bound novels and textbooks, scrolls of parchment, and stacks of newspapers. He could see ladders that looked to be smaller than his fingernail, but as he passed one, he noticed they were about ten feet in length.

Quinn glanced at Chaos as he stared at the vast wooden floor, a level down, placed with tilted globes of Cadere, and working and reading stations. He was speaking softly, expecting Chaos to do the same, "I'm not sure of who you speak, but I am able to show you to any section you would like."

Chaos dragged his awestruck gaze to Quinn for a moment before flicking to the softly painted ceiling and the clear glass in the very center. When he noticed the silence stretched for too long, he snapped back to the librarian, clearing his throat.

He narrowed his eyes, catching Quinn's lie. Or at least he hoped it was a lie.

"I can prove to you I know him." Chaos shoved his hand in his pocket and pulled out a wrinkled picture of Death. He was softly grinning, Balance at his side. Chaos, for his benefit, had folded back her half of the photograph.

He had stolen it from Death's desk when he had been talking.

They had stopped at a section labeled 'Astronomy' on the ceiling in a metal tile. Quinn leaned forward and surveyed the photograph. After a minute, he frowned and pulled away.

"Not familiar."

Chaos could feel his demeanor cracking.

"I need you to take me to the Night Market. *Richard* tells me you know the maze they call the Secret System. Will you? Please?"

Quinn shoved his hands in his trouser pockets, leaning against the shelves, "I'm sorry, sir. I don't understand you. I have no association with the Night Market. I'm a librarian."

To Chaos, that was the most suspicious thing Quinn had said so far.

Chaos smirked, "I can tell you more of Richard."

Quinn blinked blankly as Chaos continued in a hushed voice as a woman strode past them.

"He's frightened of ladybugs, although his girlfriend- I call her Lancey- loved counting their spots. His favorite subject is history, although I say it's useless. To be fair, all of them are quite useless. And has he ever told you he's awful at table tennis?" Chaos counted off on his fingers, leaning back on the railing across from Quinn.

Quinn's lips twitched.

Chaos noticed and cocked his head, "How much Pecunia?"

Quinn's subtle smile vanished at his words and he straightened, "I'll take you."

Chaos grinned, crossing his arms, "Money is incentive, then?"

"No. I don't accept bribery. I merely wanted to see how far you would go."

Chaos rolled his eyes as he pushed off the railing. He was ready to finally lay his eyes on the Night Market. He was ready to leave the parchment and ink smelling air.

"I cannot take you today." Quinn stopped Chaos in his tracks, speaking lowly, "Wait two days and return."

He paused, hesitating to ask, "What exactly are you looking for?"

Chaos paused and turned to face Quinn's implacable expression, "A rare element."

Quinn gave a soft huff of a laugh, before turning the other way. After taking a couple steps, he slowed to face Chaos, "Meet me at seven in the evening in the neighborhood past the south-west edge of Primor, just before Krise town square. If you see the castle, your compass is wrong. Do you know where that is?"

Chaos thought for a moment then nodded, "I'll be there."

"If you get lost, follow the stars."

Before Chaos could ask how, since the sun wouldn't have set yet, Quinn was already gone.

CHAPTER

SEVENTEEN

Life

The Altar.

It was a phenomenon Life couldn't quite wrap her mind around. After the whole incident with the diary, she had started to overthink everything. Why was Death so secretive? Why was Time mentioned in those deckled pages?

Nobody knew exactly who Time was except for Retribution. Everything was spiraling out of control and she needed answers. And the only person who could give her that was Death.

Tall green grass waved at her, and the breeze tickled her skin. There was something to the air that just made it feel fresher, more relaxing.

She looked at the large gray stoned house, filling her with memories. There were the tall tinted windows Death and Life painted together, the proud boulder that sat on the edge of the other side of the pond that they named 'Mighty Rock.'

She knelt down, feeling the rough stone pathways with overgrown weeds sprouting from the gaps. She looked down at the pond, seeing her reflection clear as day. She swirled her finger in the water, blurring her reflection as the fish greeted her with a nudge.

She remembered when she was first learning how to control and use her powers. She always loved the fish at the Altar, so she decided to create fish on Cadere. It was her first accomplishment and she couldn't stop smiling for days.

White yarrows and purple hyacinths bloomed in gardens along with many of her other favorite flowers. She walked through the winding paths of the Altar, with varying colored stones lining the ground. How many times had she run, walked, layed, or fell on these very grounds?

She knew this place better than she knew herself.

As she expected, Death was sitting down in a chair on the front porch, content, drinking a steaming mug of coffee.

She made her way to him and sat down at the opposite end of the table, studying him in silence. He raised his brow as he curiously surveyed her tense form. She merely grabbed an empty cup and poured herself a mug of coffee.

"I was wondering when you would show up again." He said, resting his back onto his chair as he looked at her.

Life scoffed. "That's it? Not a 'hi Life, how are you?'"

She missed being able to see Death whenever she wanted.

He grinned before looking at her. "How are you?"

She laughed nervously, "I don't even know."

Death raised his mug in a mock toast.

She smiled looking down at her steaming mug, before frowning again.

"Death, what are you still doing here?" she asked him gently. His expression morphed into a scowl and he looked into the distance.

"Here we go again." Death said, rolling his eyes.

"What?" Life narrowed her eyes at him.

"You know what I mean. Not even two sentences in and it's already straight to the point."

"Death, we've come a long way since just polite conversations. What's going on with you?"

"What do you mean?" He replied back, his voice suddenly stoic.

"You know what I mean."

"No, not entirely. Elaborate, please."

"It's been a while, Death. Eventually you'll- "

He stood up, abruptly pushing away from the table.

"Well, 'eventually' hasn't arrived yet, Life. You of all people should know that."

"I know, but Balance wouldn't want this. She wouldn't want-"

"You don't know what Balance would want," He snapped, shaking his head, "As long as I'm here, it's like... it's like I'm still connected to her."

She shook her head and stood up to face him. "We need you."

"Did Retribution put you up to this? Is that the only reason you're here? To try and bring me back?"

Life frowned, "No, I just wanted to check up on you- my family- and there's no need to be so callous to Ret. You and I know he's doing his best."

He dropped back into his chair.

"Well, I'm perfectly content here. You don't have anything to worry about." He said.

Life paused, letting the room fall into a thick silence as she regathered her thoughts.

"You know, when Krasivaya fell," she began, sitting down again in her chair. "I felt like a piece of me was gone."

Death huffed out a breath.

Life pursed her lips, "We were supposed to protect them. Guide the government in a way that wouldn't result in catastrophe." Her gaze dropped down, fiddling with the spoon in front of her. "I saw children die and heard their screams. And I couldn't do anything to prevent it."

"Life, that wasn't your fault. It wasn't anyones." Death began, his voice becoming softer. She inhaled and looked at him.

"My point exactly. You need to stop blaming yourself for what happened to her." Life interrupted.

Death tore his gaze away from Life.

She breathed in deeply, "Point is, I know how it feels to feel helpless. To not be able to do anything for the ones you love. But I'm trying to move on, and I think you need to too."

Death stared softly at Life.

"Everyone mourns differently. I'm not ready, Life. Maybe ask me again in a month or two." He whispered.

She couldn't give up on Death. Not as long as he was alive but maybe he really wasn't ready and the least she could do was give him some more time to grieve.

She shook her head. "So, what do you do here?" she asked him.

"Not much, but I've been thinking a lot."

"About?" She asked him.

"All of us, but mostly just thinking of long term strategies for the war." She nodded, when he continued again. "And you? What have you been doing in your spare time?"

She racked her brain for lies, knowing that confessing she snooped through his things wasn't the best option.

"I've been helping Retribution with a few things he needed." She said quickly.

His eyes widened, almost comically, at her words, "Retribution asked for help?"

"Why is that such a surprise? Am I not helpful?"

"No it's not that. It's just that I find it hard to believe that Retribution would ask for help with anything. He always takes it upon himself to finish what is needed alone, or with *Time*."

She mentally cursed herself. Of course Death could tell when she was lying.

142

"Just needed help with some war stuff. We're all helping him."

She technically wasn't lying.

He hummed in agreement, his eyes studying her.

"So how are things with the others? Has there been any progress lately?" He asked her.

"It's slow, but it's the only thing that's holding the war from complete havoc." she said.

A small smile traced his lips, and she wondered what he was thinking about.

The image of the diary nagged in the back of her mind. Her face fell. She just couldn't forget the eerie feeling she had when she entered his office and found the compartment. She shuddered just thinking about it.

"What are you thinking about?"

She looked up at the sound of his voice. "Hmm? Oh nothing. Just some war business."

She never used to lie to Death. Why was it so easy for her to lie now?

"How is Retribution anyway?" He asked her.

"He's good. He has a lot of work." She answered.

"Well he's consistently being wrapped in with whatever Time is doing to help. I get the feeling of having the weight of the world on your shoulders, but I could only imagine how much pressure Time is putting on him."

Her heart sank. She couldn't even begin to imagine. She wished Retribution would ask for real help, instead of having them do futile tasks.

"He's tired though, of everything."

"I figured."

Her thought wandered back to the diary she had found. She hadn't had much time to sit with it, but that didn't stop her from skimming it when she could. She didn't know what she was planning on doing with it. She didn't know why she even wanted it.

She was just hoping that this was the stroke of luck she was in desperate need of.

She sighed as her gaze shifted to stare out of the window to the Altar lake. Her eyebrows furrowed. The book had a mention of Time. Maybe the book had the answers to the mission Retribution always works on. Millions of questions swarmed through her head. But then wouldn't Death know?

She looked up at Death. The words were on the tip of her tongue.

"Speaking of Time, have you met him before?"

Death raised his brow. "You and I both know that Retribution is the only one of us that's met him, and you know how they are. Always secretive. Why do you ask?"

"Do you know what was there before we were created?" She asked quickly.

"I know that Time lived on Cadere-"

Life shook her head, "Well not that. We all know that. What else?"

Death frowned, "You know I don't know. I mean if any of us did know it would probably be you."

"It's just- so unknown. I remember when I first created life-forms on this planet. I was the first of us created. I did it alone. Of course, Time gave that letter of our purpose, but I never really knew Time until Retribution mentioned him to us."

"Right-"

"Did you ever send a letter back?"

Death set his cup onto the circular table, "How could I? I'm not even sure where he lives."

"I just wish there was something that we could find, something that would tell us what happened before Cadere." Death's tongue ran over his lips.

Bingo.

"Speaking of which, why is he always on about the mission? What about the war?" She continued, "like what is so important, even more important than Balance- might I add- than the war and all of us?"

"He is a busy-"

"But how would you know that?"

"Well, I'm only assuming based on his and Retribution's mission."

"It seems like Retribution is the only one that's working."

"You can't just say that. Life, I'm sure that whatever they're doing, it might help all of us in some way or another. Time knows best."

"Well Time created us to help, and what have we done? Fate let a war rage right beneath our noses and Chaos does nothing, I wander looking for something- anything- that can help, and you're here."

"Life, we were created for a reason."

"And I still wonder what that reason truly is. In fact, I've always wondered *how* we were created," she said, "a lot of questions and thoughts must've been put into it."

Death shut his eyes, "Definitely."

"What are your thoughts?" She asked, catching him slip up. He hesitated, not knowing what to say.

"Where's this coming from-?"

"Do you know something that I don't?" She pressed further.

"Don't be ridiculous, Life. I know just as much as you know."

"You do know that you're a terrible liar right?"

Death rolled his eyes, "Life-"

"No, but I'm serious! If Time really was that powerful, he should focus more on the war than his secret mission." She chewed the inside of her lip, deep in thought.

"Now that's a question for Retribution. Let's-"

"But that doesn't make sense. I'm sure he wouldn't just hide as the Protectors do everything. Time's smart. He would want to rule-"

"Life." He interrupted. "Enough. These are questions I don't know the answer to, and it feels awfully a lot like I'm being cornered right now."

"But-"

"Life there's nothing to investigate. We need to focus on the war."

"So there *is* something to investigate?" She asked him. He ran his hands through his hair in frustration.

"No I- why all the questions?"

Life shrugged, "It's just been on my mind for a while I guess."

"Life, you're digging yourself into a hole-"

"I don't need a lecture, Death. What I need are answers."

"Well you don't need answers. Just focus on the war."

"Why does everyone keep saying that?" She yelled. "There's something strange going on with Time and Retribution. And I'm gonna find out what."

Death looked at her, incredulously.

"Life, you should know that information is dangerous when placed in the wrong hands."

"So what? I'm the wrong hands?"

"Just- it can get used in all the wrong ways. It can spread, It can be used against you. There are just some things that are better off, for the sake of humanity, to remain buried under the surface."

She kept silent, pursing her lips. Maybe he was right. What if this investigation could get her into trouble. But she never got into trouble. She was always the one who did the right thing. This could be a point where she could prove herself and show them that a little information wouldn't harm her.

She regained her posture and continued.

"I am the oldest Death. The first protector to ever exist on Cadere-"

Death interrupted, "It doesn't matter. We all work together-"

"It does matter! Why can't you see? We can stop the war! Time was mentioned in it, and if I find out why, I'll get to the bottom of it."

Death paused. He narrowed his eyes at her, replaying her words in his brain.

Aw, Frank.

"Mentioned in *it*...?" He stared at her, trying to gauge her reaction.

"Uh- um," she racked her brain for excuses. "...mentioned in the conversation with Retribution."

His eyes shone with realization. "What really have you been doing with your time, Life?"

"What?" She chuckled nervously. "I already told you. I was attending to the needs of the war." She waved her hand lazily for emphasis.

If she told Death she found the diary, the conversation wouldn't really end well for her. Of course, she was sure that he was catching on.

"Life, you're lying. What did you find?" He snapped. He leaned forward in his chair, suddenly distressed.

"I didn't find anything!"

"Life, I-" Abruptly, they both felt a pull in the shoulders and a twist in the gut. They shared a look, knowing the feeling all too well.

"Retribution is calling a meeting." She told him. His eyes never left hers, searching for every bit of detail it could find.

"This conversation is not over, Life." He told her. She internally thanked Retribution for getting her out of this sticky mess and took a few steps back, not that she planned on attending this meeting either.

She was planning on actually stopping the war, rather than wasting her time arguing with the other protectors for an hour straight.

"Life-" Death's brown furrowed as if torn between saying something.

She stared at him.

"Be careful."

Life nodded once before closing her eyes, allowing the Altar to send her back to Cadere.

CHAPTER

EIGHTEEN

FLASHBACK

*F*ate *pulls her hair into a ponytail, letting the shortest layers in the front fall onto her face. She places her left arm over the crook of her other arm to stretch it. Switching the positions of her arms, she grins at the stillness of the manor.*

It's still dark outside, but Fate figures she can use this time to go on a run. She slowly walks to the door, careful not to make any noise.

Perhaps she also should have been paying attention to the furniture placement of her own home.

She falls to the ground in pain, her toe throbbing from slamming into the corner of the dinner table. She slowly blows air through her lips, scrunching up her face to keep from cursing.

"Fate?"

Fate freezes for a moment before shooting up to face the voice. Suddenly, she's forgotten about her injury.

Retribution stands in the hallway, arms crossed, in jogging pants and a thin jacket. He looks like he's been awake for a while.

"What are you doing?" His voice is low, so no one else hears them.

Fate frowns, "I don't see why that's any of your business."

Retribution smirks, grabbing a jacket from the hook to his side. He throws it at her. Fate raises an eyebrow, catching the jacket with both hands.

"It's cold." He merely says. He brushes past her to the door, "So, are we going or not?"

Fate doesn't know what to say. She just follows him, surprised they had the same idea.

Retribution shakes his head when she takes a step forward, "Are you going to be running without shoes?"

She looks down at her socks, dumbly. It's safe to say she's never been caught off guard this hard.

"I was just planning to put them on before you showed up." She pulls off her shoes from a rack by the door, leaning down to tie them.

Retribution watches her, a smile in his voice as he speaks, "Still need me to help you tie your shoelaces?"

Fate scowls up at him, "That was decades ago. Let it go."

He grins, gesturing to her jacket as his hand wraps around the door knob.

"It cannot be that cold." She grumbles.

Retribution proves his point by opening the door to let the frigid winter air into the heat of the Altar manor. Begrudgingly, she pulls on the jacket.

As they step out onto the porch, Fate pulls the door shut.

Feeling the cold wind bite at their faces, Fate mutters, "At least I hadn't put my shoes on the wrong feet."

Retribution starts running, calling back to her, "At least I didn't stub my toe two minutes ago."

Fate tilts her head and smiles dryly. She snatches a pillow from the porch couch and aims it at Retribution's head.

At his grunt of surprise, she sprints ahead.

"Try to be a little faster, would you?" She drawls.

His voice comes muffled through the whistling of the wind, but it's clear what he says.

"I hate you."

***

Chaos groans, pushing away from the wooden piano. He picks up a few loose pieces of sheet music off of the floor, placing it messily onto the piano bench.

Life and Death just left to check up on the autopilots, along with Fate who wants to 'observe the Rebellion', Balance is still asleep, and Chaos is bored.

Chaos collapses onto his bed, propping himself up on his elbows, staring lazily out the window.

His eyebrow quirks.

There is someone else at the Altar with him.

He pushes against the plush fabric of the bed, striding to his bedroom door.

With newfound determination he practically skips down the hall, only slowing down when he faces another wooden door.

With a grin on his face, Chaos slams the door open.

A startled yell sounds from Retribution.

"Frank! Chaos? What are you doing?" He snaps.

Chaos slowly leans against the door hinge. His eyes survey the room slowly, opting to ignore Retribution's question.

"Hello?" Retribution scoffs, pushing away from his desk, "Get out."

Chaos bites back a smile as his eyes skim over Retribution's Perry Siles vinyl.

Retribution crosses his hands, "You're infuriating. Go find someone else to bother."

Chaos hums, a smile spreading onto his face as his eyes take another slow lap of the room.

151

Before Chaos could blink, a plush toy, gifted to Retribution by Balance, comes hurling at his face.

Chaos yelps as his hands come to swat away the toy. Then with a quick shrug Chaos spins on his heels, walking back to his room.

"Chaos-"

Chaos grins, throwing a quick look over his shoulder *"What's that?"*

Muffled clattering comes from Retribution's room, "Chaos, close the door!"

"Gladly!" In a quick motion Chaos slams his own bedroom door shut, grinning to himself.

CHAPTER

NINETEEN

Life

Life was tired of doing this alone. As it turned out,
reading a mystery journal only got her so far.

A group of kids were kicking a ball back and forth as the
townspeople chatted amongst themselves. Fortem's people were
incredibly tight-knit. The country was one of the places on Cadere
that Life had always adored. The hot sandy landscape that seemed
to never-endingly stretch, the bustling of the mortals, and her
favorite part of all, Retribution.

She reminisced of the memories of them together, as she
walked through the suburban parts of Fortem.

One memory always seemed to pop up in her mind; the
time where Retribution gave her a gardenia. A simple gesture
really, but she couldn't help the smile form on her face as her mind
replayed his nervous blush when he was around her.

She walked through the town, his house becoming visible.

She needed to talk to him. It was destroying her, not being
able to talk to anyone about it. The diary, the war, Time- it was all
overwhelming.

As she walked through the winding streets, she was met
with a brown house, with colorful flowers Life had made a while
ago.

She stumbled up the two front porch steps and debated on whether to knock or not. She remembered the conversation with Death a few days ago, when he told her how much stress was on Retribution.

She took a deep breath, her hand raising to knock the door before pausing suddenly. The door was slightly ajar.

She frowned. It wasn't like Retribution to keep his door unlocked. She narrowed her eyes at the door, creaking it open and peering inside.

"Hello? Ret?"

No answer. That was odd. She silently slipped through the open door and made her way through the familiar halls of his house.

"Is anyone home?" She asked again. Silence. She made her way through the kitchen, passed one of the bedrooms, when suddenly she heard talking. She froze as a smooth voice spoke.

"Any progress yet?" The voice asked calmly. She couldn't recognize it, her body seemed to. A chilling shiver climbed up her spine.

She felt her shoulders tense up and her eyebrows scrunch together in concern. The feeling was foreign.

She didn't know whether she liked it or not.

"Not yet, but I'm getting closer." A voice, all too familiar, sighed.

Retribution. There was silence on the other end, when she heard the shuffling of feet.

"Do you know why this is really important to me, Retribution?"

"I've wondered, but I just assumed you didn't want it to get in the wrong hands."

"That is one of them, yes," the voice said, walking around as the floorboards creaked. "Control is something that many never attain. It is not something that you can just grab while you can. In fact, you and I have something in common."

"And what's that?"

"We both seek control. I asked you to help me because I saw something in you, and I still do. However, what we are looking for is beyond anything you can comprehend. Victory is in itself inevitable, now are you the one that fights for victory and control?"

No reply.

"I am dutifully doing my side of this... *scavenger hunt*, if you will, but I can't do this alone. I need you to deliver." The voice continued speaking.

"Of course, Time." Retribution spoke softly.

Her eyes bulged, and her jaw dropped.

Time?

Only a thin wall with peeling paint separated Life from the being that created them- the being they had idolized for so long.

"You've yet to let me down Retribution. I'm counting on you. I've told you all I know: it's either the caves, rivers, or underground. Anything, even the smallest thing can be significant enough to help us retrieve it. I will try to find more information to narrow the options down, but in the meantime, *search everywhere for the stone.*"

Life heard a long period of silence. Suddenly the knot in her shoulders and upper back untangled and relaxed.

Retribution groaned softly. She could hear feet shuffling, papers getting tossed all over the room, and drawers getting opened and shut.

A part of her mind begged her to stride through those doors and embrace him. She shouldn't have come.

She stepped away some more when suddenly she heard the back door shut. She stopped. She knew there was a back door that led outside from the meeting room. Was Retribution gone?

She came closer to the edge of the wall and peered from behind it, scanning the room. The room was empty. She let out a breath of air and slowly stepped into the room.

The mess of Retribution's frustration was blanketed over the room. She hesitated before going over to his desk, where a large map of Cadere was splayed out. She narrowed her eyes.

She should definitely not be doing this. She continued staring at the map.

"No. I can't. I couldn't do that to him." She whispered to herself.

Her hand inched forward.

It was right there, and besides, no one would know. Just a few steps forward and she would see a glimpse of what Retribution had been hiding this entire time.

She forcefully closed her eyes, clenching her fists. A small peak wouldn't hurt. She gave into the temptation, and took a few steps forward, the map coming into clear view.

She saw several 'X' marks scattered across the map of Cadere. Question marks and annotations littered the sides. Her eyes skimmed the map, her fingers lightly grazing the countries and X's. She remembered what Time had told Retribution some mere minutes ago, about searching for something. What were they searching for? Questions swirled around in her head. First it was the diary, and now this?

She tore her gaze away, and stumbled back. She needed to leave. Death was right, she was snooping.

She pushed through the back door and left Retribution's house.

***

Life sighed and fell onto her plush bed. Key words replayed in her mind: searching, caves, underground, rivers, and stone.

She chucked a pillow into the air.

Catch. What's so important about a stone?

She launched it again.

Catch. What is significant about underground, caves, and rivers?

Catch. Why was Time mentioned in the Diary?

Catch. If someone knows about Time, do they know about us?

She pushed herself into a sitting position.

The way Time talked about control rubbed her the wrong way. Victory? Victory to what? What's there to win?

She threw the pillow again, her mind snapping and her arms releasing too much force. It landed on the floor beside her and she groaned. Life blew away the sliver of hair covering her eyes, then stood up. Crouching down, she grabbed the pillow while looking wearily at a large box under her bed. She debated opening it and returning the diary to Death's library, but something about the book was alluring.

She would never be able to return it. It's too late now.

She heaved the large treasure-like box out from under her bed and rummaged through the century old belongings she liked to horde. Tucked away beneath a large Table Tennis paddle was the Diary. She smiled at the paddle, reliving old memories.

"You ready to lose, Life?" Chaos smirked at her, over the table.

"Bring it on."

"Winner fights me. After all I am the all time champion-" Death added in from the side. Whoever lost had to make breakfast for all six of them for a week and she most definitely was not going to be it.

"Keep on dreaming Death." Balance said, patting him on the back.

"What? I am." He replied, as they all laughed.

"Whatever you say." Fate joined in.

157

"Okay, are you two ready?" Retribution asked them.
"Ready." She affirmed.
"Ditto." Chaos added.
"Okay, start!" Balance said, and the match began.

Nostalgia burned a hole in Life's heart, as she brought the paddle down and set it inside the box, most likely never to be used again. She gingerly grabbed the leather-bound diary and made her way to her bed. With nimble fingers she flipped to the first entry in the book:

Year 63, Day 13

Powers as of now:

-Accidentally turned a bagel into a rock

-What else?

Possibilities:

[STEP 1: Learn how to harness]

-Matter into other matter

-Matter into living things?

-Frogs for ammunition

-Fish

~Roses

~Others like me?

*Would that need more
power?

Feelings:

~Shocked

~Little tired

~Exhilaration- finally!

She looked up from the book, her mind stuck on only one word: powers. She grazed the handwriting printed onto the old sheet of paper. There was no doubt it was Death's handwriting. But it didn't make sense. Nothing made sense. Death's only powers were delaying death and well... death.

She skimmed the next couple of pages, reading a couple of progress entries and a page full of brainstorming scribbles. She flipped through the diary. Some pages were bullet pointed, straightforward, and short while others were nearly incomprehensible.

This wasn't Death.

She frowned. Maybe Death copied it?

She flipped through the book again, this time flipping all the way to the end when suddenly, the words were different. There were fuller, completed sentences in a differently styled manner.

A change in author?

She creased her eyebrows together in confusion. Majority of the book was written in the same style. A jumble of thoughts as if the writer themselves was confused. The second part was more of what you would expect in a diary. Not to mention, it was significantly more comprehensible.

She flipped through the pages, seeking to find more information related to the keywords that were glued to her mind. She stopped at the very last page of the diary, reading it carefully.

Year 238, Day 59

It's unfortunate really, how she could never share the prosperity in which we now live in. Living in the Altar is going well, and the Protectors are proving themselves more and more useful everyday. We come down every once in a while, visiting our favorite caves and rivers. There is this one river that really captures the essence of balance.

She read that sentence again. Was it just a coincidence that Balance was mentioned?

It's my personal favorite so far, but no matter where I go, it's never enough. After the sacrifices we made?

She paused for a brief second, absorbing everything that was displayed on the paper. She turned the page but was met with the end of the diary.

She set the diary back down on the bed, trying to wrap her mind around everything that was thrown at her, including the map. It didn't make sense. Death wasn't there before Cadere was created. Not only that, but the way each sentence was phrased was unlike him. So that solidified it.

The book had to have been copied by death, but that led her back to her first question: Who's diary is this?

She shook her head and tried to remember the map she had found in Retribution's house.

Caves, rivers, X's.

It was all there right under her nose. She just needed to piece it together.

Time and Retribution said they were looking for a stone, but why?

"The mission." She whispered.

Life knew the stone had to be connected to 'the mission', but what if it was the mission?

Life frowned, flipping back through the pages absentmindedly. If It was indeed the mission then all she needed to know was that the stone was powerful. Incredibly powerful.

She remembered the countless times Retribution had impatiently ranted about the significance of the mission and how it would bring control and peace. So that was a strong possibility. Time and Retribution were searching for a stone that could grant them control and peace.

She looked at the cover of the book.

It could mean they had found a means to end the war.

But why did a stone hold that much power? And why didn't Retribution tell the other Protectors about it?

Life's brows drew together in confusion as she shook her head frowning. It didn't make sense. Why place all bets on a stone?

It had to have been a strong enough lead for Time- the all knowing creator of the world- to chase it down.

Life bit her cheek as she stared at the book.

Taking someone's mission as her own was something Life couldn't do, yet the hunger in her was itching to attack at the opportunity. But she wasn't stealing his job. Retribution would still work on it, and besides, Life has an additional source that he doesn't. Why let that go to waste? After all she was doing Time and Retribution a favor.

Life flinched at the sound of a slamming door.

Her eyes widened as she slammed the book shut, scrambling to hide it beneath her pillow when a voice called out.

"Life! Are you home?"

Retribution.

Life rushed to make her bed look more slept in. Her foot hit a hard box, and, with a thud, the wooden box- previously holding the diary- fell off the bed.

"Oh, Frank!" She whispered shakily. She reached under her pillow and shoved the book into the box which was now lying on the floor.

Footsteps echoed through the house.

In a sharp motion she kicked the box under the bed and rolled into the covers. Retribution opened the door and met her with a small smile.

"Hey." He whispered.

"Hi." She said slightly out of breath, blowing a strand of hair out of her face.

"So, I was wondering if you wanted to take a stroll with me? We could even visit your favorite river?" He rubbed the back of his neck, waiting for her answer.

"Oh!"

She looked out of her window. Moonlight lit the ruins of Krasivaya.

"Sure Ret, let's head out." She said, needing to get out of the house.

***

"How have you been?" She asked him, as they wandered through the ups and downs of the river Onda in rural Riqueza.

He sighed, " I've been better."

"Well, what happened?" She asked, even though she now knew exactly what was weighing him down.

"Just- a lot of things." There it was again. Always holding back.

"Well… how is the mission coming along?" Life asked, adopting an innocent face. He glanced at her, then swallowed, his Adam's apple bobbing with the force of it.

"I- It's fine… let's try and talk about something else. How are you doing?"

"Hey, if you need to talk, you can always talk to me."

"I know. I just don't really want to talk about the mission." He said, his voice tense.

"But don't you want to get it off your chest?"

He slowed his walking as if hesitating, "How do you know I have something *on* my chest?"

Life frowned, coming to a stop. "Ret, you're constantly stressed about everything. Maybe it would be good for you to let some steam out."

"Life, you know I can't tell you-"

"Well, I know that, but-"

"There is no but. I can't afford to lose Time's trust and there is just too much going on for you to understand-"

Life's eyes widened, "Understand? Wait, let me remind you that *you* were the one who called me for a walk. And when I ask you a simple question, you shut down."

163

Retribution clenched his eyes shut. "I know. I'm sorry. I thought we could talk about something else. I didn't mean it like that," Retribution said, his voice becoming soft.

Life couldn't care less, scoffing at the fact he would say something like that.

"Then what did you mean?" Her eyes narrowed as his eyes darted around nervously.

"Life, this is a lot for me to handle and I'm sorry if I made you mad, but I don't want to dump all of this on you. If I can't handle it, you certainly can't."

Life scoffed, starting to walk again. "You are such a hypocrite Retribution."

Retribution drummed his fingers against his thighs as his face twisted into frustration. Life turned to stare at Retribution as he paused, checking his watch, as Life waited for him to retort back.

Life rolled her eyes, "I guess you need to leave huh?"

"I'm sorry, we'll continue this later." He replied softly.

"What are you gonna do?"

"I can't tell you, Life! Just drop it."

"Retribution, why did you call me out here?" She said, her voice growing steely. She stepped towards him. "Because you needed to clear your mind." She mocked slightly. "Is that all I am to you? A distraction?"

"How could you think that?" Retribution sputtered.

"You keep running away from *all* your problems and you won't let us help you. Let *me* help you! Like now, you always go on about the 'mission' because you follow Time around mindlessly? You think you're some untouchable man that can do it all by himself, but he can't open his eyes and see that the people who actually care about him want to help! You're not a burden to me. It's exhausting! Do you want me in your life or not? Because it sure seems like you're doing fine without me."

Retribution remained silent, his mouth ajar in disbelief. His gaze lingered on hers for a second before looking back to his watch.

"I'm sorry." Retribution's voice wavered slightly.

"You don't need to be sorry, just let me help you."

"And you think I don't want your help? I would *love* your help. But you can't. It's not possible."

"Why not?"

"You know why Life. It's complicated."

"Then explain it to me." She said, "Go on."

He blew out a puff of air, the darkness around the pair was suddenly daunting. He checked his watch again, and closed his eyes.

"Tell me what you have to do. Prove to me that I'm trustworthy."

"You know I trust you Life…"

"Do you, though?" Her voice had a bitter edge to it.

"Life." Retribution said, clasping her hands in his gently before she yanked them away.

"Tell me, Ret." She said, her voice cracking.

"Don't make me choose between you and Time. Some things are meant to be kept secret, and you need to just stop. I mean it, I don't want you caught up in something. Just stick to going through Death's things. Speaking of which, I have yet to hear anything about that because you refuse to come to a single progress meeting!"

"Stop lecturing me."

Retribution sighed, his head drooping towards the ground. "You're not giving me a choice here."

Life's eyes widened as he disappeared.

Retribution's words pounded in her mind.

He chose *him*…

CHAPTER TWENTY

AAHI

"She should be dead in mere minutes."

Aahi peered down the shadowed streets, the humid wind whipping at her armored suit. Her eyes lifted to domed structures rising above the village streets- Hikma's presidential palace. Compared to hers and, especially, to Casimir's, President Inaya's home seemed quaint. It was detailed in white stone, revealing its antique nature. Upon the highest visible dome, was a flag violently flailing in the harsh wind.

Fallen merchant's stands, broken glass, discarded bullets, and the echoes of horrified screams littered each bricked road. Casimir's army, collected from the captured kingdoms and those from their own countries, scoured the deserted streets, a hand on either a rifle or a blade. They waited for an attack of some sort, although they knew it wouldn't come.

What was left of Hikma's measly army was destroyed. Riqueza and Mahana's armies had attacked from the rear, taking months to travel through Fortem for an unexpected surprise, instead of where Hikma's army was stationed by the ports. While less than a fourth of Riqueza's total army fought at the border already doing maximum damage by capturing war prisoners and thoroughly destroying Hikma, control wasn't theirs until President Inaya stopped breathing.

The war for control over Hikma had only been raging for a mere week. With the full force of an army from 5 different countries and a strategic plan, adding the fact Hikma stayed independent- which meant their resources were only what they could gather- the odds were in their favor. Fate was in their favor. *Bhaagy mahaan ke lie mudata hai.* A mahanan saying- Fate twists for the great.

She and Casimir had traveled to Hikma, after the brunt of the war in the capital, to be present as the country fell into their hands. She remembered, when she was young, visiting Azhar with her mother for a council meeting. The streets then were bustling with citizens, rosy cheeks and bright smiles across their warm tan skin. She could picture her leaving her mother's side and running through the streets, feeling more at home in Hikma than she ever felt in Mahana, regardless of the fact she was next in line for the throne. She could still smell the faint aromas of baked flatbread, much like the ones at home, of their rice dishes, and their nutty pastries.

Any trace of what used to be, was now snuffed, buried below a mountain of terror and bloodshed.

She couldn't help but think that her mother would have been unbelievably disappointed in her.

"The rest of our army dwelling in Hikma is breaching the fortress of the presidential palace at this very moment." Casimir-Riqueza's king- spoke, turning to Aahi. His face was unreadable under the shadows of the dark clouds above, "Once President Inaya is disposed of, Hikma is officially ours."

"Kill the head…"

"Kill the body." Casimir nodded at her as thunder rumbled from the distance. Aahi couldn't tell if it was an agreement or a warning from Fate.

They stood together in silence again. Aahi could visualize what once was a symbol of power in Hikma, fortified by the remaining army to keep safe their leader - who hid like a coward- in ruins. The blood of her and Inaya's people would pool together as a symbol of their unity.

What once was seven separate kingdoms and countries would soon be one.

Globs of water, their impact as hard as rocks, collided against the brick, against the shops, against the housing buildings, against her and Casimir's bodies. She looked at him.

Shockingly, she trusted him. He had brought her to victory. He had brought her country prosperity and well being. He was her partner in war.

He taught her how a ruler led.

How one kept power.

With fear, with force, with strategy.

She was loved; she was feared.

But all that mattered to her was her own country. The one her mother had failed to lead. The one Aahi had built up over years after her mother was murdered.

An internal clock ticked in Aahi's ear. Her heart pounded, with apprehension or exhilaration, she wasn't sure.

"How do you feel, Aahi?" Casimir's brown hair now coated his pale skin in a wet mess. A thin band of gold that rested on his head, the symbol of a king, glinted in the dim light. His eyes, sharp and clear, looked at her, waiting for her answer.

"Ready." The wind tugged on her coat.

"Ready?" Casimir's gaze fell down on her, heavy.

"Ready for this to end. For the war to be over. For peace." Aahi kept her unfaltering gaze trained on Hikma's flag above the dome.

Casimir tisked softly, as he followed her line of sight. He rolled up the sleeve of his long coat. "Peace will never come. Not in our lifetime. Not for us."

Water dripped down her face, blurring her vision, but was unmistakable when Hikma's flag lowered.

Minutes later, a dark green and red flag, and a deep purple flag under it, flew across the darkened sky. As if on cue, lightning tore through the darkness, the white tendrils branching across the clouds.

Inaya was dead.

All Aahi could do was stare at the flags. Hikma was theirs.

"Hikma is ours," Casimir said. There was no victory in his voice, no glee.

The wind howled.

"All that's left is Lucror." He continued. Aahi could feel Casimir try to catch her gaze.

Lucror was the last step to success.

Her people would be safe, and soon when *her people* consisted entirely of Cadere, they would all be safe.

As long as she won, as long as Mahana prospered, she would be willing to destroy the world.

And it seemed, that was exactly what she had done.

CHAPTER

TWENTY-ONE

CHAOS

Krise was a perfectly average looking suburb where it seemed as if its residents dutifully visited the grocery market each week and were not dutifully hiding an entrance to the most illegal market on Cadere. Chaos walked on the pavement, occasionally kicking a pinecone. His eyes were up, looking for Quinn.

The neighborhood's streets were empty but for the bronze rays of the sun which spanned down the roads like carpet. Through a few windows he could see figures seated at their dining tables or lounging on the couch. It was the only sign that the street wasn't completely uninhabited.

Chaos sighed as he stopped, turning in place. Perhaps trusting some random man- a *librarian* at that- wasn't the best idea, nor was failing to ask for clearer direction and establishing a form of communication.

Meet me at seven in the evening in the neighborhood past the south-west edge of Primor, just before Krise town square. If you see the castle, your compass is wrong, Quinn had said.

Chaos couldn't see the castle and this was the only neighborhood between the capital- Primor- and Krise's center portion. He had to be in the right place.

Chaos was now sweating. The summer heat didn't stop bearing down on him although the sun was halfway gone. There was no chance he would wait for Quinn longer than another ten minutes.

Perhaps Quinn was playing a game. If Chaos was doing something illegal, he wouldn't openly give directions. Chaos dropped his eyes to the plates of pavement beneath his feet. There was a small carved star at the corner of a plate a couple feet ahead.

If you get lost, follow the stars.

Chaos grimaced. He'd have to give Quinn tips on his 'clandestine' clues.

Hurrying ahead, he *followed the stars* until he stopped at a house deep into the turns of the neighborhood. The house was painted a light blue, the wreath placed on the door in the outline of a star. The curtains were drawn shut, the lights all turned off.

Chaos scoffed and muttered something along the lines of, 'inconspicuous' and 'stupid'. He still had no idea what he was doing here. Was it Quinn's house and he'd take him to the entrance further off? Or was this the entrance? He inhaled and decided there was no other way he could spend his time since Fate was busy locked in her apartment alone; he strode to the door and knocked.

The door flung open in a moment and inside stood Quinn.

"Hi-"

"Inside. Shut the door." Quinn spun, leaving Chaos on the porch to obey.

Chaos stepped in the dim building, annoyed, shutting out the small ray of light and plunging the room into darkness. Without a second thought he followed Quinn down a set of stairs.

"Is this your house?" Chaos squinted his eyes to look for photo frames along the wall.

"Yes." Quinn twisted around the wooden handrail as he reached the lower level.

"The entrance to the Secret System is in your home?"

Quinn paused as he reached a metal padlocked door. He glanced at Chaos finally, "We call them safe houses. A few of our Travelers keep entrances in their homes and the vendors use them at their discretion- well, on the weekends when the market is open."

He reached down into a box by the door and tossed Chaos a flashlight, "Is that what you'll be wearing?"

Chaos grabbed the torch and glanced down. He was wearing a half sleeve shirt for the summer heat and his usual pair of pants.

"What do you mean-" Chaos glanced up and then only did he see the man's boots and a coat slung over a sweater vest.

It appeared he hadn't accounted for the temperature below ground.

Quinn sighed and pulled a bronze key from his coat and began working on the lock. Chaos focused his attention on Quinn's home. The level only consisted of a single couch across from the door. The only other thing the room had were shelves of books, which spanned floor to ceiling on all the other walls the metal door was not on.

Why a librarian would need his own books was beyond Chaos. Perhaps these were collectors editions.

There were no signs that there were other inhabitants of the house.

"Does your family live with you?" Chaos walked around to face Quinn, watching his fiddle with the key. A click sounded and the metal door swung open. Chaos widened his eyes at the incoming door and sidestepped.

Quinn waved Chaos into what seemed like a dark abyss with dark concrete stairs. Chaos hesitated, wondering if the man had heard his question, but Quinn was walking fast down the stairs after telling him to shut the door behind them.

The librarian was right. The tunnels were absurdly cold. Chaos felt like he was walking into a cooler. His skin prickled from both the cold and the echoing noises of each step.

Chaos pivoted and pulled on the steel handle. The door boomed throughout the tunnels, the soundwaves clapping at his ears. Disorientated, Chaos shuffled back down to meet Quinn, who had switched on his torch. But when Chaos reached for his own, Quinn held up a hand.

"Use yours when and if my torch stops working or if we get separated. Mine should suffice." Quinn gave Chaos a quick unplaceable smile as he shone the light straight forward. The light didn't fall on an end, making it seem as if the tunnels went on forever. Or perhaps they did. "It'd be in your best interest *not* to get separated."

Chaos mocked a smile, "I'll be sure to remember that."

The tunnels were about ten feet tall and fifteen feet wide. A pure absence of light for miles. The walls and flooring were all made of the same painted concrete with no wall art, no maps, or symbols. There was nothing there except a thick coating of dust.

Although if he turned back he could still see the door, he was already exhausted from the absence of- well- pretty much everything. When Chaos opened his mouth to supply some commentary on the frigid silence, Quinn finally answered Chaos' question.

"My family does live with me. We've had a family business down here since the Night Market's existence. So I've been a Traveler my entire life." Quinn spoke softly, his voice echoing like whispers in their ears, "I no longer partake in the trade, but my younger sister and parents do."

"Sister?"

Quinn laughed softly as they continued forward, Chaos with his arms crossed to provide heat to his bare skin, "When she's not at school, she's selling banned books."

Chaos gaped and paused in his tracks, "Your family is part of an illegal market and they sell cloth-bound sheets of *paper*? So you decided to be a librarian to keep with novels but preserve your morality? Am I getting that right?"

Quinn spun around, glaring, "Walk faster or we won't make it before midnight." He spoke again dryly, "But that's correct."

Chaos shook his head in disbelief, increasing his pace, "Midnight? That's in four hours."

Quinn didn't respond as they slowed at a sort of fork in the path. There was the road that they were walking on, that led straight, and two arched holes in the left side of the concrete that led somewhere else. They took the second arch on the wall.

"Let's hope my memory still holds." Quinn quipped, walking forwards.

"What?" Chaos asked unamused as he slid in after Quinn.

This tunnel was narrower but just as tall. Just as endless and dark.

"How much do you know about the Secret System?" When Chaos shrugged, Quinn continued, "It was originally an Old Caderian idea that they could dig these tunnels under the oceans and get to more land. When they realized the ground wasn't deep enough to hit the ocean floor, they moved these tunnels inland to stabilize the ground so Lucror wouldn't collapse around the edges. Due to the uselessness and the hazard of these tunnels, they patched up the entrances and never spoke of it again. It wasn't until a century ago that Lucrians found them and repurposed them after stabilizing them with concrete. Since then it's been expanded and used to get things in and out of places they shouldn't be."

Chaos nodded with respect, "Smugglers."

Quinn's tone wasn't as admiring, "Smugglers. And the infamous underground market we all know which is named after the pitch black tunnels it takes to get there and the time when the market is opened- Night."

Chaos couldn't feel his fingers anymore and it had only been about thirty minutes, "And the Night Market? How did it come to be?"

Quinn scoffed, "When the smugglers realized they needed a place to sell those items."

They grew silent and thankfully the shuffling of their shoes was enough to fill the absence.

Chaos didn't know how long it had been as he followed the shaky movement of Quinn's torch as they strode. His legs were growing weaker and he only snapped from his daze each time they stopped to turn down another pathway in the forks and fell under the haze again as they continued.

"Are we there yet?" Chaos groaned, his mouth feeling dry. He rubbed at his forehead wearily.

Quinn responded simply, "No."

And they kept walking.

At a point, Chaos had gasped loud enough to echo for minutes when he heard something scurrying. He had only taken a breath when Quinn pointed the light at a horrifyingly large rat and dragged him forward.

About two and a half hours later, Quinn stopped. He hadn't stopped at a fork in the tunnels or a large cavern with a bustling crowd and colorful tents. He'd merely paused on the path.

"Go forward about fifty feet and take the first exit on your right. I wish you luck." Quinn nodded to Chaos, "You can use your torch now."

Chaos blinked through his daze, confused, "Are you not joining?"

Quinn seemed to pale and shook his head, "I told you. I don't associate myself here anymore. You can get back by finding the tent selling banned books and hand them your torch. See that star emblem? My family will know how to take you home from there."

Chaos was quite sure he would not be taking the tunnels back above ground.

"Be very careful. This market isn't fit for young people or the faint of heart. Take watch of your surroundings and what comes out of your mouth. Don't buy what you don't need."

Chaos nodded along with Quinn with disinterest. An unknown burst of energy had rejuvenated his limp, weary body. He was ready to see what he called the only world wonder of Cadere.

"One more thing," Quinn smiled gravely, "You say you're looking for an element? Find the elemental dealer. He has what you want."

Quinn nodded to him once and turned the other way. Just like that, Chaos was off to steal from a thief.

CHAPTER

TWENTY-TWO

Life

Retribution's words pounded her head. Her own words swirled around in the mess.

She scratched at her head, the thoughts of the diary, the map, the argument with Retribution, the altar, replaying over and over in her head.

Caves.

Forgotten.

X's.

Time.

Stone.

He lied to her. He never trusted her for even a fraction of a second. And she couldn't trust him either.

She thought about the other protectors. Did they still trust her?

Life clenched her eyes shut. She missed how life was, where all of them were, at least, somewhat close to happy.

Life frowned. It was like she didn't know who Retribution was anymore. Why couldn't he just tell her a general gist of where he was going?

Her mind replayed his conversation with Time.

Control and peace...

She was sure the stone could end the war. She was sure that she could end the war.

She had to do this. If the war ended then peace would come back. Balance would come back.

A small smile spread onto her face.

She would finally be able to see the grin that used to adorn Death's face, Retribution would finally get the break he deserved, everyone would be relieved.

As far as she was concerned, there were more pros than cons with her plan.

She got up suddenly. It was solidified. She would find the stone and end the war. She needed that map– no matter what it took.

She opened the diary, her fingers skimming past the lines, anything that mentioned a specific river or cave.

She thought of the map and the X's that were scribbled on there. If she could get her hands on the map, it would be easier for her to track it, on top of getting clues and hints in the diary.

She took the diary into her hand again, flipping to the page where the cave and river was mentioned. As she read each word, only one thing stuck out to her... the mention of Balance.

She continued scrolling through the book, looking for a mention of Balance's name anywhere, but it was nowhere to be seen... odd. It felt as if the answer was on the tip of her tongue, waiting to be solved like a puzzle piece, inching together as her mind worked.

"Caves, rivers, underground, and Balance" She whispered to herself.

What did Balance have to do with anything?

Life's face flickered.

If someone knew about Balance, they knew about the rest of them. It couldn't just be a coincidence that she was mentioned.

She bit at her lip.

It didn't really narrow her options down any further whether it was in a river or cave, but at least she was already closer to finding it than Retribution.

Life furrowed her brow and stood up, walking towards her desk. She needed a location. She ran through images of rivers and caves she had traveled to. She scoffed. What was she looking for?

A place where balance-

Her eyes widened. It felt like her mind clicked for the very first time. A puzzle that fit perfectly. Almost everything made sense.

Heping.

Balance chose Heping as her country- her home. It was the only place in the world to truly capture the essence of harmonies blending together in the wild. The blue rivers that carved through rock and sand. The perfect swaying willow trees that dance in the breeze. Cracks in cave walls, allowing darkness and light to shelter the animals. And that was only the caves she *had* seen. What of the ones she hadn't?

She needed the map.

She jerked her head to the clock, reading half past midnight. Retribution would most likely be sleeping right about now. She couldn't afford to do it tomorrow night; this was the perfect opportunity. Life rushed downstairs, her palms sweaty, and a grin on her face.

She couldn't let them down, no matter what it took.

She turned off all the lights, pulled the curtains over the windows. With a fleeting glance, she left the house.

A sense of determination surged through her veins.

She didn't realize that droplets of rain were pelting down on her till she was shivering. She looked over her shoulder at the sight of the late Krasivyan Queen's ruined home. The dead trees, yellowing grass, and toppled stones stared back at her.

She raised her chin as crumpled leaves whipped around in the air with a gust of wind. Her eyes shut as she imagined Retribution's living room.

And then she was falling.

***

Retribution's house: one of the few places where she felt like she wasn't free-falling - like she didn't have to feel, or hear, but just be. The place where she felt safe and secure. But this wasn't one of those times.

She landed on the wood floor with a thud. Her eyes clenched shut, as she mentally cursed herself.

She looked around the house, the curtains lazily moving with the wind, papers splayed everywhere around the room, and Retribution slumped into the couch, his eyes closed and his breathing even.

She slowly made her way towards him, the floor creaking slightly. She winced at the sound and stared at him.

She never noticed how peaceful he looked as he slept. His chest rose up and down in even beats.

She tore her gaze away from him.

This was wrong.

But she had to do it.

She had to help Retribution, get the war to stop, bring back Balance, and save the mortals. She was already too far in to stop now, everything she was doing was for them. She needed this.

If Retribution found her snooping- she shivered, not wanting to even think about what might happen.

Yet, it was a risk worth taking.

Life scanned the room briefly.

The map had to be in the meeting room.

She took a deep breath, her heart beat slightly steadying. She pursed her lips as she moved away from the couch, her mind set on one thing.

Find the map.

She tiptoed across the living room and into the hallway, her eyes quickly adjusting to the darkness.

She reached for the door handle on her left. Her fingers gently pressed the handle, opening the office room and tip toeing in. She closed the door behind her and made her way to the office table that sat in the middle of the room.

Her heart dropped.

The map wasn't on the desk.

She dropped to her knees and frantically searched for the parchment under the desk. She then stood up and opened the drawer left of Retribution's office chair. Near the very back of the wooden nook lay a hastily rolled paper.

Life grabbed the paper with a grin on her face. She clung onto the map like it was dear life and opened it up, revealing the annotations.

She stared at Krasivya's section of the map. There were many X's she never noticed until now. She was surprised Retribution had visited a lot of these places. Some of these, even she hadn't visited. She continued looking.

There weren't a lot of rivers in Fortem, although there were a lot of caves. Most of the locations were marked with X's, only a few question marks placed here and there.

Her gaze flitted to Lucror. There were only a few crosses on this part. She visited Lucror numerous times, but as far as she knew, there were very few rivers and caves. It was a cityland, buildings and roads built in almost every corner.

She looked at Hikma. Every cave except for one had an X' on it. Retribution and Time evidently didn't find the stone there.

How long had they searched for it again? She shrugged to herself.

Mahana was next. There were more waterfalls than serene rivers or caves. Plus Mahana only had large winding rivers, none of which would run through a cave.

Life turned her attention to Riqueza. She frowned. Riqueza used to be different. It used to be peaceful. Ever since the new ruler, king Casmir, came into power, everything went downhill.

Riquezas section was littered with 'X's.

Her brows furrowed. Why would Retribution and Time search the kingdom who started the war for a means to end it?

She finally turned her eyes to Heping, her best guess as to where the stone was, had several 'X's. What caught her eye on this map was that 7 caves were circled, in addition to the question marks.

She beamed. This was all the confirmation she needed. If this was a game of parieur, all her money would be up for betting.

She looked around the map and saw a note that was messily scrawled onto the side in Retribution's handwriting. *Caves, Rivers, or Underground?*

Which one was it that she needed to search for?

She bit her lip, as she scanned the map again.

It had to incorporate Balance. How-

Her eyes widened.

She gasped lightly, *of course,* she thought. *Balance. It's a balance!*

She tried remembering what she saw months ago on a pamphlet that got passed out to her in Heping. There was a park. A national park if she remembered correctly. The pamphlet had boasted about the glistening river running through the length of the cave. She had wanted to go ever since she saw the pictures, but what was the name?

She wracked her brain. Her fingers tapped against the smooth table.

"Endless... endless something?" She murmured to herself.

182

She snapped her fingers, grinning, "The Sans Fin Caverns—the endless caves!" She whispered. Everything was fitting into place: the caves were underground and the rivers flowed through it.

She heard a mumbling sound coming from the living room. She froze, her breath catching. Retribution didn't typically wake up in the middle of the night.

She frowned. He must have been sleep-talking.

She shivered and quickly rolled up the map, taking the back door out when she abruptly froze midway.

She turned her head to the side, to stare at an open ink jar. She chewed the inside of her lip before letting out a shaky breath and walking back to the office table.

She got out a blank piece of paper, and a spare fountain pen.

Dear Ret,

There is so much I want to explain to you, but not enough time. I don't want to leave you, please know that much, but I'm doing this for you. For all of us. I need to do this for myself as well. This will set things right, I'm sure of it. You can relax now, take a shower, sleep in, I'm handling it. I know you might never forgive me, and that's a risk I'm willing to take.

Yours Truly, Life

She set the pen down on the paper, then swiftly walked to the back door. She pushed it open quietly, and before walking out. she looked down at the grass, puddles becoming wider and deeper, the raindrops falling from hundreds of feet and landing on her soft skin.

"I'm sorry…" And with that, she stepped out into the pouring rain, closing her eyes as she fell.

CHAPTER

TWENTY-THREE

RETRIBUTION

He lurched up, sweat clinging onto his dark skin.

His eyes jumped to the moonlight shining through the windows. A slight breeze brushed past his skin, as he pushed himself into a sitting position.

He sighed, as his hands ran over his short curls. Retribution eyed the house wearily. He groggily stood up, the floor creaking as he made his way to the kitchen, staring at the clock through squinting eyes. He scoffed and rubbed at his eyes, trying to push the sleepiness away.

Retribution cracked his knuckles and took out a cup from his cupboard, filling it with water and emptying it, letting it slide down the drain.

He paused, staring down at the ceramic mug. With a sigh, he set it back into the cabinet and turned around and walked slowly to his office.

Pushing past the door, he turned on a light. He squinted as he stepped further into the room and froze.

A letter sat on his desk. From whom? It wasn't like Retribution wasn't accustomed to receiving mail. On the contrary he practically expected a letter daily from Time and other Riquezan officials, but he had just seen Time.

Just seen Time kill Fate.

Retribution shook his head. There was no chance this one was from him.

He reached out a hand and gripped the sheet. The ink glistened in the dim light. He squinted as his eyes moved to the start of the letter. The handwriting laid in swirls yet it was clearly rushed. As if written by someone who clearly had somewhere to be.

Retribution frowned. He knew this handwriting. He shook his head, focusing his gaze to read the letter.

His eyes widened as he made his way lower on the page. "No…"

This wasn't happening. This couldn't be happening. He wasn't in the right mindset for this. He couldn't lose another Protector. Not after Death was practically unreachable. Not after Balance. Not after Fate- not after what he did to Fate.

His hands shook at the thought. He wouldn't be able to deal with Life gone too.

He wouldn't be able to deal with the thought that he pushed her away too. He wouldn't be able to deal with another death on his hands.

The paper grew heavier by the second, the words branding into his mind.

He froze. In the letter Life kept insisting that she had to do 'it'. That she had to help.

Retribution felt bile build up in his throat.

He dropped to his knees, whipping opening the top drawer. This was the one thing he tried to keep everyone away from. This was the one thing that would surely destroy them.

This was all he had.

"The map." He muttered quickly. His heartbeat spiked, his mind distorted, all his work gone in a single night.

What was he going to tell Time?

What was going to happen to Life?

"Frank." He cursed, his voice trembling.

He clenched his eyes shut reaching for those familiar strings in his mind to pull. He needed to talk to her. Talk her out of whatever she was planning. He yanked repetitively on Life's string.

"Come on Life ple-" His voice broke.

He pulled more, until he felt a slight pull in return. He put his head in his hands.

There was nothing he could do but wait.

Chapter

Twenty-Four

DEATH

He glided the knife against the soft skin, watching the red flood out. In a slick motion he tossed the inside of the tomato out and layered the slice onto his half-built sandwich.

He knew he should go back to Cadere. He knew he should be helping, but he just couldn't. How could he do anything knowing that the only good thing in the world was gone? Not to mention, what use was a world that had no peace- no Balance?

He layered thinly sliced avocados onto the bread, finding himself thanking the old them for planting such an abundance of fruits and vegetables before being kicked out. In all honesty, Death was quite surprised to find their garden still there. He knew that time worked strangely on the Altar, yet it managed to surprise him every time.

It was as if whenever on the Altar, time was on your side.

Between seeing Chaos and Life, Death knew that it had been at least half a year since he had come to the Altar. However, it had only felt like a month or two. Although he had physically looked better, the time passed- or lack thereof- did nothing to encourage him to return to his duties.

Death put the second bread over the now completed sandwich, slightly pressing it down. Even though he didn't technically need to eat, there was something so comforting about being back in the Altar kitchen, doing something as simple as assembling a sandwich. Death adjusted it in his hand ready to take a bite.

He felt his stomach twist as his shoulder seemed to pull forward slightly. He frowned, putting the sandwich down. In a fraction of a second a disgruntled figure appeared in the living room, slamming into the edge of the couch and doubling over in pain.

"Oh, Frank." The figure grit out through bared teeth.

Death frowned. He definitely knew that voice. He quickly strode out of the kitchen peering over a counter to stare at the sprawled figure.

"Retribution?" Death grinned.

It was about time that Death saw Retribution. Even though he made no attempt to leave the Altar, that didn't change the fact that he desperately wanted to know what was happening on Cadere with the war, and more than that: Death missed his brother.

Retribution whipped his head up, craning his neck to look at Death incredulously. "Death? What? How?"

He shook his head, pushing himself off the ground, "Where-" He froze. His head moved to quickly survey their surroundings.

Death shook his head, chuckling as he made his way to Retribution, embracing him in a tight hug. Death felt Retribution's tense shoulders unfurl in his embrace. His hands came to wrap around Death's frame.

Death didn't know how much he needed this hug, nor did he know how much Retribution needed it.

"Are we at the Altar?" Retribution pulled away, gaping. "How are we at the Altar I thought-"

"I don't know." Death finished quietly, "I'm not sure. After Balance, it just brought me here. I didn't ask it to or anything, it just kind of..." He gestured with his hands.

Retribution nodded as he looked around, absorbing everything until his eyes focused on a frame mounted on a side table. He laughed softly walking over to pick it up. "I was so upset when I realized the only copy of this photo was here. I swear I remember making everyone go through all of their things to see if anyone had a copy of this back on Cadere."

Death smiled softly, walking up to Retribution. He looked down at the photo. Retribution was right: it was a really nice photo. Chaos had his hands under Retribution's, hoisting him up by his shoulders. Fate was cradling him almost like a baby with one hand under his back and the other on the underside of his knees while Death was bracing his legs, keeping him suspended in air. Balance sat under Retribution, a cake in hand. Life was next to her with a sign that read, 'Milestone Birthday- 287 years old' in swirly orange lettering. Retribution had the widest grin on his face. His normally short, coily hair was instead tightly braided back in slick rows. He had a cone-like party hat strapped lazily to his head.

Death grinned, clapping Retribution's shoulders, "Take it back with you- assuming that you are going back."

Retribution's smile flickered, "Yeah- yeah I'll be going back. I mean, I have to." His voice quieted as he gently folded the picture.

Death pushed Retribution's shoulder to face him. Retribution was never the most cheery Protector, especially with all the pressure being put on him. However this was different, Death noted. He was always well with handling the load.

"What's wrong"

He frowned, his shoulder almost caving away from Death's touch. His eyes moved to look past him and into the door near the kitchen.

Death bit at the inside of his cheek and opted for an easier question. "Coffee?"

Retribution smiled softly, "Yeah."

Death turned on his heel, walking back towards the kitchen. He peered over his shoulder at Retribution following a few paces behind.

"Sit." Death eyed the chair in front of Retribution that was pushed up against the kitchen island. He filled a small pot full of water and placed it on the stove to boil. He spun around to face Retribution and slid his previously made sandwich across the table.

"Eat. I just made it." He turned around again, grabbing an old tin from a shelf above the sink. In rusty letters's Death could barely make out the word 'coffee'. Not that he needed to read it. Lately Death had been consuming far too much of the bitter liquid. He would probably be able to make himself a pot of it in his sleep.

"How did you do it?"

Retribution's question shook Death out of his thoughts.

"Do what?" He questioned, pouring a scoop of coffee powder into the boiling water.

"How were you so good at keeping everything running smoothly? How did you make everyone listen to you? How were you so put together? I remember before Time, you were our rock. You were- you." He groaned, massaging the spot between his brows.

Death stared down at the sandwich in front of them. He knew what Retribution was feeling. Before Time, Death was the unlabeled leader, but he was more than happy to let Retribution fill the role. In all honesty, Death wouldn't have been able to handle it all.

"Do I seem put together now, Retribution?" Death whispered, a small smile on his face.

Retribution frowned, dismissing Death's question as he looked down at his fiddling fingers. "I don't know what I'm doing."

He laughed bitterly, "Frank, Death, I could use your help back on Cadere."

Death turned away from Retribution, opting to add some sugar to the coffee instead.

"I don't know what to do, Death." Retribution whispered, dragging his hands over his face.

Death frowned, turning to stare at Retribution, "Then let us help."

Retribution scoffed sadly, "I think that ship has sailed." He picked at the sandwich.

Death's face twisted. "Don't be like that Retribution. We've spent years insisting you take our help, why wouldn't we help you?"

Retribution set the sandwich down, decidedly not hungry. He pushed out a deep breath, "You're here. Fate is engrossed in her plans. Chaos is Chaos and Life won't even spare a second to talk to me I-" His voice choked.

Death's eyes fluttered, "What do you mean Life won't spare you a second? What is she doing?"

Retribution shrugged, miserably, "I haven't the slightest idea. She was supposed to find you and I have no idea what happened because suddenly she was avoiding everyone. Death, she wouldn't even come to progress meetings."

Death's brows together. Fate or Chaos disappearing for weeks at a time wasn't unheard of but Life?

"Well, is she okay? That isn't like her."

Retribution shook his head, "Yeah, she's fine. It isn't like I haven't seen her since Balance, it's just that I have to go looking for her and she's never keen on staying for too long."

Death turned around, his lip between his teeth as he thought over what Retribution had just told him. He had seen Life a few times when she had come to visit him. The most recent time she had visited had left him a bit lost. She had clearly lied to him. That in itself wasn't like her. She definitely had the diary, but that couldn't have impacted her actions. That diary was just a jumble of thoughts. In fact it was so useless that Death had decided not to share it with the group. That and the fact that Death was pretty sure that he was either sleep deprived or quite strongly under the influence when he had first seen it. It had appeared to him first in a sort of projection. At least he's pretty sure it did. Turned out booze and coffee was not the brightest mix.

The diary was solid. It looked like a real book, but inside the cover was a note that said, 'Copy this down word-for-word. This copy of the diary is the last one in the world and it will disappear at the end of the 24 hours.'

Death shivered, brushing off the thought. It was ridiculous. A sure waste of time that Death must have created at three in the morning while not in his right mind.

He heard Retribution sigh from behind him. "I feel like everything I'm doing is wrong."

Death nodded, "The mission?"

Retribution bit his lip, hesitating before he nodded, running his hands down his face.

Death put the gas on low heat before he pulled a chair across Retribution and took a seat. Retribution was always closed off about the mission and all of them knew it. Unlike the others though, Death had never pushed the matter too far. Retribution was never one to hide things from them, so very quickly Death realized that it must have been something truly impossible to share.

"Do you want to talk about it?"

Retribution peaked at Death from between his fingers. In that moment Death realized that just maybe he was about to figure out the secret Retribution had hoarded for so long.

A plethora of emotions flickered past Retribution's face. He shook his head, clenching his eyes shut.

"I'm looking for a stone."

Death raised his brow, leaning forward. "A stone?" He shook his head, confused, urging Retribution to continue.

"Can't tell you much more than that." Retribution cracked his knuckles. "It's just a really important stone that I need to find for Time."

Death bit his lip, staring at Retribution, "Can it stop the war?"

Retribution hesitated as if considering whether he was sharing too much, before he closed his eyes, nodding slowly.

Death frowned, "But you've been after it since before the war."

Retribution's face constricted as if in pain at the mere thought of the mission. He moved his gaze to stare out a window, "With this stone we would be able to ensure peace. Forever. It's very powerful, but it's equally dangerous to try and find. Time and I have been struggling with it for quite some time."

He shook his head, "But that doesn't even matter because I can't find the blasted thing. But past that-" Retribution paused again. He frowned, debating whether to continue.

"Remember how I told you about Life being... distant?" Retribution started slowly.

Death frowned, his finger tracing shapes in the table's wood, "Yeah?"

Retribution sat up a bit straighter, determined to look at anything but Death. "Well she's not just ignoring me. She left."

Death's brows pulled together, "Left?" Given that Protectors could teleport, Cadere was a pretty small planet. Their world truly wasn't big when they could cross the planet in less than seconds. So, when Retribution said she left, Death was confused.

"What do you mean left? Where is she?"

"She's trying to find the stone."

A silence stretched out.

"The same stone that you just said was incredibly dangerous to find?" Death asked, much more calm than he felt.

Retribution merely nodded in response.

Death pushed away from the table, suddenly remembering the coffee he had on the stove.

"She took my map." He shook his head, chuckling out a defeated sound. "I mean I guess it's partially my fault."

Death turned around, meeting Retribution's gaze.

"All of my work trying to track down that damn stone was written on one map." He laughed again bitterly, rolling a piece of bread between his fingers. "I mean who puts decades of work on only *one* source?"

With gentle fingers Death opened a coffee strainer, setting it on a cup. Life had always been the most eager one to help Retribution, but she would never go behind his back like this. Not when she could see how much he insisted on keeping her in the dark about it. Or perhaps that was the motivation. She never did take well to being unincluded.

"Do you think she'll find it?" Death muttered.

Retribution was quiet. Death didn't know if it was because he didn't know or if it was because he was scared of the answer.

"I think she's going to find it or die trying."

Death's hands shook as he poured the steaming coffee into the strainer.

"You need to stop her. Tell Time and find her."

Life had come to him and asked him what to do. She had pried for information even he didn't know. At the time he didn't know what it had to do with. He was pretty certain it was concerning the diary. Retribution had mentioned that Life was tasked with finding him so it only made sense that she had paid his house a visit which would explain how she got her hands on it in the first place. If she had already left and was looking for this 'stone' then that meant she had a decent amount of knowledge beforehand. Retribution said Life had stolen his map. That already limited the options for her. And then the diary.

Death clenched his eyes shut.

Life wouldn't just leave and follow a few loose threads of a plan. There must have been something in the diary that had stood out to her.

"It's fine. There were only so many ca- locations left." Retribution nodded to himself, "yeah I should be able to track those last few ends down. I'll tell Time and we'll get moving-"

If Life was close then that meant she was much closer to being in danger.

Death turned around handing Retribution a steaming mug. "Why doesn't Time just spin the clock back? Isn't that his whole ability?" He questioned.

Retribution slid his hand into the handle of the mug, "No, even his ability has limitations. It's been too long."

Death felt his stomach sink. Balance was gone, and now Life was in danger. He couldn't lose another one of them- he wouldn't

He clasped his head with his fingers, "She- she has this diary."

Retribution took a sip from his cup, grimacing at the taste. "Oh, yeah?"

Death shook his head, frowning. He needed to do this. Life being in danger overrode his unsaid obligation to keep her secret.

"It's not her own diary. It's one that I kept in my office."

Retribution drank again, peering at Death from over the rim of the cup, "Whose is it?"

"Not sure, but I got it back when the only country was Lucror."

Retribution raised his brows, "Lucror? That was before the first 100 years."

Death nodded, "Mhm, I don't know how I got it and I don't know how anyone could find that jumble of a mess useful, but I think Life might have."

Retribution shook his head holding his hand up in an indication to slow down. "Did you give her this diary?"

"No. I'm assuming she picked it up from my office when she was looking for me."

"Wait, how do you know she has it in the first place?"

Death winced internally. If Life ever caught wind of this conversation Death would never hear the end of it.

"I saw her. She visited me a few times at the Altar."

Retribution sat up a bit straighter, something unreadable crossing his face, "You knew she was trying to figure something out and you didn't think to tell me?"

Death took a sip from his mug, "Why would I? Life is always about investigating something. I had no reason to suspect anything."

A half truth.

Retribution shrugged as he slumped back onto the table, "Can't really argue with that."

Death stared at Retribution as he absentmindedly drummed his fingers against the table. He knew Retribution's side. He was trying to keep everyone safe. He felt a sick feeling twist up his body. Retribution was right he should be back on Cadere. He shouldn't be here.

"You should go."

Death said the words before he could even process the thought.

Retribution scoffed, "You kicking me out of my own house?"

Death smiled as he pushed away from the table, "No, nothing like that. It's just, don't you have a daily progress meeting with Time?"

Retribution's brows furrowed in confusion, "Yeah, but it's only been like half an hour. I've got time."

Death shook his head as he walked around the island, holding his hand out for Retribution to clasp. "Time is working a bit differently here right now. It's already been a day or two back on Cadere."

Retribution's eyes blew wide, "What? How has it been that long?"

Death shrugged frowning, "I have no idea. It's actually bad. It's making handling Balance's-" He trailed off.

A thick silence fell over the pair.

Retribution clasped Death's outstretched palm as he stepped off the barstool. "I get it. It's really hard for me too, Death. I mean for at least a couple months after her cessation I didn't know what to do with myself."

Death nodded, his eyes glued to the carpet.

Retribution's other hand came to rest firmly on Death's shoulder, "Hey, I'll see you, yeah?"

Death smiled as he squeezed his hand, "Yeah. Yeah, I'll see you."

CHAPTER

TWENTY-FIVE

FATE

Fate's every waking thought was the same: a search for a solution.

The days were passing faster than she could understand. She could only tell it was a new day because her eyes were continuously trained on the floor-length window across the couch. She watched as the sun set, as the moon rose, and as the sun returned to haunt Fate with its tiresome enthusiasm.

Her hands were occasionally occupied with a wooden pencil, sprawling her plans onto blank sheets of paper- all of which ended up blanketed across the floor. Ever since Lucror, she hadn't left her cramped apartment for more than a day every two weeks. She was scoping, planning, *thinking*.

She was forgetting what life used to be like, what *she* used to be like before the war.

At least she had until Chaos kept mailing her letters. She didn't understand why he cared what she did. She left the unopened notes stacked on the kitchen counter, forgetting about them until she received a new one. Each time the mailman slid the new envelope under her door, she remembered flashes of her past. It left her in a daze strong enough to bring her back to the Altar 200 years ago, as if the last 2 centuries had vanished from her mind.

She couldn't understand why Balance hadn't knocked on her door and coaxed her into an embrace. She couldn't understand why Death hadn't talked her through her thoughts, helping her find the perfect solution. She couldn't understand why Life hadn't plopped beside her with a hand on her shoulder, or why Retribution hadn't dragged her to his room to listen to his records in silence.

Slowly nostalgia's bitterness would fade and all of that would feel like someone else's memories- a story she had imagined, a dream she had woken up from. Something she would never have.

That was what she was fighting for though. An impossible bargain, a dream, a wish. She didn't know why a part of her held a pulsing desire to restore something that was clearly irreparable.

Was it to regain her abilities, to bring back Balance, or to do penance for her guilt?

However long she pondered this question, she had found no answer. Although, months later, she did find a solution to the larger problem.

She found a way to save the world.

***

Fate had always been sure of a decision. Sure, there was always a chance- a possibility- that the probability of something occurring would spike at the last moment and she would end up being wrong. However, the way her ability had worked was fortunately similar to gambling. She had gotten good at making bets- at taking chances..

But whatever crutch she once possessed as a Protector had abandoned her. Suddenly, her choices had no longer held the same guarantee of success she once had.

This solution wasn't a gamble she was willing to take if she wasn't entirely confident in its benefits.

And the more she sat, back to her couch, the more her apartment's walls pressed towards her, the faster the breaths left her lips, and the more she itched to tear the hair from her scalp.

Fate held her head in her hands. *She had no idea what she should do.*

The thought was suffocating, so suffocating in fact, that the room was spinning. The ground was sinking. And she was falling.

She knew what was happening.

She didn't *want* to leave her paper puddle of misery, but her body was moving of its own will. She couldn't continue being locked in her mind in the overwhelming silence of her home. She needed-

Her hands met cool wood. She was bent over a table, her arms propping up her body, and her hair falling wildly over her face.

She took a shaky breath. This was...this was *Retribution's* table.

Something cleared in her mind; it was as if she had just gained consciousness. As if she had been dipped into frigid waters while she had been sleeping.

She desperately needed to talk to someone- talk to Retribution. She needed clarity.

Fate pushed her hair back from her face with her palm. She waited for a moment, staring blankly at the papers scattered around the table- much like ones on the rug of her home in Mahana. He would understand, more than anyone else would.

Pushing away, she stumbled slightly. Her legs struggled from disuse. Awkwardly, she continued to the door frame, leaning only her head past it to check for any signs of Retribution.

It wasn't like her- to ask for help. Not that she had been anything like herself these past couple of months. What other choice did she have other than ask his advice? She might have been too proud to rely on him, but she was also too proud to let her destroy herself.

She knew what she was going to look like to him. Frail, exhausted, *out of her damn mind.* Her hair stuck up around her head, her eyes were hollowed and dark, and she was stumbling over her steps.

But what choice did she have?

Fate pushed herself through the frame, gripping it tightly. Retribution's house was grand in comparison to her dingy apartment. He had a balcony, revealing a top floor, that overlooked the spacious living room and a curved wooden staircase.

She had been in his home enough times to know where each door and turn led. Yet, the home's size shocked her each time she stayed longer than for a progress meeting.

A sound of rushing water drew her eyes from the staircase to the kitchen. She exhaled slowly as her arms went slack against the frame. She moved herself towards the corridor on the left, leaning against the wall as the kitchen displayed through an arch.

Retribution had his palm over his face and a half filled glass of water in his other hand. He inhaled slowly and dragged his hand down his face before lifting this glass to his lips. As he drank, his eyes drifted to the archway of his kitchen. Fate watched calmly as his eyes bulged and he spluttered, coughing into his elbow.

"*Fate*? What the Frank, Fate? Do you have news about the war?" Retribution coughed again and gave her a second glance, "Are you...are you *okay*?"

Fate couldn't manage a disarming smile. She just opened her mouth to respond, her body slack, "I just...I wasn't sure if- it's not..."

She had forgotten the sound of her own voice, of anyone else's voice. She had forgotten how it felt to form coherent thoughts.

She forced herself to respond again at the silence that followed, "I lost my abilities."

Fate froze. Retribution went slack.

She had not meant to say that.

He placed his glass on the granite counter gently and spoke slowly, "What do you mean?"

The air was roaring in her ears.

She was scared to open her mouth again. She wasn't in the right mindset for this conversation.

Closing her eyes, as if that was going to protect her from her disconnected thoughts, she gritted out, "I can't predict the future, Retribution. What else do you think that means?"

The anger she tried to push into her words fell flat, and she knew Retribution had noticed it as well.

She felt an arm around her shoulders as Retribution leaned her against his body. He walked her over to a stool under this kitchen counter. She opened her eyes wearily, avoiding eye contact, as he helped her sit.

"Is that why you…" Retribution murmured, keeping a hand on her shoulder.

She narrowed her eyes at the counter, "Look so weak? No. I'm just exhausted. Trust me, this isn't what happened to Balance."

"That's not what I-" Retribution stopped himself. He placed his hand on the back of Fate's head since she hadn't looked up, "Look, I'm making you something to drink."

Fate shook her head once before he let go and spoke, "I wasn't asking you. Clearly you need energy, and clearly, you haven't been eating. We used to go on morning runs together at the Altar, remember? You know how important energy is for the body."

She scowled at herself, "I can take care of myself."

Sure, he was practically her brother, but he didn't need to act like it. She would be fine. Soon, at least.

Retribution merely glanced at her, "Then why come here?"

Fate fell silent, picking at the skin around her nails. She heard Retribution swing open some random cupboards, muttering to himself, after grabbing her a glass. She looked up to see him slicing a lemon on a cutting board with horrible technique.

"Does Chaos know?" He threw over his shoulder without glancing at her. She looked away anyway.

"No. Just you."

"How…long has it been?" He asked hesitantly, turning around with his quarter slices of lemon.

"A bit after Balance." She muttered.

He exhaled slowly, swallowing more questions. He threw some spices in the lemon-water mixture and slid it over to her. Fate, not arguing she needed the fuel, tilted the glass into her mouth.

Her face twisted in disgust, "What the Frank did you put in here?"

She coughed, feeling as if she was swallowing sand instead of spices. Retribution grinned and patted her arm, "Drink up."

Fate felt the edges of her lips tug upwards, then fall. She was wasting time here.

"I know a way I can bring my abilities back," She assured him, "but…" She forced herself to push out the rest of her sentence, "how do I know if it's the right decision?"

Retribution furrowed his eyebrows, "You won't, Fate. There's no way to know unless you try."

Sighing at her disgusted expression, he continued, "Can I know what you're planning to do?"

Fate idly slid her glass on the granite between her hands, "I need to remove the root of the problem, but is one life worth ending for the fate of the world?

Retribution's jaw dropped in horror, "What are you talking about?"

Fate scowled at him, trying to push herself from the counter, "I thought you would understand. You deal with difficult choices all day, working with *Time*, right?"

"Fate- okay, wait," He slid a hand down his face, one that was getting harder to see as the bright colors of sunset faded into a deep blue, "I mean, it depends, but, *probably* yes. One life is nothing compared to the planet of billions of lives we have on our shoulders, but-"

Her voice was frigid when she interrupted, "I need to do this, Retribution."

He paused, clearly not sure what to say, and rubbed the back of his neck, "I can't help you if you don't tell me the entire story, Fate."

Fate gave him half a smile, "You already did help me."

Retribution processed this and shook his head, "No, Fate, *no*, you can't-"

By the time he finished talking, she was already gone.

CHAPTER

TWENTY-SIX

CHAOS

Chaos was grinning from ear to ear as he stepped through the tunnel's cement arch. The Night Market was nothing short of its legend.

The market took place in some sort of hub where smaller, narrower tunnels all led to a large hollow space. Varied vibrant cloth tents and wooden stands were packed along the floor, leaving mere feet in between for customers to walk by. His eyes kept flying, attracted like a moth to the bright colors, to the loud cackles and to the slogans of multiple vendors.

"Get high *for the* low *price of 455 pecunia."*
"Need a helping hand?*"*
"Travel far… *in one of our rooms."*

The walls of the hub were all plastered with advertisements for the businesses as well. He couldn't read them well enough, though, due to the dim lighting and the mass of people.

The longer Chaos stared, the more he noticed: the masks vendors wore over their noses, the specificity of each stand- secret files of government officials, human organs, peculiar looking animals- and the children running between the legs of the customers. He could see people entering and exiting from the narrow tunnels, suspicious looking packages in their hands.

Not only was the route to reach the Night Market complicated, but the span of the hub was large enough to be considered a maze itself.

This was Chaos' type of place- illegal, disconcerting, and downright horrifying.

As his eyes followed a shine of light from a torch, his eyes widened, remembering Quinn and that Chaos had dropped the torch Quinn had given him somewhere in the narrow tunnel.

Shaking his head, he remembered he was here for plutonium, not to stare adoringly at severed body parts and shiny weapons. What had Quinn said?

Find the elemental dealer.

Chaos looked, half amused, at what felt like a never ending mass of people and colored tents. It wouldn't hurt to look around while he searched. He practically bounded forward.

The moment Chaos joined the crowd of people, he could hardly hear his own thoughts. His eyes were roving from left to right, peering inside tents and gaping at the displays on the stands. His legs were struggling to keep up, following the flow of the horde of people. It was because of both those things that he had tripped over a small child.

Wincing, he set the confused child upright and patted her on the head before swerving into a random tent. Pushing through the red diamond-patterned fabric, he set his eyes on a pale, rounder man. Surrounding the man on a stand were small bags of powder and rolled up bundles. The store smelled horribly of smoke and another foul scent.

"Oh dear boy, would you like some? Ask anything and we should have it. If you're wary, we have chocolate bars." The man smiled at him, his eyes crinkling. He gestured to the display in front of him.

Chaos gazed closer for a minute then shook his head and spoke breathlessly, "Do you know where the elemental dealer is?"

"Oh!" The vendor's eyes brightened, "I do indeed. It is a purple tent, past Emmett's designer brands. No, perhaps…straight from here, then take a right, go further, take another right..then another right? No, that's a circle."

The man tapped his chin, "It's a purple tent, lad."

Chaos, after attempting to understand, decided that asking a substance dealer wasn't exactly the best option. He left with a curt 'thanks' and stumbled back into the crowd. He found he could finally breathe the air for about two seconds until someone pushed him forwards from behind.

"Sir, would you like one of these poisoned arrows?"

Chaos kept walking, his eyes still caught on the arrows.

"Move, boy." A gruff voice said, pushing past him. Chaos scowled.

Seconds later, he turned to a tap on his shoulder.

"Excuse me! Would you like to try a miniature cake?" A woman, her face shredded with scarring pushed her tray into Chaos.

Chaos smirked, noticing the tactic, "What's in those?"

The woman smiled eerily before Chaos turned away.

Scrambling ahead, he kept his eyes trained in the sky for a sharp point of purple.

After turning about a hundred times, dodging multiple vendors, and pushing past ridiculously slow walkers, he found himself, soaked in sweat, in front of a purple tent. Sure, it hadn't been the only purple tent in the entirety of the Night Market, but the others he had stepped inside contained either illegal substances, a group of undressed people, or a magic trick booth.

This tent was widely different from the others. The customers surrounding it kept a wide perimeter, as if it was radioactive.

Chaos assumed he had found his elemental dealer.

He slipped through the purple fabric.

The interior of the tent was incredibly organized compared to the surrounding businesses. Stacks of acrylic encased elements, shaped into cubes, lined the walls on metal shelves. Other elements at the stand, at the very end of the tent, were put in mere plastic containers. The containers were possibly determined on the level of danger each element possessed.

The dealer leaned lazily on the stand in front of him. A hood was pulled low over his face.

Straightening at the sight of Chaos, the dealer pulled down his hood for extra bravado, smirking. Or *her* hood.

The dealer had a jagged scar from her temple up to the choppy hair that fell just above her shoulders. She wore a ragged bandana wrapped around her pin-straight hair like a headband and seemed of Heping origins.

At Chaos' shock, she grinned.

"My name is Element. What can I do for you?" Her voice was raspy as she spoke. Calmly, she appeared from behind the stand. The dim lighting of the lanterns hung on the wiring of the tent revealed a small scar on the edge of her top lip.

Slowly, a smile appeared on Chaos' lips, "I'm just browsing."

"Browsing?" She raised an eyebrow, surveying Chaos carefully. She crossed her arms as Chaos let his eyes travel carefully around the room for something labeled plutonium. Unfortunately, it didn't seem like stealing was going to be that easy.

He nodded with too much enthusiasm to be buying science class materials.

"Where are you from?" He asked, staring into the elemental cubes as if he was at a museum.

The girl scoffed, amused, "South-east side of Lucror. And you?"

Chaos walked around the room, feeling her eyes on his back.

"That's surprising. I am as well. I mean, my family's from Riqueza, but we've moved a lot," He lied.

"Oh, really?"

Chaos could see her disbelieving reflection as he stared into the one element he could truly differentiate. Gold.

He nodded, seeing how far he could take the conversion, "Do you sell illegal elements for a living?"

"Do you spend your free time shopping for illegal elements?" She quipped.

Chaos grinned, turning back to her, "Only when things become too peaceful above ground. Speaking of peace…what are your most dangerous elements?"

All Chaos knew of plutonium was that it was dangerous and rare.

Element's expression changed to a wry smile, "To your right, you see that liquid metallic substance? That is mercury."

Chaos followed her finger to a substance encased in an acrylic cube. He didn't have to try hard to feign interest.

"Mercury can be absorbed through your unbroken skin or easily inhaled. If it gets inside your system, it can damage your organs, enough to where you can't even sell it here."

"Pity." Chaos drawled.

"Not only that but it can affect your memory, muscle coordination, and strength. And in large doses, mercury can be deadly." Element was clearly amused by the explanation, "That one further off, near the entrance is plutonium."

Chaos' heart nearly lurched out of his chest at the name. He had to take careful care to make sure none of his excitement bled onto his expression. He strode forward, pointing at the shelf of small metal cubes inside a larger clear rectangle.

"This one?" The corners of his mouth were twitching as he surveyed the element. How much did the Rebellion say they wanted? Did they tell him at all?

Grimacing, he just decided he would take multiple.

She nodded, "It's a highly radioactive element capable of high scale destruction. It isn't as toxic as polonium, which I will tell you about later. It wouldn't kill you outright, but it can expose you to radioactivity, which *can* ruin your life."

"Ruin your life? How?"

She tilted her head. "Cancer. More than that, it's a very powerful explosive."

Element rolled up the sleeves of her zippered coat as she continued, her back to Chaos. Chaos' shoulders lowered at the absence of her gaze. Carefully, he put his fingers around the acrylic, taking care not to make a noise as he pulled it from the shelf. Quickly, he shoved the rectangle into his back pocket.

"Now of polonium. I would say this one is my favorite." She glanced back at him after gesturing to a brownish looking metal. Thankfully, he had turned back to her in a position that made it seem as if he was still paying attention.

She continued, looking away, "It's 250-thousand times more toxic than cyanide. A single gram, if inhaled or ingested, could kill about ten million people."

"That might be in my top three elements as well."

"Nice to know." She mused.

Chaos had gone and slipped another prism into his pocket before she turned his direction to point out another element. Unfortunately he was still touching the next container of plutonium he was to take as she faced him.

Element frowned, waving her hand, "No touching unless you intend to buy."

As Chaos backed away, faking surprise, she held up a clear cube with a sort of white powder inside.

"This is arsenic. It was a popular method of poisoning an enemy in Old Caderian times. It's colorless and flavorless. It disrupts the amount of energy your cells receive and can cause cancer. And in large doses, it's deadly." Placing the Arsenic back, she strode to the front of the room, adjusting her bandana. Her eyes were no longer on Chaos in this position.

As she spoke of more elements like lead and francium, Chaos had slipped two more boxes of plutonium into his front pockets. He had responded each time, keeping her focus off him.

Needless to say, he was having fun. That was until her rant slowed to a stop.

"Anything pique your interest?" She looked at him, amused, leaning against the front counter.

"With how much you know about elements, I'm curious, do you also poison people for a living?"

After hearing her speech, this was probably the most attractive person Chaos had met in his entire existence.

"I've thought about it."

Chaos smirked, "What a surprise. So have I."

Noticing her expectant eyebrow, Chaos tilted his head, "I've enjoyed the information, but I should get going."

Chaos pivoted and got three steps in before she stopped him.

"Before you leave, I have a small request." Her raspy voice was calm.

Chaos didn't turn, "Oh?"

"Empty out your pockets."

Chaos halted.

"What's wrong?" She taunted from the other side of the tent.

Grinning, Chaos reached into his shoe, grabbing a Kostco bag- a Lucrian membership warehouse club- and flicking it open. As Element stared at him, disarrayed, he grabbed an acrylic prism from the shelf with his free hand. He chucked it at her. She cried out as it hit her square in the nose.

Before she could yell any further, Chaos swiped the entirety of the plutonium supply from the shelf and sprinted from the tent. Thankfully, since people were avoiding the tent, he didn't run into anyone this time or smack anyone with the large bag he was hauling over his shoulder. After whipping his head both sides to decide his next path, he groaned and squeezed into the small crack between Element's tent and another one.

Quickly, he willed himself to disappear. The tents spun purple and green strings in his mind as he panted. He shook his head slightly in disappointment.

He'd had better theft days.

***

Chaos stumbled into an Abuvakeli alleyway.

Due to the time differences between the countries, Fortem was just coming to midday. It was *great* for Chaos, who was used to the darkness of Lucror's tunnels. When he pulled open his eyes, he grimaced, covering them with his hands, before they adjusted.

Peering through the bright sunlight, Chaos walked onto the warm streets, dragging the Kostco bag with him. This was another difference. From the frigid underground to Fortem's warm spring. This change, Chaos preferred.

He needed to find the Rebellion again. Chaos decided he would just attempt what he had done last time. Asking around before they kidnapped him again.

As he turned a corner, his eyes fell on a boy with warm brown skin. He was holding a cloth bag, looking intensely at a display of apples. As Chaos walked nearer, he realized he recognized the boy. He was one of the three Rebellion members he had met when they had knocked Chaos out.

Kasim.

"Oh, hey! I know you." Chaos snapped and pointed at the boy as he jogged to stand beside him, "Kasim, yes?"

Kasim's head whipped to him and his eyes widened dramatically.

"Tell your Chief I have your plutonium."

"No wai-"

"Here, I'll show you." Chaos stumbled to pull out all four cases of the metal and open the bag simultaneously.

"Are you kidding?" Kasim hissed, stepping closer to Chaos to hide it from the vendor's view, "We are a secret organization. Do you know what that means?"

Chaos looked at him dryly.

Chaos had opened his mouth to supply a response but suddenly his body was overcome with the strangest urge to head to Retribution's house. Retribution was calling another progress meeting. Scowling, he shoved the bag of cases of plutonium into Kasim's hand.

"Give this to Sarki, tell him I will be back soon to discuss our aid. I have to go."

Retribution had the *worst* sense of timing. The only reason he was hurrying to meet his friends was because Fate would be there and they hadn't talked in a while. He was ready to finally tell her what he had accomplished. He had acquired the help of an entire organization.

Kasim shook his head incredulously, "Where did you get these? And why do you look like you've spent hours rolling in dirt?"

Chaos glanced down at his outfit, which was indeed covered in dirt, probably from the debris in the tunnel system.

He winced at his lack of time, then grinned, "The Night Market."

Kasim gaped.

"I'll return with Fate."

With that, he turned and ran back to the alleyway he had come from. He, being named *Chaos*, was going to stop a war.

He was finally going to help.

CHAPTER

TWENTY-SEVEN

FATE

"I hate to place 'Chaos' and 'right' in the same

sentence, but there is no reason for progress meetings back to back." Fate leaned against the red wallpaper intertwining her arms over her chest. Her conversation with Retribution had vitalized her. She was close to ready now to follow through with her plan.

Nothing had ever seemed so desirable.

Retribution looked up from whatever piece of parchment he was reading, subtly placing his hand over it to hinder her view. Whatever secret project he and Time were working towards, she didn't care. It was probably something useless.

"It's been human *months* since I last called a meeting, Fate." He said, looking at her weirdly.

Fate blinked. He was right; it had been months. On top of their large lifespan and her planning every waking moment of the day, she hadn't noticed. She was getting close. She was getting *too* close to a solution. The question was- was she ready to go through with it, and if she was, was she ready to go through with it *alone*?

Chaos blinked into the room, tripping over his legs, somehow managing to catch himself before he fell. His eyes were wide open and his normally disheveled attire was even more

216

chaotic. He tried wiping off the mask of dust on his face, but he just ended up smearing it.

Retribution stared at him, gaping, but shook his head, slowly pulling his gaze away from Chaos, and rooted his eyes on the parchment again.

"I think Aahi just blew up a primary school."

"What?" Fate and Retribution demanded simultaneously, as their heads whipped up in unison.

"Oh, don't worry," Chaos muttered airily, "No one was inside."

"What were you doing at a primary school?" Retribution asked at the same time Fate asked, "Did you hit your head?"

"I'm fine, thank you for asking." Chaos brushed the sides of his clothing with his hands, frowning at the streaks of dirt.

She knew Chaos was lying. Aahi had indeed blown up a primary school...years prior. She guessed it was part of the mission the Rebellion had sent him on. One she no longer cared about.

She only cared about one thing.. It was exhausting, overwhelming, time-consuming, *unhealthy* to be so...obsessed with getting her powers back.

"Where's Life?"Chaos asked, rubbing the back of his head.

Retribution's look to Chaos was leaning towards a glare, "She's chasing down a lead for me."

Chaos gave him a glance of mild respect, "You let her help you? What about the times I asked."

"Well, I can trust *her*." Retribution smacked the back of Chaos' head. He yelped and rubbed his curls with a grin.

Retribution crossed his arms, wearily meeting Fate's eyes. *Don't ask*, Fate willed.

"Any progress with the alliance?" What he meant was 'any progress getting your abilities back?'

Before anyone could say anything else, Fate spit out, "We're working on it."

Chaos, still recovering from whatever new traumatic event he had been through, shook his head slowly, "What do you-"

"I have it under control, *Chaos*."

Chaos looked at her for a minute, then laughed. "No you *don't*. Where have you even been? I've been..."

Chaos stopped himself before he could reveal the meetings with the Rebellion.

Retribution caught the implication, "You've been *what*, Chaos?"

Fate noticed Retribution hadn't asked what *she'd* been doing, but he gave her a sideways look that meant to say 'we need to talk.' She hadn't left him on a good note after the conversation at his house.

Chaos adjusted a ring, "I've been in a support group for cannibalism, anarchy, you get it-"

"*What?*" Retribution exclaimed.

Chaos looked lazily at him while Fate remained silent, raising her eyebrows.

Chaos turned away from Retribution to glare at Fate, "You spent the past months plotting something."

It wasn't a question.

Chaos was referring to her absence after Lucror. His letters were still littered in her kitchen, unopened.

Fate needed to do this by herself. Needed to prove that she could win without her powers. Perhaps then they'd come back. When she stopped the war, when she finally proved to the world that she was capable. She couldn't keep losing everything she had. Everything that made her, *her*.

"I said I'm handling it." Fate gritted out. "At least I'm not spending my time getting beat up in Fortem."

Chaos glared at her.

"Again?" Retribution groaned. He slid a hand down his face.

"We could have gone back, Fate. More prepared. We haven't failed yet."

She knew he wasn't mentioning the Rebellion plan so that they both weren't subjected to a lecture. Fate was a minute away from spilling that was never going to use that option anyway. She didn't particularly have a great history with the Rebellion.

She didn't need their help.

Though Chaos had said the words with a scowl, Fate felt surprised at the assurance in his words, as if he knew precisely what words she had been drowning in these past months.

"Favian wouldn't have agreed. I *know* he wouldn't."

Chaos cocked an eyebrow.

Fate clenched her jaw. She hadn't been thinking. With her ability, she should've known Favian was going to reject their idea before they even stepped into Lucror.

She had been too arrogant to think that Favian would have agreed to the alliance.

"I have a lot of work to continue, if you'll let me." Fate snapped, pushing away from the wall.

Chaos scoffed, "Care to share your plans?"

"I have a strange feeling it wouldn't be to your liking."

Retribution's head turned back and forth to follow the speaker like he were watching a table tennis match.

For a moment, Fate couldn't look away from Chaos. Her vision was swaying, feeling like the scene before her was some dream. Her body felt entirely unlike her own.

Her hand placed itself at her hip.

No, not yet.

She felt her heart beat rapidly in her chest. It was time. She had to test her theory when she had the chance. She was done feeling useless, feeling weak, feeling foreign in her own body.

With a step, Chaos' wrist was in her hand and they were falling. *Krasivaya.*

Ruins, overgrown greenery, empty scenery for miles.

Krasivaya, Krasivaya, Krasivaya, Krasi-

Her feet hit the ground, just as Chaos made an effort to pull his hand from her grasp. Her eyes flicked open, however the motion was quite useless. Under the crumbling ruins of some citizen's home and the endless black sky, she couldn't see much until her vision adjusted to the limited moonlight.

She twisted Chaos' hand behind his back.

More, *more.*

Chaos cried out in pain. His foot swept under hers to tip her balance, which was a smart move on his part considering their similar height. A move she had consistently used against him during their lessons in combat. She placed her foot on the outside of his to stabilize herself and kicked the inside of his knee to drop him to a kneel as he tried to pull his arm free.

"What-" Chaos tried then yelped as Fate pushed him to the ground. She placed a knee on his back to keep him down. Her free hand gripped his chin and forced his face to her as his eyes widened. He knew what her next move would be.

A strike to the chin.

And his head fell limp against his shoulders, his curls curtaining his eyes.

Fate waiting, slowly releasing herself from him. It was a tactic he had done before, feigning to be unconscious until she had loosened her grip.

She pulled away, breathing heavily, although it had nothing to do with the exertion.

Rope.

She was able to see well now under the gleaming moonlight. Her eyes tracked to the pile of wood on the very corner of the ruin, that had been a set of stairs. Carefully, she lifted a piece of wood reaching for the rope she had placed hours before.

Days.

Weeks.

Months.

This was the only solution that had a chance of success.

Twisting the rough braid in her sweat-coated palms, she ran back to Chaos' limp body. Was she ready?

She had to be.

Her hands quickly tied the rope around his limbs, knotting it multiple times over. Pulling her dagger out from inside the belt inside her pants, she sawed the rope, watching as the threads snapped, knowing the feeling all too well. Once she had two parts, she hauled Chaos over to the side of the wall to a large chunk of stone painted with moss. She inhaled the cool air with a trembling breath.

Slowly, she took the other part of the rope and winded it around the stone and him multiple times over, securing it with knots at the back.

She stalked back to face his form. His eyes were closed, his eyelashes rested against his flushed cheeks. His face was so utterly peaceful.

Kill him.

Five centuries together…

He ruined your life.

He's your brother.

Kill him. KILL HIM.

Her hand tightened against the hilt of the blade. The blade glinted in the moonlight like the shine of his hair.

His throat.

His throat was bent to allow his head to rest against his shoulders. Air flowed through his throat.

His heart.

His chest rose and fell. She felt like she could hear his heart in her ears- or was that hers?

Beat. Beat. Beat. *Don't do it.* Beat. Beat. *Do it.*

The blood supply to his body.

Her hand gripped his shoulder, feeling the thin cloth under her hand. A white dress shirt. A red dress shirt. Red.

Her hand switched to his throat, feeling his pulse under her fingers. The dagger pushed closer. The point against the base of his neck.

She cried out in refusal.

"Do it, Fate."

Fate gasped and pulled the knife back.

Chaos didn't smile. He wasn't joking.

"You think I want this? To be the protector of everything *wrong*. Balance's cessation was because of *me*, people's lives are ruined because of *me*. I…"

He looked away from her.

Fate shook her head slowly.

"No-" Her voice cracked, "You didn't…"

Chaos managed a small sharp laugh, "Before you kill me, I just want to know. Why did you hide that vision from us a decade ago?"

At that, the thread in her mind being pulled in opposite directions snapped. Her legs fell from under her. She fell to her knees at Chaos' tied legs.

Why had she? The question she had been asked day after day. Was it her own fault for all of this?

A Krasivayan woman. Her voice, whenever she spoke, was always thick with the Krasivayan accent. Her eyes, bright with youth, sharp with challenge.

A woman.

She had collapsed the fate of the world for a *woman*.

Carrilea.

Red running down her chest, a steady stream.

'A young woman- Carrilea Zaitsev- killed by gunshot tonight on 1718 Krasny Lane. The murderer, a patrol guard, shot Zaitsev after she was discovered to be in league with the uprising rebellion group against Queen Katya. Ruled justified.'

Fate felt the burning tears pouring across her cheeks, warm as blood. The metal in her hands warped from the water in her

222

eyes. She could taste the salt on her tongue as she opened her mouth to speak. She tried. She couldn't tell him.

No. She owed him as much, to tell him. *Then* she would kill him.

She *would* kill him.

"A woman," Fate choked out, "The woman I loved. Killed- justified...."

Chaos remained silent.

Fate shut her eyes, trembling, "They ruled the murder justified. She tried to *fix* the society in Krasivaya."

"A rebellion?" Chaos asked, softer than she had ever heard him speak.

"Yes." She kept her eyes closed and her head bent, hiding behind the strands of dark hair. She didn't want to see the expression on Chaos' face.   Whether it was pity or anger or empathy- she didn't want to see it.

She was sure the world would end before she ever admitted her motive for hiding her vision.

She pried her eyes open, her tears becoming those of anger, "I couldn't protect her, *we* couldn't protect her. If I couldn't save the person I loved, then what use was saving the others?"

Her eyes lifted from the blade twisted in her hand to Chaos' face. His eyes had opened at some point and his face was horribly implacable.

"Do you regret it?" Was all he asked.

She paused and searched his face.

And she admitted to the clawing feeling of guilt she had tried to keep caged.

"Everyday."

At that, he seemed satisfied, "Do it."

And she obliged.

Her knuckles went white around the hilt of the dagger and she pierced it through the air at Chaos' body.

Her body shook as she unraveled her fingers from her grip. The blade was embedded in the stone, hairs away from Chaos' throat.

She couldn't face Chaos' eyes. She examined the shine of the hilt in the moonlight as she heaved. She couldn't do it. She couldn't kill him.

She could have killed him and gotten her power back. But it was impossible. She was being selfish. She couldn't kill him for her own benefit.

How had she *ever* thought that this was a good idea?

Fate was silent as she gathered herself up, standing. When she spoke she could feel her cheeks stretching against her dried tears, "You understand now?"

He gave a small nod, but didn't say anything. Fate turned away.

"Fate." He said, shattering the chilling silence of the night sky.

She paused, then turned to face him. If he was going to ask for her to untie him…

When she met his eyes, her eyebrows raised in shock. The mischief had returned to his eyes and his lips were twisted in a smirk, "Did you really think I wouldn't notice you lost your ability?"

Fate gaped.

"Please," He grinned wearily, "We both know saving lives wasn't your motivation behind building the coalition or sending me to that death threat of a Rebellion to get some random element that I actually do ha-"

Fate scowled and turned her back to him, not listening to his words over the thumping in her mind, "Shut up."

She shut her eyes. Nothing was going fast enough- the end of the power, the reinstatement of her powers. Just as she felt her surroundings melt together, she heard a cry from behind her. Her plan now was obvious, and it was going to destroy Cadere before it could save them. She just had to hope the shattered pieces left behind were enough to be placed together to form something better.

"Fate, wait! I have the-"

And with that, she left Chaos tied in 1718 Krasny Lane.

She told herself she would end this. For Carrilea.

For Chaos.

CHAPTER

TWENTY-EIGHT

FLASHBACK

Fate can't help but stare at the girl with blond hair. Fate would never get tired of staring at her.

Carrilea.

She sits, crouched next to a smaller girl, both giggling. The two girls shoot quick glances and giggles at Fate. The Protector smiles and walks towards the two girls.

"Shh! She's coming here!" The younger girl loudly whispers, pushing Carrilea towards Fate. Carrilea throws her head back, laughing.

Fate grins as she braces the laughing woman. Fate turns back to the starry eyed child, "Well, hello, Evora." A fond smirk spreads to her face. "Get into any mischief with Eli recently?"

Carrilea shoots a scolding look at Evora.

"No." She mutters begrudgingly, kicking up dirt with her shoe.

"Evora!" A small child wearing a big smile and extremely short, jaggedly cut hair stumbles forward, barrelling into Evora, sending them both to the floor.

"Get off Eli!" Evora giggles, rolling the thrashing counterpart off her. Carrillea grinned broadly at her siblings, intertwining her fingers with Fate's.

Fate's jaw dropped comically, "Eli! Have you cut your hair?"

"Yeah! You like it?" The child grins at Fate, exposing a set of pearly white teeth.

Carrillea grins widely at Fate, "I told her not to do it!" She laughs.

Fate smiles as she leans down to stare the child in the eye. "Well I think you look positively handsome Eli."

Fate winks at Eli's shy grin. Her gaze shifts, resting on Carrilea's ivory face.

As usual, bruises and cuts lay scattered on the mortal's jaw, cheek, neck, and hands. Though she will say, there seems to be more today than usual. Were her eyes this sunken in the last time Fate had seen her?

Fate's smile wavers. Her hand raises up grazing Carrilea's jaw. "Evora, Eli, could you give your sister and I a moment please?"

Evora and Eli look at eachother giggling before running away to the crowd.

Fate turns back to look at the mortal, her expression suddenly serious. "You've been spending more time with that Rebellion haven't you?" Fate accuses, her brows furrow in disapproval.

"Okay, do not start this-"

"You say you have it under control but you're injured. You're getting too involved. You're losing sleep. You're bleeding on your face, there are no healers here-"

"It's just a scratch, and that's exactly why we need this! We don't have healers. We don't have anything. Fate, I am their leader. I started the rebellion. I can't just sit there while people are dying. I want to help- I will help. I made this decision because I knew what I was getting into."

Fate stares into her eyes, "You're too rash-"

"You're one to talk." Carrilea pulls away. "I can take care of myself," She snaps.

The pair quiet, staring at each other. Fate sighs "You're right. I'm sorry I just worry for you."

Fate brings her hands up again, cupping the skin of Carrilea's face. This time Carrilea doesn't move away, instead opting to close her eyes and nestle closer.

"I know you do Fate, but please trust me."

"Of course." Fate whispers. Carrilea grins, leaning forward to steal a kiss from Fate's lips. The Protector's eyes flutter shut, her hand flying to the base of Carrilea's neck to keep their lips interlocked. Fate feels Carrilea's finger rest on her cheek, drawing small circles on her tan skin. Fate sighs as Carrilea pulls away.

"Fate?" Carrilea whispers. Slowly, Fate's eyes open, immediately coming to rest on Carrilea's face.

"I trust you Carrilea. I always will, but I don't trust them. Accidents happen. Just be careful. Please."

Carrilea smiles, leaning her forehead against Fate's.

"Of course."

***

Chaos shoots up with an icy gasp, his heart pounds into his eardrums. He frantically jerks his head around, scoping his surroundings. A wooden upright piano, papers littered across the floor, a large window overlooking the Altar lake...

He sighs out a breath. As he plops back down into his plush bed. A chill runs through his frame as he recalls his nightmare.

It was something following the lines of 'Death turned into a large dragon-like monster with pink fur and tentacles then presumed to chase him around the Altar.' Then the scene had changed, and then something happened to Fate and then she was gone for eternity, and he wasn't there to stop it.

Chaos runs his hands down his face. He pushes the back of his head into his pillow as he turns to the left, practically glaring at a bright red clock on his bedside table.

2:17 am.

He flinches back suddenly, scrambling into a sitting position. He could swear that he saw something next to his window. A large dark figure. Shifty.

Chaos blinks.

"Oh." He whispers curtly. "It's just a jacket on a hook. Nothing more."

His chest constricts in panic. He shuffles back, his back hitting the bed frame. He flinches again as his head swivels to look towards his piano: creaky and old.

"Just old."

Chaos lays down, pulling his blankets up to his chin as he clamps his eyes shut.

No. No he can't do that. His eyes open again. If they're closed then he won't be able to see if someone were to sneak up on him.

Chaos groans quietly, burying himself deeper into the blankets. He wishes he could just sink into the bed. More than that, how dearly he wishes in this moment that he had made an effort when the others had tried to teach him how to fight. Not that he would ever tell them that.

He shoots up. He can't do this. It was too much. The creaking, the shadows- he can't.

Chaos swings his legs over the side of the bed. He stands up, quickly walking to the door. He softly opens it and steps out of his room.

To his immense disappointment, the halls of the Altar are dark. No candles are lit. Just the faint light from a few stars through the windows. Chaos tip toes forward, leaving his room.

He doesn't think. His feet take him forward. He doesn't realize he has stopped walking until all the shadows seem far closer to him than before.

He looks up at a sturdy wooden door next to a portrait of a fruit in a cornucopia. Chaos' gaze flickers. Then slowly he raises his hand to meet the wood in two sharp knocks.

He steps back, as he hears shuffling behind the door.

The door swings open. "What? What do you want?" *A voice groans.*

Chaos stares at Fate's tired form. Oh, good she's not dead. *Fate rubs her eyes tiredly.*

"Nightmare." *He whispers.*

She pauses, looking at Chaos. She sighs as she looks back into her room, stepping to the side to let Chaos in.

"Come on."

Chaos shuffles in quickly.

The room has different fighting tactics taped to the walls. Pencils and papers on her desk and floors, and the picture of all the Protectors sitting in a small frame on her bedside table wraps everything up nicely.

Chaos turns to look at Fate as she quietly shuts the door.

"So... what was your nightmare about?" *She asks calmly.*

Chaos' hand travels to rub the back of his neck. "You know. The usual."

Fate nods simply in reply. She knew she wouldn't get anything from Chaos if he didn't want to say it.

She walked past him tiredly before collapsing onto her large bed. "Well I'm tired, so either get in bed or get out."

Chaos rolls his eyes as he walks to the other side of the bed, sliding into the soft cotton covers.

The two lay on their back quietly, staring up at the ceiling. It's a good silence. One full of mutual understanding.

Chaos relaxes, his shoulders untensing as he feels himself sink a little deeper into the bed. His eyes flutter shut as he feels fatigue seep into his bones, his adrenalin running thin.

"Can you move?" Fate snaps.

Chaos feels his eyes roll under his lids.

"You're taking up the whole bed, can you move?"

Chaos smiles ever so softly, as he hears Fate's exasperated tone. She jerks up, glaring at Chaos.

"I know you're not asleep, I will kick you off this bed."

Chaos groans comically as he rolls over to the right side of the bed.

"Better?" He mocks.

"Much." She mimics.

Chaos grins, as he closes his eyes again. Perhaps this time he'll dream about turning into an enormous pink furry monster with tentacles instead of Death. His first action as tentacle furry monster will be to traumatize Fate by chasing her around the Altar. It will be a nice change of pace.

Chaos smiles at the thought as he feels sleep over take him.

CHAPTER

TWENTY-NINE

FATE

She hadn't been sure if killing Chaos would have any effect at all on the war, so she had come up with a secondary plan. One that threw diplomacy out the window. If she succeeded, world-wide damage would be inevitable. It would, however, allow the citizens to build up and reshape the world on their own. For better or for worse.

She found the root of the problem, and she was here to terminate it.

The royal Riquezan castle was breathtaking. Architectural gilding framed every edge of the building glinting under the moonlight. In the sunlight, the gold speared outwards, resulting in a stunning glow. But even under the dim lighting, the tall turrets and the multiple stories of gilded windows that seemed to reach higher into the sky than the mountains were a sight to behold.

Though it was quite aggravating, without her ability she had to watch the castle for weeks after she had made up her mind, noting the guard switch times, oftentimes even stepping foot in the castle in place of a throne room guard to scout her area. It wasn't as difficult as it should have been. And Casimir hardly resided in his throne room. He was oftentimes seen in the halls, speaking to his advisor or general, or even Aahi.

Every six hours, a new shift of guards would take station in front of and inside the castle. It happened at differing times at different entrances throughout the castle, so it wouldn't be left unguarded. *Smart.*

The guards in the throne room switched at 2300 hours, which was the simplest time to catch Casimir unprepared and unprotected. Obviously, she only had seconds before the new batch of soldiers walked in, but a few seconds was enough to watch the life leak out of someone's eyes.

The murder would never trace back to her, considering she had no DNA, and the western countries could be free from Casimir's grip. Win-win. Aahi, well, Aahi…Fate could determine her future at a later date. She wasn't contributing as much to the level of destruction as Riqueza was, and Aahi still had empathy she tried to conceal.

There was nothing to lose.

Except maybe her cover. It would be very time-consuming to tie up the loose ends, but it would be possible. She would 'take care' of every citizen in the entire country if she had too.

Her eyes glanced down from her position above a ledge on the throne room's tiered dome. Combed brown hair on top of pale skin. Black clothing under red and green robes. The throne he sat on, plated in gold and adorned with sculptures of dragons.

Casimir.

A mortal man- flesh, blood, a lifetime less than a mere century. It'd be simple- she'd just have to be precise.

Her gaze flicked back to her wrist. The hands on the silver watch ticked closer to 2300 hours. *Chaos'* silver watch that she had stolen from him before she tied him up. He would probably kill her when she got back, for multiple reasons that was.

Five, four, three.

Her heart pounded in her ears. This was it.

Two.

One.

The guards stationed along the walls of the throne room filled out. It had never been so silent and yet so loud at the same time. Their shuffling movements echoed through the hall as they exited through the grand doors and into the corridor.

Eight more guards.

Five. Four.

Two.

Her stomach twisted, her palms felt warm and sticky. No, *no.* This was the absolute worst time to be nervous.

Just as the door shut, and Casimir was left completely unprotected, she shut her eyes.

Her hand gripped her knife with such intensity, she was surprised she hadn't broken it.

She felt the ledge disappear from under her feet.

Her eyes flicked open, she could feel the clock hands' movement on her wrist. She could hear the ticking in her ears.

Fate spun, pulling away her fingers from the hilt, steadying herself to disappear the second after it embedded itself in Casimir's heart. The blade spun in the air. Growing farther from her, and closer, closer, closer to Casimir's body until...

The dagger collided with Casimir's body.

The motion was done, but her task was not. The blade bounced off his chest like hitting rubber and fell at his feet.

Something was wrong. Someth-

Her face paled. The room spun.

There was only one being she could not kill.

One being she could not harm.

It wasn't the mortal Casimir.

It was- it was-

"Time." Casimir said, raising his eyebrows, "Pleased to finally meet you, Fate."

Casimir- Time- stepped down from his dias, leaning forward to pick up her blade. Fate only stared, completely unable to move. This couldn't be.

She had never even *glimpsed* Time and here he was. Ruling almost the entire planet. Where was he when she begged, her hands stained red, cradling Carrilea in her arms? Where was he the moment after their creation as they struggled to protect an entire planet?

All she could do was stare as he stalked closer. His eyes were deep and dark, a pool of secrets. He was tall, taller than her, but only by a few inches.   Too much, *too much.*

Time placed a hand on her shoulder, handing Fate her dagger in an open palm.

"Calm yourself, Fate," Time said as she bore her eyes into the blade on his palm.

Calm? How could she even *fathom* being calm?

She had almost killed Chaos.

Casimir was Time.

And there she was- alone in front of a being created at the beginning of existence itself. Who controlled existence itself. Who created *her.*

Without thinking, her fingers wrapped around the hilt on the dagger on his palm. Her leg twisted in the air aiming for his chest, but he simply stepped aside.

He reached into his robes, with a pitying frown, and pulled out a gold knife. The traditional *Riquezan* dagger.

This fight was impossible to win. The safest option was to back out, run back to Krasivaya, untie Chaos, and stay hidden from the public eye.

But, she couldn't.

He had made her existence torture.

He had bestowed her with such power, such power that only came with the burden of an entire planet's future resting on her hands. He had never shown up when her family had needed him. Instead, he commenced a war, gathering countries under his rule like they were fruit, killing and kidnapping innocent humans, ending Balance's existence, and taking away her future sight.

It wasn't Chaos who had ruined her existence.

It wasn't herself, who she had to blame.

It was Time.

She would find a way to kill the unkillable.

And their blades clashed. The dome echoed their sound like the ringing of Altar bells. Strike. Parry. Feign. Twist. Strike.

"Put down the weapon, Fate. Come to your senses." Time reprimanded. He spoke in an awfully indifferent voice, a tone of cruel amusement.

Kick. Parry. Punch. Duck.

His lips curled up as he continued to divert her attacks.

"Why? Why build an empire? Why do you *need* an empire?" She swept her foot under his, her voice thick with disdain.

He faltered slightly, but brushed himself off, "Sometimes, Fate, there is no reason to do so."

Her tied hair whipped along her neck as she pressed her blade into his. Such *lies.* Her foot slid along the tile as he pushed back against her dagger. They both pulled back.

She was breathing heavily, but he just crossed his arms.

"You fight well. Those miniscule motions revealing the next attack, you use to your advantage. Try striking with less force, however, and be more precise, Fate."

Gone, she wanted him gone. Blinked out of sight, like his existence had never occurred. If she heard her name on his lips, even once more, she would fall into insanity.

They fought once more, but his motions were increasingly forceful. His blade hit the skin on her wrist, on her face, on her neck.

Her blade lifted to strike his upper arm but just as she did, a small smile curved up his lips.

236

Her limbs slowed- stopped almost- as if she was moving through concrete. As if her limbs were held back by resistance bands. She could only watch as the weapon in her hand slowed as it glided through the air at his arm.

He merely pushed her hand aside a couple of inches as her sloth-like motions reached for him. And just as it came, her motions returned to normal and her force titled her weight onto her toes, almost toppling over.

Oh, she had forgotten he had abilities. *A dirty play.* She, like her fellow protectors, could only use her abilities on mortals, but *Time* - it seemed- was exempt from their restriction.

She turned, aiming for skin, but her effort was futile, and she found herself facing the floor, on the tip of her toes, once more.

"What-"

"Less force, more angle." Time chided as he watched her flail. If she could, she would carve out the disapproving frown that seemed to be permanently etched onto his face.

And the cycle continued, for what like hours, her attacks hit nothing but air and she was never allowed further from her initial position. Over, over, again, again, repeat, repeat, *repeat,*

The back of her neck was damp, her arms were sore, and the blaze in her step snuffed. Time simply stood and scrutinized her every move. It was *awful.* She made moves, planned attacks that either seemed to never exist, or never reach her destination. In other words; each attack was only wearing her out, draining her energy.

"Now, show me your technique."

Her limbs seemed to defrost, gliding through the air again once more. She *wanted* to kill him. But, it was hopeless. She had broken into the Riquezan royal castle expecting a mortal man- one fairly easy to kill- and she had gotten an all-powerful, unkillable god.

It was over- it had never begun. He had *known* she was coming. *How?*

That wasn't important, however, because he could overpower her with a mere thought.

"Will you let me," Fate gasped as her blade collided with his, knocking away his weapon from his hands, "leave?"

Time's lips quirked up as he pulled yet another dagger from his robes, "A wise question."

He hit her skin again, this time it was deeper, a stream of red snaking down her arm. She gritted her teeth in pain.

"Unfortunately," He twisted around her, grabbing her arm and holding it against her back. His pressure was too much for her to budge.

"Not." His free arm held the point of his blade to her neck, his feet firmly holding hers in place, shoving her against the wall between the room's two windows. Fate slowed her breathing, certain that the skin that rose when she inhaled would hit the metal.

She closed her eyes, focusing, focusing...

She couldn't focus on disappearing, not when a knife was at her throat. Honestly, it was bold of her to assume he wouldn't just reset time if she had managed to disappear from his grasp.

She was completely defenseless. She could feel his calloused hand on her arm, his frame caging her against the wall, the cold metal against her skin. She blinked, spots appearing in her vision.

Her mouth. Her *words*.

"Will you tell the others? Does Retribution know his *beloved* mentor is nothing but a power-hungry man?" Fate sneered, twisting in his grip.

"Hm," He mused, "why don't you ask him?"

She scoffed. She turned her head as Time pulled his weapon away just enough to allow for some leeway to meet dark eyes. Her heart dropped. Dropped, then shattered.

"No!" Fate spat.

No, no, no, no, no.

238

Retribution stood and watched with a sway in his stance. He never stepped forward, never pulled out a weapon, but his eyes were blown wide. He shook, his mouth wide in horror. Almost mechanically, he turned away and pushed past the grand doors.

"No." She whispered, pulling her limbs away with even stronger force. It only tightened Time's grip on her and pushed the blade deeper into her skin. She heaved, shutting her eyes for focus. She searched her mind, knowing if they could feel her connection, there had to be some way to turn it off. It was better that way. She didn't want them to see her like this. Defeated.

She found something hidden far in the maze in her head. Four remaining strings. One for Death, Life, Retribution, and Chaos. Strings representing the bond for feeling the other's existence. She wrapped her mind around the end of three of the strings and pulled. Pulled with the entire force of her focus, until they simultaneously snapped, rebounding waves in her head.

Retribution would feel her die. It was only fitting. She would let the denial of guilt build up in his mind, corroding the edges of his brain for all eternity. Like it had to her.

She had trusted him, she had come to him in her time of need, he was her *brother*. How could he leave?

Time squeezed her tighter, placing his mouth by her ear, "Give Carrilea my greetings, will you?"

The blade slashed across her throat. Her body collapsed to the ground at Time's feet.

She could feel the warmth spreading down her blouse. She could smell the copper, taste the copper even.

Her vision blurred. She could feel the rising weight in her lungs. She could hear the blood rushing down her neck, louder than Cadere's waterfalls.

And yet, even louder in her ears were Time's receding footsteps.

"Perhaps, Chaos, I should have tried the diplomatic approach."

Blood filled her lungs, then her throat, then her mouth.
And she finally got an answer.
She couldn't have future sight if the world had no future.

CHAPTER THIRTY

Life

She had to make it to Sēnlín National Park– Heping.

That was where her journey really began.

The actual caves of the park were quite well hidden. Now, she just had to find them because the Sans Fin cave system was where the stone was.

Life frowned. It was probably where the stone was…

Her eyesight cleared as she scanned her surroundings. Confirming that she had made it to the path there. She unzipped her backpack and took out the map.

It felt heavy in her hands. What had this map cost her?

She shook her head and unrolled it, her eyes scanning for her location and then the Sans Fin Caverns that she needed to get to. It was almost twelve miles from here, which would mean around seven hours of walking.

She sighed deeply.

It was moments like these where she wished she had explored Heping more. Protectors could only teleport to where they've been or where they could vividly visualize. This rural part of Heping was foreign to her.

"Alright, come on Life. Twelve miles, that's not bad." She muttered to herself. She remembered when all the protectors had a 7 mile race. She shuddered even thinking about it. It was basic torture they had forced her to do. After that day, she never participated in the runs again.

"This is just walking, It won't be that bad." She looked at where she was standing on the map and then her destination again.

She brought out her compass, lugged her legs toward the arrow pointing North-West, and walked.

***

As the minutes grew, her morale continued to shrink. She had made friends with a pet rock. It wasn't her best moment.

She checked her pocket watch, only four more hours to go. She felt like her legs were going to disassemble and collapse beneath her.

"So, Tabitha, tell me about yourself." She mumbled to the rock.

"Well, I like rocks and I have a personal collection of pebbles!" Life replied to herself, forcing her voice to jump several octaves higher.

"Fascinating! You should show them to me sometime! In fact, I have a personal collection myself."

"Really?" She replied as Tabitha.

"Indeed, I collect fossils. It's a nice little reminder."

"What's the best one you've collected so far?"

"Oh, that's an easy one, I-" She paused.

What am I doing?

She shook her head, and chucked the rock as hard as she could.

She turned around, walking down the winding path before freezing, her eyes widening.

Frank, Tabitha! She groaned as she scrambled toward the direction of her throw.

That rock was practically the only thing holding her together. She checked under leaves and behind trees before dropping onto her knees and searching fervently.

"Yes!" Life held up Tabitha victoriously. At least, she thought that was Tabitha… it had to be.

"Sorry." She smiled as she pocketed Tabitha in a small pouch and continued walking. She could hear the sounds of a village not too far away.

She smiled.

That would be her one-fourth point in her journey.

The sun began to dim behind the clouds.

She checked her pocket watch again, displaying six o'clock in the evening.

She knew that she was making this journey much worse for herself by constantly checking the time, but she was uncomfortably close to losing her mind. Every minute that passed seemed to stretch on. At this rate the war would be over by the time she reached the caves.

A soft crunch of footsteps sounded to her left. Her eyes widened as she quickly crouched. There was a cluster of sticks and branches leaning against the bark of a tree, some leaves covering the top. At first glance Life would have just brushed it off as a fallen tree, but the more she stared at it the more she noticed the intentionally placed pine and sticks.

She tilted her head. A tent in the middle of the woods? She inched closer.

She flinched at the sound of wrinkling leaves under her foot.

"Hello? Is anyone there?" Life wiggled between the trees, revealing a largely impressive space beneath the canopy.

Two loud voices yelled right next to her ears, "Boo!"

Life screamed as she scrambled back, misplacing her foot. She slipped, landing with a thud.

The two figures laughed, clutching their stomachs. Life huffed, quickly standing back up.

A boy that looked around the age of nine was hunched over, laughing at her. He had wavy dark hair, and his brown eyes crinkled, complementing his smile. His red shirt hung low and loose on his frame, and his dark brown pants and shoes made him look taller, but not by a lot.

The second was a short girl with silky long black hair. Her skin shone brightly as her cheeks flushed. She looked much cleaner than the former.

Life frowned.

She looked like Balance.

"Very funny." Life snapped, dusting her clothes off.

"It is funny, thank you for being our victim in our hilarious prank." The brown haired boy spoke. They both giggled again and shared a high-five.

Life felt her stomach twist. The two children reminded her of the antics of her and a certain Protector who always wore a watch.

"Name's Diego.

Life scanned the boy, "A pleasure." She offered, shortly.

"More like, a pleasure to scare you!" He laughed again.

Life grimaced at the joke. She turned to look at the girl. "What's your name?

The girl smiled, "Mei. What's your name?"

"I'm Li-" Life paused, " I'm Lily."

"Did you just stumble on your name?" Diego snickered at her.

Life rolled her eyes, "I have more than one name."

Diego stepped forward, "Wait, so are you a top secret spy or something?"

"Are you undercover?" The girl continued.

"How did you guess?" Life mused, the smallest smile cracking onto her face.

"I'm just naturally smart."

"Wow, I'm speechless." Diego smiled and nodded, folding his arms and looking toward her, clearly showing a look of approval.

"So what's your mission?" Diego asked her, moving to wiggle out of the structure.

"Top secret."

"Then count me in!" Diego said, his arms behind his head, supporting it. Her eyes widened.

"What-? No. It's dangerous." She picked up her pace as Diego and the girl started to jog to keep up with her.

She groaned at the realization that they were not leaving.

"Don't you need to get to your family? It's getting late, your parents must be worried about you." She asked them.

Mei's eyes widened comically, "Oh yeah!" She turned to Diego, "I gotta go. Bye!"

He smiled a thin lipped smile and waved at her.

Life stared at Diego, "And what about you?"

He frowned. She had a feeling she had accidentally hit a nerve.

"Don't got any. Not anymore." He mumbled. "My parents died in the Krasivayan attack."

Life slowed down as she stared at him. She felt like a hammer had dropped on her. She couldn't even imagine being so young and having no one other than a five year old friend to keep him company.

"Oh." She started, "I'm sorry. I know a thing or two about loss. Were your parents Krasivayan?"

"No. They were Riquezan."

Life's eyes widened before nodding slightly.

"Did they believe in Riqueza's cause?"

Diego shrugged, staring at her. "I know that look."

Life frowned, "What look?"

"That look people get when I tell them I'm Riquezan."

Life shook her head, "One of my closest friends is Riquezan, and I'd trust him till the end."

"Are you sure?" His voice was barely audible now, "I guess everyone just abandons me at some point." He mumbled to himself, but it was loud enough for her to hear.

Oh, she knew what game he was playing. And unfortunately, it made her hesitate.

She rolled her eyes, stopping and staring at him.

"Is this you trying to guilt-trip me or something?" She mused.

"Yeah, is it working?"

She turned around. "Yeah, a bit."

He grinned skipping infront of her, "So can I help you on your mission?"

Life frowned. How many times had she asked that same question to Retribution? It would be hypocritical to not let Diego come.

"Well?" Life said.

"Well what?"

"Are you coming or not?"

He grinned as he jogged to her side.

"Now where are we off to?" He asked her.

She looked up, the darkness had started bleeding into the sky. She took out her pocket watch.

"7:15" She tilted her head to look at him, "Can you walk for a bit just until we get to the streets? It's not far from here."

"Lily, my friend, I walk all day, everyday. In fact, one would call me a walking expert."

"Uh huh." She smiled.

"I know the ins and outs of this forest, I can get us out of here quicker than you can say Chaos."

She paused before shaking her head. He was Riquezan. They were loyal to Chaos. He couldn't have known.

"Really?" She slowed down.

"Mhm."

"And this isn't one of your pranks?"

246

"That was one time okay?" He insisted, "And many before that, but that's not the point!" He ran in front of her and stopped her from walking.

"This is for your top secret mission right?"

She chuckled and nodded.

"Alright, and when do you need to be on the streets of the town?"

"Preferably before it gets dark."

"Okay, I know the perfect route. Follow me!" He spun around, striding forward.

She hesitated.

"Come on!" He urged and continued marching.

"Alright, alright." Life sped walked to catch up with him.

"So, how old are you?" He asked over his shoulder.

"I'm- uh-" She racked her brain for numbers that would suit her well. "Twenty-three."

"Wow, you're old."

"Yeah, I know." She scoffed, "So do you just sleep outside?"

She didn't want to intrude on a sensitive topic, not that he didn't seem to care.

"I lived in a group home for a few years. Finally got the guts to bust myself out of that mess."

"What happened there?"

"The beds, the elders, oh, and the food," he shuddered. "It sucked. But the main reason was the other kids. They… they didn't like me all that much. I was tough though. I stood my ground… most of the time."

Her brows furrowed,"I get it."

"I know you do," He looked at her, "I can tell."

Life was silent for a moment, "Where do you live now?"

"That place at Hua park in the tent. I feel like I'm camping all the time, it's great. My parents never took me before."

247

Life exhaled slowly, "Why don't you go and live at a friend's house?"

"Are you kidding? I've probably pranked every single person I know. They were good pranks though, it was hilarious but they were mostly annoyed at me. All the parents thought I was a 'bad influence'."

His face constricted in thought, "Okay, maybe I am a little, but what's wrong with a few harmless pranks?"

"Nothing at all."

"Exactly."

Life grinned, "You know, when I was younger, I was a bit of a prankster myself."

"Really?" He laughed.

"Mhm! My pranks would sometimes be... *potentially* harmful, *but* everyone enjoyed them."

"What kind of pranks?"

She bit her lip, "Well let's see, there was the classic banana prank, the ice bucket prank, oh can't forget the fireworks one-"

"You pranked someone with fireworks?!" He asked her, looking up in awe.

"Yup. My friend, Chaos and I-"

"Chaos? Like the god?"

She had slipped up. She closed her eyes for a beat.

"Yeah you could say that. His parents were very religious I guess."

"I see." He nodded solemnly.

The pair walked in silence.

"You know you're different than I thought you were."

She raised her brow, "What did you think I was?"

"Boring."

Her jaw dropped. Her? Boring? She was *not* boring.

"Well you're very wrong. I am, in fact, the opposite." She said, grinning at herself.

"Sure." He said, sarcastically. "Oh, and hot-headed. You would probably be the kind of baby that threw a lot of tantrums as a kid. Boy, I feel bad for your parents."

Life's jaw dropped. She was probably the least troublesome out of all the Protectors. She winced slightly. Well maybe not least likely, but between Chaos' aptitude for trouble and Fate's need to medle the Protectors had their hands full without her adding fuel to the fire.

"Hey! I do not throw tantrums. You shouldn't even be talking. You're like what? Three?"

"I'm eleven! I already told you."

"Yeah, yeah, same thing."

"In fact, I'm gonna be eleven and a half in a couple of months." He shot her a look of annoyance and she chuckled. They both walked in silence. She felt her mind start to wander again. This stone would stop the war. Balance would be back, and retribution would no longer have the burden of a mystery mission on his back. Everything would go back to normal. She was killing three birds with one stone.

"Are we there yet?" He whined, "My feet are burning."

"Well, I don't know! You have the directions."

Diego gasped before breaking into a run.

"Diego, what?" Life quickly followed.

Diego suddenly froze, turning around grinning.

"Welcome, my dear friend Lily, to the busy streets of Sēnlín."

Life straightened out her back in relief, cars and carriages roaming the suburban streets outside of Sēnlín National Park.

"Isn't it wonderful?" Diego asked her.

"It truly is."

He turned to her, "So, I helped you. Obviously I'm trustworthy and know my way around here much better than you. Will you tell me where we're headed now?"

Life paused, staring at him. She shouldn't involve him. This was her mission.

Maybe she was starting to get Retribution's side now.

She sighed, "Sēnlín National Park."

His eyes lit up, "Well why didn't you say so? I know a shortcut!"

"You know, I don't know how much I trust these shortcuts of yours."

"Hey I'm good for it."

She rolled her eyes, following as he started to walk down the street.

"Do you even know where you're going?" Life asked him.

"Trust me, I've been here countless times. Have you?"

She grumbled.

"Maybe we should go tomorrow. Do you want to find somewhere to sleep?"

She looked up. Hues of purples, blues, and oranges lit up the sky.

Protectors didn't technically need to sleep. It was helpful though. It gave their bodies some time to recuperate.

She fished her pocket watch out, scanning the face of it for the time. She nodded, "Sure."

"Then I know the perfect place."

She puffed out a breath of air and followed him begrudgingly. She didn't know why she was following an eleven year old, but he seemed to know the area pretty well. Much better than her.

"Do you sleep at that... tent every night?" Life asked him.

"Most of the time. I usually only come to Sēnlín Park for food." He responded. "Since it's been annexed by Riqueza, and I obviously look Riquezan, the soldiers are pretty nice to me. The townspeople on the other hand..." He trailed off. He grinned at her expression, "It's no trouble though! Not all of them are mean, and the soldiers give me enough food to live on. They even offered a barn for me to stay at!"

"Then why the tent?"

"I don't want to live in a Riquezan barn. I'm not trying to be more hated by the people here than I already am. Plus, the tent's closer to Mei's house!"

She hummed in understanding.

"Do you go to school?" Life said.

"Geez, what's with all the questions?"

"Well, you're a kid. You should be living in a nice, comfy home."

He shrugged, "It doesn't really bother me anymore." He said, coming to a stop.

Life wished she could do something more to help the people because these living conditions were unbearable. It wasn't like she could just stop making life. She would never hear the end of it if she disrupted the natural flow. She supposed that was another reason she had to do this.

Life scanned her surroundings, a small creek ran through a little garden of flowers and foliage. There were great pine's surrounding the garden, covering it from the public as Diego and Life wiggled to get inside.

"Wow. I'm impressed." Life stated.

"I know." He collapsed dramatically onto the warm, soft grass.

She smiled, sitting down next to him.

"Thanks for bringing me along." He muttered.

Life looked up at the sky, and took out her pocket watch. Diego rolled over and opened her backpack, rummaging through it. He took out her blanket and her compass pouch, his brow furrowed.

"Why do you have a rock in your pouch?" He questioned.

"Don't you know it's rude to go through other people's things?" She snatched her pouch and Tabitha from his thin fingers.

"Who do you think teaches me manners?" He deadpanned, "So about that rock…?"

"It's complicated, okay?" She ran her thumb over the rocks smooth surface.

Diego's face scrunched in mock disgust. "I'm gonna sleep."

"Yeah, that's right. Isn't it past your bedtime?" Life grinned, "Don't want Diego to get grumpy, do we?" She set the rock down inside the pouch, wished it goodnight and closed it.

She looked at her pocket watch again. "It's quarter to nine, which means if we sleep now, we'll get around… 8 hours of sleep." Life whispered.

Diego stole her blanket and laid down.

"Hey, my blanket!" Life yanked the blanket from underneath him as he started in protest.

"Didn't you say that I deserved a nice, comfy home not too long ago?"

"Well-"

"Of course I don't. A poor child with no parents… even a small blanket is too much for a person to give. A life so hard that-

"Don't be dramatic, I was going to give you half of it?" She sighed, throwing the plush fabric over both of them.

He grinned happily and laid down again, turning onto his side. His back faced her.

Life stayed sitting as Diego curled into the ground, as if this was the comfiest thing he had ever laid on.

There were a couple of beats of silence before he started again,

"You know, there are a lot of things that I haven't told anyone. Like sometimes I really wonder what my life would've been if my parents were still here."

"Well, It would resume wherever you left off before your parents died. But all of this only made you stronger. And I know you're hurt, so am I, but we are strong. We know how to survive.

252

I'm telling you, you have an amazing life ahead of you, just you wait." She whispered.

He took a deep breath, "I'm a kid, I wasn't supposed to be stronger, I was supposed to be safe."

Life frowned.

The two sat in silence.

"How do you know?" He asked, finally.

"How do I know what?"

"That life has something in store for me?"

"I just do."

He nodded slowly, "Thanks."

"No problem."

"Oh wow, what a long day of pranking. I guess I have to go to sleep now. Good night." He said, shifting in his place one last time before shutting his eyes.

"Goodnight." Life said, frowning when he didn't respond.

There was no way he slept that fast. She refused to believe it. She was pretty sure he was faking it.

***

He wasn't faking it. He really did fall asleep in seconds.

Life groaned, turning onto her side. All she could think about was Retribution. She wondered what his reaction was when he saw the letter this morning.

Did he tell the others? Were they all searching for her? Was Retribution relieved or angry?

She turned again. Her frame shifted against the soft grass.

One time Fate, Balance, and Life had camped outside. It had been just like this.

Life smiled.

She missed Balance. She missed Fate and her being that close. She missed the days before the war had started. It was just another reminder that she was doing this to get it back. To get everything back.

She thought about the map and the diary, questions replaying in her mind.

She looked over at Diego, frowning. She felt like she was being thrown into an infinite hole, getting dirt thrown in her face as the darkness ate away the light.

She needed to get going if she wanted to get the stone before Retribution and Time.

She frowned at Diego's figure, curled up.

She was doing this for him as well.

She had to leave. She would have left him at some point, besides he seemed to be surviving by himself pretty well.

Her eyes shut.

She didn't want to leave.

For the first time in so long, she wasn't alone anymore.

She shook her head. She slowly got up, throwing on her backpack. She bent down, about to pull off the blanket from him when she stopped. She withdrew her hand and looked at Diego, his young features worn off by dirt and grub. She stood up straight again, leaving the blanket for him as he cuddled into it.

"I'll be back… after I make everything right. I promise." She whispered under her breath and turned around, wiggling through the trees and getting back on the midnight road.

CHAPTER

THIRTY-ONE

CHAOS

His least favorite thing about being tied to a rock was that it made teleporting surprisingly difficult.

Once his mind had wrapped around himself and the rock, his stomach lurched, feeling as if he was plummeting through space itself. He could almost guarantee that with his luck he'd land face side down, the boulder pinning his flattened body. At least then, he wouldn't have to deal with Fate and her recent upsurge of homicidal tendencies.

Chaos felt cool tile against his pants, his eyes -that were clenched in fear- blinked open, allowing harsh sunlight to flood his vision. He squinted harshly until dark red wallpaper, plastered on the sides of the room, was clear in his vision.

"Well, if it isn't my favorite *brother*." Chaos threw on a smile, knocking his head back against the rock, as he addressed Retribution, who seemed to be shuffling through parchment.

"Cha-" Retribution spoke dryly, then lifted his head, "...os."

"It would help generously if you would stop gawking and untie me."

Retribution blinked in front of Chaos, a frown lining his lips. He merely stared at Chaos' lazy grin before daring to ask, "Who did this to you?"

"What? Can't I tie myself to a boulder?"

Retribution's eyebrows drew together, "Answer the question, Chaos."

Chaos' cellar of bottled up anger spilled into his laughter. One bottle after another. His laughter didn't stop pushing the walls of silence, until his stomach felt sore, and the cellar consisted of nothing but broken glass. He didn't care if Retribution had somewhere to be, he didn't care that he should've been searching for Fate before she plunged Cadere into pure havoc. He didn't care that he had almost been killed. He didn't care.

When his lips pulled with strain, and his eyes burned like acid, he forced his gaze back to Retribution's clenched jaw.

"It was Fate." Chaos shifted his back against the hard, uneven planes of rock, "She wanted me to stay out of something."

Retribution's jaw ticked. In fact, his entire body tensed.

"And what was that?" Retribution asked, his voice low.

Chaos frowned mockingly at him, "I don't owe you my entire life story, Retribution. Would you also like to know about the time we broke your Perry Siles album?"

He was distracting Retribution, and they both knew it.

"Well. As much as I enjoy being tied to a boulder...get on with it, will you?" Chaos shrugged his shoulders around the rope. He leaned his head back once again, as Retribution leaned down, surveying the knots. Chaos could hear the knife slip from a sheath at Retribution's side; he began sawing against the piercing strands of the golden snake burrowed into his skin.

"You look horrible." Retribution muttered, as his eyes were trained on the snapping thread.

"You as well, but that's not any recent revelation."

After minutes of pounding silence, the rope bonding his figure to the boulder dropped lifelessly on the tile. His eyebrow itched. His feet spiked with loss of movement.

"Great job, Retribution. One down, and about 50 more to go."

With each bond releasing, breaths became easier and his shoulders fell in relief. He twisted his wrists around to regain circulation, as Retribution finished sawing the last strands around his ankles. Before Retribution could even push himself from the ground, Chaos jumped from the tile, wincing at the weariness in his limbs.

Retribution straightened, standing beside Chaos and running a hand over the curls tight against his head.

Chaos grimaced, glancing behind him at the door. "I have to go."

Retribution fixed Chaos with a disapproving frown, "Don't get into any more trouble."

Chaos smirked, raising his hand in a salut. Instead of giving Retribution a chance to leave first, Chaos saw his surroundings spin in strands of multicolored string.

"Wait- what do I do with the boulder?" Came Retribution's muffled yell, "Chaos!"

Chaos shut his eyes, and gave a wicked grin that he knew Retribution couldn't see.

As to where he was going? He knew where Fate was. He knew her plans.

And he had to make sure, if only to calm the sinkhole in his stomach, that she was still safe.

***

If Chaos remembered one thing Fate had taught him, it was to appear in washrooms when breaking and entering. His lips tilted as he surveyed the royal castles' bathrooms. A title on the flooring alone had more wealth than the entire country of Hikma.

Pushing the stall door, not even stopping to check his appearance in the mirror, he rushed into the corridors, each with gold-lined pointed arches of glass, revealing an endless black. He didn't know the guard surveillance times, he didn't have a Riquezan guard uniform, he wasn't coordinated.

He wasn't Fate.

His legs moved a little faster, his eyes flicked a little more rapidly, he strained his memory of the throne room's placement a little harder.

He wasn't going to think about what would happen if he was caught. He wasn't going to think about what would happen if she had been caught.

They'd been a team for as long as he could remember. Ruining their family's days, ruining each other's days...

Sure, there wasn't going to be permanent harm to her physically, but it would reveal their secret if her captors found out she was unkillable. *Then,* they would have a large problem. One Chaos wasn't willing, or able to, solve.

His heart slowed in relief as his eyes fixed on two double doors a few corridors down. His hands curled into fists. As much as he wanted to break out into a run, it wouldn't be wise. What would he find past those doors? A body on the floor? The royal crown of gold separated from its head of display. Would Fate be there? Shocked at what she had done? As much as she pretended not to care, Chaos had known her for too long to be tricked.

Would Fate have left to meet with him, only to find him gone?

All he could take comfort in was that he didn't hear any commotion, nor did he feel the sharp plunge pain of a Protector's death.

Perhaps Fate hadn't gone through with it.

His feet slowed at the ten-foot tall doors. Something was wrong. Something was missing.

Chaos' eyes quickly scanned his surroundings.

Guards weren't stationed at the doors. Now that he thought of it, guards hadn't been *anywhere* in the entirety of the castle that he had been in. *No one* had been in the corridors at all.

Had Fate killed them all?

With shaking fingers, his hands rested against the wooden door, as claws dug into the lining of his stomach.

Click.

The door of engraved, weathered gold released a draft of frigid air, prickling up his back.

Before pushing the doors further, Chaos clenched his eyes shut. It was Fate he was thinking of. The same Fate who could best each protector in sparring, the same Fate with a wicked mind.

The same Fate who no longer had the aid of her powers, the same Fate who fell prey to her anger.

His fingers brushed the gold, pushing the door enough for his body to slip through the crack.

And when his eyes fell to the body on the ivory tile, pooled in red liquid- it's copper stench attacking him from every angle- there was no circlet of gold by the body's feet. There were no robes of red and green.

There was only hair spilled like ink. A woman's broken body.

A woman.

A Mahanan woman.

His legs froze.

A joke, a lie, a prank...

As he reached her body, a laugh bubbled in his throat. "That's funny, Fate."

His shoe moved to nudge her arm, "We have to leave-"

He nudged her again, "Fate."

Chaos' body was frozen.

The world shook, blurred, darkened, and spun.

His knees collapsed into the blood, still slightly warm. It soaked into his pants, coated his hands. He shook her shoulders. Everything he touched stained red. The color of blood. The color of the Riquezan flag.

It was impossible.

Fate wouldn't let herself be killed, by a mortal man nonetheless.

How-

It was impossible.

Chaos shook Fate's shoulder, "Fate, come on wake up."

Fate's blouse was darker than the midnight sky, her hair was a mess, haloing around her head, sticky with fallen blood. Her mouth was left open, dripping red from an incision in her throat. Her eyes were shut, resting against her cheek.

For once Fate wasn't in order.

Chaos clenched his eyes shut as his hold on her increased until his knuckles turned white.

With every throb of his head, her form felt less solid. And Chaos couldn't bring himself to look. Just hold.

Hold.

The wristwatch.

Slowly, he raised his head, forcing his slightly trembling hands to unclasp the watch along her wrist. He grasped the watch in his hand. Just like the rest of her, it was painted with deep red blood.

Chaos sat kneeling next to her figure, forcing himself to watch as her body matched the color of the air. Watched as her edges blurred, until nothing but his tear-stained face in her blood remained.

"Fate?" Chaos whispered- a strained whisper. His fingers reached for her body, as if she had merely gone invisible. But they hit the cool stone.

His expression hardened, as his hands shook more fervently.

He would *kill* Casimir.

He didn't care. And if he got himself killed while doing it, so be it.

Was he going to take everything from Chaos? His entire family?

Is it better, Chaos? She'll no longer hold you back. You can cause all the havoc you've dreamed of. Why would you want *to stop the war? Stop the destruction?* Frank laughed.

Chaos' knuckles bloomed white around the wristwatch, her last remains. A promise.

And he shut his eyes, and let the pull of pain guide him.

CHAPTER

THIRTY-TWO

FLASHBACK

"How much for the wristwatch?"

*At this point Chaos has already broken rule number one-
don't show interest in the goods one steals. Fate had told him it
was a direct ticket to conflict. Unfortunately for everyone, Chaos is
all about conflict.*

*The man scowls at Chaos' blindingly innocent eyes, "This
isn't a store, boy."*

*He's right, of course. It isn't. Chaos knows he's standing in
a gambling hall. Which means everything is fair game if you have
enough wits to get it.*

*Chaos pulls cards from his pockets with fluid ease, as if he
planned for it, which he did- well, if a person could call glancing at
the first thing they saw and thinking "I want it" a plan.*

"I win, I get the watch. You-"

*"I win, you give me all the gold in your pockets, rich boy."
The man's scowl turns up into a twisted smirk. He leans back into
the peeling wooden chair that seems to bend under his muscular
weight, and pats the wooden stand in front of him, an invitation to
sit. The man unclips the watch from his wrist and drops it on the
table as Chaos slides on the chair, dealing the cards through the
shadowed lighting and the heavy cigarette smoke. When there are 2*

cards in front of Chaos, he shoves his hand into his pockets, making a show of pulling out every coin he has.

"Ah, 25 acunars. 26-no-27-no-32-no-" Chaos drops more clinking coins on the table's glaze, paying more attention to the gold disks than the man's rising grin, "50?"

"Liar." The man stares, as if his eyes were a gold detector, right into Chaos' pockets.

Chaos gives a thin, mocking smile, "You caught me."

He reaches into his pockets yet again, pulling out 10 more coins which pulls the total to 100 acunar. Is Chaos going to win this watch? Probably not. It doesn't hurt to try, though.

"Good. We play." The man snatches his cards like a selfish child and fans them out in front of him, squinting hard.

Chaos grabs the deck and places three cards in front of him, face up.

"Ah...ha, ha!" The man places down his hand. Ha, Chaos knows he can easily beat him, if he has the ace of spades he was already perfectly set up for a flush. He glances at his new card, and his smile wavers.

He blinks. There's no way he's going to win this.

And they play, the man growing his grin, which becomes larger than his mustache, and Chaos spouts out arrogant nonsense to make it seem as if he is just as likely to win.

"Will you really add more chips to your bet?" Chaos leans back and scoffs, "Alright, then."

He finds it amusing to watch the sweat roll down the man's face. Perhaps it is because the smell of sour alcohol is a strong cloud around the man, that he believes Chaos' taunting.

"Do you have a wife, sir?" Chaos asks, eyes flicking to a woman watching intensely from the side.

The man laughs, slapping his leg, "Of course, I do. She's waiting for me, just over there. Linda, my love."

He does not glance at the woman, too intrigued in the game.

"Oh, but don't worry, boy. You'll get one soon enough. What're you, ten?"

"Fourteen," Chaos *slides more parieur chips into the middle, "You have a friend here, Mr…?"*

"Frank. Though it's sir to you." He laughs wildly while *Chaos waits patiently, "All these men are my buddies. Though that Petey- oh, he makes me question it sometimes."*

"Petey? The man with an eyepatch?"

"You know him?"

"I know he seems to be running his hands all over this woman. Just over there. *Linda..was her name?"*

Frank drops his cards, suddenly a lot less interested in winning Chaos' pocket money. He storms over to where Chaos had noticed Petey- the bartender with a name tag- pulling at the woman's shirt to dry off the spilled drink. From his angle, it seems a whole lot more scandalous.

Noticing his leeway, Chaos swipes the silver wristwatch and his acunar off the wood, pocketing them in a swift motion. He hears Frank roar at Petey and hears pleas from Linda as he strides out.

While Chaos pushes the door, Frank yells, "Boy! Come back here!"

Chaos turns around, letting an acunar catch the light, "Apologies, did you want this?"

Rule number two- don't aggravate the seller. Rule number three- don't admit to thievery. Rule number four- leave as fast as you can.

"Thief!" Frank yells and as soon as it leaves his mouth, five other muscled men push up from their seats. It hits Chaos that perhaps it's time to leave.

Chaos flips the coin on the floor, "For the troubles."

Then he runs. Or tries *to run. The second he's two steps into the cool air, a calloused hand grabs his arm.*

Chaos tries to twist from the grasp, instead glancing up to see he's cornered between masses of muscle and a blanket of body odor intertwined with pungent alcohol.

He chuckles nervously.

Frank's face twists derisively, "A foolish attempt."

He and his companions shove Chaos into a damp, mildew coated alleyway. Chaos stumbles in the dark.

"Come now," he says as the men advance, holding up his hands, "my voice hasn't even deepened yet. I believe this is actually quite illegal."

"Legality don't matter when no one is looking." Another man, this one with a dragon tattoo, sneers.

"You won't pay acunar for your theft, boy. I'll take the price another way," Frank assures, his eyes glinting in the moonlight.

The side of Chaos' jaw spikes with pain. He can taste the metallic blood in his mouth from biting down on his cheek.

"Ow." Chaos spits, rubbing at the side of his face.

Frank grabs his shirt and shoves him to the floor. His ribs take the impact, his teeth clamp down on his lips to keep from screaming at the stabbing pain in his side that assuredly came from a fracture.

The men laugh. And laugh. Chaos can't see from his bruised eyes, his face is swollen, his body is limp and broken. He knows blood runs down his nose and lips and yet the punching throb of every breath lets him feel nothing else. Pain had been a foreign feeling. It isn't anymore.

He only knows they are gone when the burn of their lashing laughter dims.

It seems as if he's there for days as the sun rises and falls, as if full years have passed while he's barely breathing and alone, tears dripping down the sides of his chin.

His pockets keep him anchored to the ground, silver and gold. He knows what Death will shout at him, how Retribution will *be conflicted between concern and disgust, how Fate will mock him when he's healed.*

That is if he sees them again at all.

When he can't tell the difference between reality and the screams in his mind, he hears voices through his growing nausea. Voices that are too muffled to be in his head.

"Chaos?"

"What in the Altar's name-"

"Is he alive?"

"Did he jump *from this building?"*

"Did he get *jumped?"*

He forces his eyes open, though he can only see from a narrow line in his vision.

"I broke your rules, Fate." He slurs.

He doesn't know if the words were understandable until the voices continue.

"What rules?*"*

"You idiot."

Then he cannot hear anything at all and his vision returns to black.

Guess it does hurt to try.

Chapter

Thirty-Three

Chaos

He only knew he wasn't still kneeling in a pool of blood when a stray leaf brushed his hair. He scrambled back, expecting his hands to slide around the cool tile, but instead grabbed fistfulls of weak grass. In front of his heaving mess of a figure, were cobblestone walls. Cracking walls of stone and glass, strangled with vipers for vines. Limp grass waved tauntingly in the feeble breeze. As if to say hello.

As if to say *welcome back.*

Chaos whipped his head back to the endless field of waving grass. Hello. Hello. Hello.

He bared his teeth, pointing into the blank gray above, faulting the Altar for his appearance. Faulting what had once been their home.

He had been perfectly content experiencing twisting nausea at the taste of Fate's blood on his tongue, he had been perfectly content sinking in the well of red beneath his legs. He would have been perfectly content never returning here. Never again witnessing his past.

His warped memories of what had been Fate.

He knew if he looked five yards to his right, he would see lifeless carved stone in the protector's shapes lined around a silver pool of water.

Statues. Statues of them all.

Balance. Fate.

He wouldn't look at them.

Her dark skin, that was instead carved in chalky stone, her challenging smile, the arches of her lashes, the twinkle stolen from her umber eyes.

He couldn't look.

His eye caught on a shadowed figure turning around a pillar. Dark wispy hair, wading in the wind, at his chin. Eyes that used to be shadowed, now brighter around the drowsy atmosphere. Eyes he hadn't seen in more than half a year.

He winced as Death came closer. Of course, Chaos wasn't alone. Of course, Death was exactly where he had expected him to be.

Feet stopped at his sprawled body and a hesitant voice rang out, "What happened?"

What happened? What hadn't happened?

Death had abandoned them for *months*. It had felt as if his entire world had fallen in ashes in the time he had been gone.

So for once, to Death's question, he was speechless.

"What *happened?*" Chaos tilted his head with a smile dripping poison.

Death ignored his accusatory tone, pushing forward, kneeling beside Chaos. He flinched as Death's fingers brushed the top of his arm, "Who's blood is that?"

Just a random guy on the street I killed.

Was what he would've said.

"Chaos?" Death prodded, not removing his dark eyes from Chaos' expression. Searching through the sharded glass of his many masks- searching for the right story.

"Doesn't matter." Chaos pushed himself off the grass, atleast, attempted pushing himself off the grass. Apparently his legs had decided to root him there, forced to fall prey to Death's questions.

"I think that rather proves the importance." Death's expression darkened, half-heartedly waving at the air. A motion describing Chaos' failure to even stand on his own two legs.

Chaos scowled, sliding his hand off his cheek, to cease an itch to bathe for days to remove the thick coating of crumbling blood. He pulled his gaze from Death's own, staring into the fields of flat plains dotted with willow trees around the manor.

How could he tell him? Where would he start?

But what he was more terrified of, was the consequences of Chaos reliving his memory of the limp body bathed in wine-red liquid.

What he would say. What he would do.

He felt Death's hand firm on his shoulder, sending a shudder throughout his body. His touch, much like hers.

Her cold, clammy fingers...

How Death could bear to keep his hand on the black layer of blood on Chaos' shirt, he didn't know. The shirt was now pressed against Chaos' skin with the force of Death's hand. The hardened blood turned his stomach, flipping repeatedly like a coin. Chaos shrugged free of the reassurance on his shoulder.

"Chaos." Surprisingly annoyance had not leaked into Death's voice. A different Chaos, a different Death.

Chaos forced his gaze to Death's expectant one. The downwards tilt of his lips and the worry etched into the lines between his eyebrows, bubbled laughter in Chaos' throat. He tilted his head back, his laughter echoing in the hollow cellar, rebounding off the shards of anger.

A voice that seemed to be too harsh to be his own, spoke from his lips, "You didn't feel it either, did you?"

"What didn't I feel?" Death had his arm over his raised leg, still waiting for an acceptable answer.

Chaos hummed, a wicked grin now plastered on his face. He pointed to Death's heart.

"That."

Death's eyebrows met as he glanced down at Chaos' finger, his lips parting in dread. His head whipped up, "Who-"

Chaos' grin slashed in two as understanding crossed Death's gaze.

He hadn't been there to save her.

And it was *his* kingdom. She had died on the grounds of the country that worshiped him, the country of people who had his appearance. Died at the hands of his people.

Chaos pushed himself off the dirt, using the force of his anger. He was done. He wouldn't wait around anymore stuck beside someone who had abandoned them at their very time of need, with an expression of false concern. He wouldn't wait around bathed in her spilled blood, without avenging it first. He scooped up the wristwatch that had fallen out of his hands at some point, shoving it in his pockets and ignoring the faint red fingerprints along it.

He turned away as Death pulled himself up, still blinking in shock.

"Where are you going?" Came Death's choked voice.

"It doesn't concern you." Chaos visualized the throne room once again, the heavy press of copper-scented air, the gold throne carved of dragons, the ivory tile split with a red and green carpet trailing to the throne. As much as he willed, the slight nausea that came with the spin and fall never came.

Riqueza.

Throne Room.

Royal Castle.

Chaos felt the wind grip the side of his face, as if mocking his inability to leave. His nails pressed into his palms.

Ivory tile, the tiered domed ceiling.

Nothing, nothing.

When Chaos opened his eyes in a blaze of impatience, he turned on Death's aggravatingly placid face, "Will it let *you* leave?"

Death leveled his gaze at Chaos, "I wouldn't know. I haven't tried."

Chaos gritted his teeth, stomping through the grass. First the Altar wouldn't let them return, now it wouldn't let him leave.

"What are you doing?" Death spoke to his back, his tone dry. Chaos would find his way back to her. Even if he had to walk through kingdoms and over oceans just to avenge her murder.

Not that he even knew where the Altar was, geography wise.

Chaos continued briskly, feeling the strands of grass wrapping around his ankle, pulling him back to the stone manor of the Altar. But he kept walking into the line where the gray sky met swaying green.

Each step felt like climbing stairs to a reservoir of anger.

Step. Fate. Step. Blame. Step. Death. Step. Casimir.

If he would've looked back, he swore he would be able to see Death and his disapproving frown. The same frown that he had been given to him constantly throughout the centuries.

The same frown he had seen each day he had lived in the Altar with his fellow protectors.

The same frown that was reserved for his and Fate's antics. Antics that had them doubled over with laughter as the others stood dripping wet, or with matching piqued expressions. Or both.

Oh, how different they had grown since then. He missed seeing the soft smile brushed on Fate's lips, rather than the cold edge of her scowl.

He missed her.

The thought folded in the stairs, tumbling his process towards fury, to the depths of sorrow underneath. Heat burned his eyes and then cheeks, as tears poured down his chin and neck. His knees buckled underneath him, holding him like gravity to the surface.

He stared into the dull gray above, allowing tears to roll down his cheeks in silence.

How could he be alone?

He sat in place, feeling the caress of warm tears on his face, wishing- wishing that all of it had just been a bad dream.

***

He hadn't known how much time had passed out in the fields after he had gotten up and continued to walk. The fields started losing their color. Duller and duller with every step. Just as he had taken his fifth step forward, his body warped and stretched. His eyes dropped down to his figure, without shock, having no control over the strange feeling. His limbs felt like limp noodles. A feeling he had grown quite accustomed to over the years.

He shuddered when it ceased, fixing his gaze on the horizon again, only to stumble backwards in fury. The Altar was back in view once again. The stone manor, the wide silver lake, the white blocks of carved stone further off.

Would it honestly not let him leave? Not when it mattered the most?

Leaning against a pillar was Death, his arms crossed as he raised his eyebrows in Chaos' direction.

"I was wondering how long it would take you."

Chaos whirled on Death, "Were you honestly waiting for it to happen?"

Death gave Chaos a slight smile, "Are you ready to talk?"

***

"Well?"

"Well what?" Chaos kept his arms tight across his chest, sinking into the hug from the chair.

Death kept his steady gaze on Chaos as he sat on the opposing chair, sipping coffee from a delicate looking teacup.

272

"Do you want some?" Death gestured to his flowered teacup.

The only thing Chaos wanted was blood. Casimir's blood.

"No." Chaos trained his eyes around the Altar's manor, viewing the ledges of the floors above, the wood and stone as they connected to form a structure, the stacks of books along the walls. He could almost see the shadow of what used to be. Him and Fate. Balance.

What once was a completely occupied house, now left him shuddering with want for his family.

As Chaos glanced back, Death stood before him, shoving a steaming cup of coffee into his face, "What-"

"You're shaking."

"Am-" Chaos glanced at his leg, which was bouncing rapidly, "..not." He put a hand over his leg, scowling down at it.

"Please don't make me burn my hand, Chaos." Death was now holding the handle with the ends of his fingers, scrunching up his face.

"Will that not make me burn *my* hands, then?"

Death sighed at his sullen tone and walked over to the wooden side-table at Chaos' right , placing the coffee upon a cork coaster. Always one for propriety.

He sat back down in the brown armchair, opposite to Chaos.

Death placed a knee over the other, "Now, tell me what's going on, or I'll ask Retribution."

That was assuming the Altar would let Death leave, of course. Which, Chaos assumed, if only to spite him, it would.

"He wouldn't know." His words were true, he hadn't spoken to Retribution after, nor did he see him standing in her puddle of blood.

Death fixed him with a long look, "Please."

Chaos looked away and didn't speak for a long time. His mouth opened multiple times, trying, but nothing came out.

But the silence was a ticking clock for Death's next words, a silence he felt he should take advantage of. He shut his eyes and blurted, "She was trying to kill Casimir."

Brown eyes, the color of splintered bark, bounced off the walls of his mind, piercing his vision. It turned what was a distant cousin of peace, to red streaks of anger.

Casimir had left Fate's body in a show of disgrace in the middle of his throne room, claiming the murder.

Claiming Fate.

He could almost smell her blood again, almost see her face that- for once- was peaceful.

He gripped the sides of the armchair and shoved himself off the chair.

"Where are you going?" Death's voice came hesitantly, as if he was still trying to process Chaos' last statement.

This time, to his question, Chaos gave him an answer, "To kill Casimir."

"What? Be rational, Chaos."

Chaos laughed, a sound of pure disbelief, "Kill the man that killed her. It's only fair"

He pushed past the chairs, stepping out of the side-room to the door, its glass revealing the waving grass and the snaking stream.

"And how do you propose to do that?"

"Knife. Poison. Acid. Bullet. It doesn't matter. Don't try to stop me." Chaos gritted his teeth without looking back at Death.

"Chaos."

"Please, Death!" Chaos whipped around only to find Death's face pale, "...What?"

"Humans can't kill us."

Chaos stilled.

Death was right. He was right. Of *course*.

How had he not remembered? It was so completely obvious, and yet...

He hadn't stopped for a second to think it might have been one of them. Might have been one of the other protectors.

One of his friends. One of their *family*.

Would he be able to kill any of them, even to avenge Fate? Retribution, Life, or Death? They'd grown apart, all of them. What once was camaraderie, was now few stumbles from hatred. But he couldn't, he wouldn't. If Fate couldn't stick a knife through his throat, then neither could he.

And Chaos remembered.

He remembered the night he found out they were invincible to humans. The night he had been caught up in dangerous activity while he had been young and arrogant. A black, damp alleyway made of mold and terror flashed in his mind. Men, two times his size, chuckling, smelling wholly of pungent alcohol. A silver watch still tucked into his pocket, as they took it upon themselves to make him pay the price of it. The price of blood.

He remembered who Death had been as he had lectured Chaos afterwards, in sharp tones, about responsibility, then forced the entire group to learn combat, mainly to teach him a lesson.

He remembered who they all had been. Young and reckless.

And he knew, knew that whatever happened, he couldn't kill any of them.

Chaos pushed himself up against the wall, feeling cracks run through his body.

"Who could have-?" Death trailed off, his lips pulled back in disgust.

"I was with Retribution right before." Chaos closed his eyes tightly, "Her blood was still warm."

Death didn't say a word.

"No one but me knew her plans. How?" Chaos allowed the dim light from the windows to fill his eyes again.

Death had turned a slight shade of sickly green, "Wait you were with Retribution?"

275

Chaos nodded.

"Perhaps, it wasn't one of us…"

"What do you mean?" Chaos felt too queasy to move anything but slight movements of his mouth. His head split like shocks of lightning, thumping periodically.

"You say only you knew of her plans. She had gone to kill Casimir." Death took a breath, "So, the only being who could have possibly killed Fate, is Casimir himself…"

"His throne room, his castle was barren of guards. He knew. *How?*" Chaos swayed, "But it doesn't make sense, humans can't kill-"

Punches of nausea.

"Time." Chaos met Death's eyes.

"Which could only mean…" Chaos started.

Death finished his thought, eyes flashing, "Casimir is Time."

CHAPTER

THIRTY-FOUR

Life

She stared at the map in her hand.

She was getting closer. She only had an hour left to go. Her feet moved swiftly. Anticipation was a heavy weight in her stomach. After a two minute increment of walking, she checked her pocket watch for the hundredth time.

"4:23" She whispered.

If she kept up this pace, she would be able to get there, grab the stone, and make it back before Diego woke up. Hopefully, that was.

Lost in thought, she hadn't noticed a horribly placed stick in the way. Her foot hitched behind the wood and sent her sprawling towards the ground. Whirling her arms, she balanced back on two feet. She continued walking, numbly.

Why was this taking so long? As someone who felt the human world run much faster than the mortals perceived, long for *her* was numerous weeks, not numerous hours.

She just stared at the dark horizon before her. Still, unflinching, silent. Her mind lulled, not thinking. She absently rubbed her thumb over Tabitha.

A mental exhaustion tugged at her frame. It was getting harder to control her thoughts. What if this didn't work the way she wanted it to? What if she made the situation worse?

Life shook her head, "No, I am helping."

She was taking a burden off Retribution. She was ending the war in the best way she could.

Her mind wandered to Diego. She breathed in sharply, forcing him out of her mind. She was doing this for him as well.

Leaves crunched under her foot. Her stomach flipped at the unexpected noise.

She sighed, a long, weary exhale.

This stone had to work. It had to stop the war. She wasn't going to start thinking about what would happen if she was wrong. She *couldn't*.

Her thoughts wouldn't yield to her determination.

She continued walking, the cool night wind pushed her blonde hair back. What would she do if the stone wasn't there? Keep searching, just like Retribution, for all her life? A race to see who would find it first? There were so many places on the map that hadn't been X'd out.

She had to. Whatever it took. She lost Balance, Retribution, Diego, herself.

She couldn't lose anyone else. She wouldn't. But all of that felt like empty promises.

She checked her pocket watch reading 5:01.

She was almost there, but she could already feel herself breaking down. Her feet burned, her core and arms burned.

She trudged forward. She felt her stomach churn slightly. She couldn't take a break now, not when she was so close. She could see dark outlines of colossal boulders towering over the horizon, the moon's reflection on soft streams, winding through rocks.

She had reached. She stepped forward, squinting, surveying the mounds of stone. A tunnel appeared dimly in her vision.

Carefully placing her feet on the tops of the slanted rock, she grabbed any protruding stone to lift herself up. Sweat beaded at her forehead, as she pulled herself into view of the tunnel.

She paused, the hair bristling on her neck.

It was so… dark.

She shook her head, "Come on, Life."

She looked up, and took a deep breath, she gripped the sides of the tunnel for support and heaved herself into the Sans Fin Cave Systems. Her legs wobbled as she stood.

"Alright, now the real challenge begins."

***

She didn't know how much time had passed.

She couldn't check her pocket watch because it was far too dark to possibly see anything. She was hoping- no- praying for a sliver of light because she was sure she wouldn't last much longer not being able to see where she stepped.

The tunnels were endless. The only reason she wasn't spinning in circles was a tugging sensation in her stomach. It coiled around her insides, practically dragging her forward. It slowly grew more intense, becoming impossible to ignore.

Every time she thought she was getting closer, she was met with a solid wall blocking her path, a seemingly endless drop, or a narrow space only a rabbit could have fit through.

Hours later, she let out a frustrated sob, yanking her hair. She was alone, with no company but her slowly deteriorating thoughts. She was far into an unexplored section of the caves. What if something horrible had happened while she was here?

She wished she was outside again. She could easily teleport out, pretend this field trip hadn't occurred, but that would mean admitting defeat. She'd know, then, that Balance was never coming back. She'd know the world was doomed. She'd know she could've been minutes away from solving all their problems. That a single decision would have cost them *everything*.

Life sobbed for a second, her ragged breathing echoing in the dome, before composing herself. She had to focus on what she could accomplish now.

She tried checking her pocket watch, but was met with the cracked, broken face of the clock. She threw the watch at the floor, stomping on it, and resuming her jagged breathing. The sound of her own anger broke her heart. When had she *ever* felt this hopeless?

Life exhaled shakily, dragging her fingers down her face. She pushed her hair out of her face and lifted her chin, taking another breath to calm herself.

Her eyes widened slowly.

"No… No- Frank." She cursed. Her hands fidgeted with the fabric of the pocket that once held her watch. Her hands came to harshly clutch her head. She couldn't help it; hot tears rolled down her face.

How long had she been in these caves? How long, how long, how long-

"Where are you?" She screamed, her voice shuddering under the force of her yell. Her arms grew limp, as she lugged forward, having no other choice. Life felt the heavy force of resignation on her shoulders as she continued, forcing her pace to significantly slow.

Simply keeping her eyes open took more energy than it was worth.

It was probably the walking draining her will power. How long had she walked already? More than she ever had in her existence, that was for sure. She felt her limbs numb with each step she took. The pull in her stomach, as persistent as ever, was doing most of the heavy lifting.

She looked up blankly as her arms, that were propped against both sides of the wall, fell to her sides. The pathway she had been following split into two different pathways.

Before she started debating which path to take, her body lurched forward subconsciously. Towards the left. She could feel it.

There was a stronger pull there.

Her brows furrowed as her shoulders relaxed. Life hesitantly continued, wondering if she was being ridiculous for trusting some inner sensation she couldn't prove. A small step at a time was all she could manage, hoping she wouldn't fall into a massive hole. As she edged her left foot closer towards the strange sensation, an icy chill sank into her shoes. Something *wet*.

Life gasped softly, stepping back, and peered at the ground. It was *rippling*. Some sort of large stream…some sort of *river*.

"Do I go forward?" She whispered.

Life waited a moment, begging for an answer or a sign. She shook her head and turned around, walking the other way.

She gasped, horrified, as her stomach curled, and she clutched her chest. She felt her body weigh down with every step. There was something wrong. Protectors had increased activity. They could technically go for hours running. So why was Life this near to unconscious?

It was as if her energy was draining everytime the hold on her stomach pulsed. She turned to face the way she had started before, fighting the way her vision blurred. Every step she took in the 'right direction,' the ringing in her head quieted.

It was a sign.

She stretched out a hand to stabilize herself against the wall as a wave of nausea hit her. She stumbled forward, her fingers twitched as she didn't hesitate to wade into the water. She felt the added weight of water in the crevices of her clothes drag her down. There were moments her heart lurched as something skimmed the bare skin on her legs. There were moments she questioned resisting her urge to stop swimming and allowing herself to sink into the river's depths.

At least she finally understood what the diary's author had meant by the river being peaceful. It made her want to put herself out of her misery.

The river was cold enough to the point she could feel nothing. She couldn't reach her sensibility, her drive to continue, or her fear for the world. Somehow, the river was a great mercy.

She slowly shut her eyes and allowed her limbs to go slack. The river's numbingly frigid water climbed up her neck, kissing her cheeks with a promise. The world would still continue to spin; she no longer needed to help.

It soothed her red and puffy eyes, washed the grime from her hair, and comforted her. What more did she need?

Life relaxed her shoulders, letting the river take everything from her. It was pure bliss.

Well, it was, for the most part, pure bliss. A burning sensation filled her lungs, growing urgent.

Life scowled, wondering what was interrupting her peace. Her eyes flew open. Now her eyes were burning, *burning.* Her lungs were scalding.

Where was she again?

Her arms were spasming, her legs were kicking. *Was this a seizure?*

Something was wrong. She pushed against the weight dragging her body down, her limbs gliding…in the air?

Oh.

Oh, Frank.

She had never gotten out of the river.

She sobbed, bubbles escaping from her lips, as she swam upwards. Everything was hurting. Her mind was pounding. Her body was straining to keep up.

The moment she was sure her life was lost forever, her head broke through the water's surface.

And she gasped. Her heavy breaths were classified more as wrangled sobs. *What had she been doing?*

Life had to get out of the water before she wished she was back under the surface again. However weary, she forced her body past its limits to pull herself to shore.

Using the last of her strength to promptly heave herself as she dripped over the stone, she collapsed at the river's bank.

And she didn't move.

***

It had been long, very long, before Life mustered enough strength to stand again. Although she was almost completely dried, a piercing chill had embedded itself in her. However many times she rubbed her arms together to feel the warmth, the chill wouldn't vanish, but there was nothing she could do but continue.

She hauled herself up gingerly into the mouth of a smaller cave.

Her hand shook as she reached forward.

A stone wall.

Tears of exhaustion rolled down her face. She turned around only to be met with more dark walls and an inky black river bellow.

She wanted to yell, or scream, or do *anything* but walk. Her body slowly slid down the wall, her legs finally giving out.

She glared at the wall- no. Her gaze softened slightly.

"It's a boulder." She whispered.

She could never move that boulder, not with her powers. Not when she could barely move herself. She took a deep breath and crawled forward, looking for gaps or anything she could wiggle through.

She touched every crevice and corner, seeing if there was a hole big enough for her to fit through. She tilted her head as her hand reached through a gaping hole near the bottom left side.

It was small. Very small.

She just needed to do this. She could feel the energy that had a hold on her pulsing powerfully, begging her to push again.

Life crawled into the opening, her limbs screaming as she squeezed herself through.

She couldn't breathe. Everything was crushing in on her. And then it wasn't.

Her eyes flew open as she finished pulling her leg through the space. She gasped in shock, a laugh bubbling in her throat. Her limbs seared, the ringing in her ears impossibly loudened.

She scanned the stone room with lidded eyes. Blood rushed through her body.

Mere feet away laid a black glimmering stone, waiting for her.

She lurched forward towards it. Her cheeks flushed a violent red. Dark spots inched its way across her vision, as she clenched her eyes shut.

Her mouth betrayed her relief, sobbing into the silence. She was so tired. She had found it. She didn't have to worry anymore.

Life could hardly breathe. Was this what it felt like? Victory?

She glanced at the stone, feeling another wave of relief, and a pull in her stomach a hundred times stronger than it had been at the river.

She remembered when Time spoke to Retribution in his house, the moment before she saw the map for the first time. She remembered the feeling Time's presence gave off.

An unexplainable pull. As if she was experiencing gravity for the first time. It had felt like this but much weaker.

She opened her eyes slowly, crawling to the stone. The stone's aura was almost palpable. With a final push, Her hands shook before gripping it white-knuckled. She shook.

She was laughing. A hollow, echoing noise of pure anguish. Of relief, of *triumph*.

The crystal black stone glimmered in her hand, pulsing with energy.

"The stone…" Her voice trembled. "I did it…" She whispered breathlessly. Her eyelids were heavy as black overtook her vision.

A shiver ran down Life's spine.

"Yes, you did," A silky voice whispered, "Hello, Life. It's been a long time, hasn't it?"

A strange lull wrapped over Life, much like the one at the river. Her fingers twitched as she barely pushed out the words, suddenly incredibly drowsy.

"Who are you?"

The voice took a moment before it spoke as if it were grinning.

"You can call me Reality."

TO BE CONTINUED...

ACKNOWLEDGMENTS

First and foremost, thank you to each other for always being there and working tirelessly to publish this book.

Thank you:

Parents for always being our number one fans. For standing by in any book related endeavor we approached. For listening to our lengthy discussions about the beloved characters. For encouraging and supporting us, every step of the way.

Friends for always encouraging our book obsession and pushing us to publish.

FaceTime for allowing the three of us to keep in touch through Covid and now through our long distance friendship.

The kind banker for his advice and his determined attempts to make our publishing process easier.

Our highschool history classes for teaching us all we know about war and google, for what we forgot from history.

Google translate for helping us name so many places on Cadere.

Everyone else who supported us through our journey.

Most importantly, thank **you** for picking up this book.

ABOUT THE AUTHORS:

Dvita Kini, Vedha Kodagi, and Ava Mandhare are currently 11th graders in high school. You can find Dvita Kini and Ava Mandhare in Novi, Michigan, and Vedha Kodagi in San Francisco, California. Even with the distance between them, they have never given up on their friendship and all consider Novi home. They have been creating stories since day one and have finally put their hard work and passion into *The Remains of Reality* as their first debut in a two-part book series. They started this incredible story at the age of thirteen and have since then considered it a fun-filled adventure. You can email them at theremainsofreality@gmail.com. You can also find Vedha Kodagi on TikTok at ViaKodagi and YouTube at Vedha Kodagi.

Dvita Kini   Ava Mandhare   Vedha Kodagi

·

Made in the USA
Monee, IL
17 September 2023

42886881R00173